THE
DAY
I LOST
YOU

Also by Ruth Mancini

The Woman on the Ledge

THE
DAY
I LOST
YOU

RUTH MANCINI

C

CENTURY

CENTURY

UK | USA | Canada | Ireland | Australia
India | New Zealand | South Africa

Century is part of the Penguin Random House group of companies
whose addresses can be found at global.penguinrandomhouse.com

Penguin Random House UK,
One Embassy Gardens, 8 Viaduct Gardens, London SW11 7BW

penguin.co.uk
global.penguinrandomhouse.com

Penguin
Random House
UK

First published 2025
001

Set in 12.5/17.38pt Times New Roman
Typeset by Six Red Marbles UK, Thetford, Norfolk

Printed and bound in Great Britain by Clays Ltd, Elcograf S.p.A.

The authorised representative in the EEA is Penguin Random House Ireland,
Morrison Chambers, 32 Nassau Street, Dublin D02 YH68

A CIP catalogue record for this book is available from the British Library

ISBN: 978–1–529–90978–4 (hardback)
ISBN: 978–1–529–90979–1 (trade paperback)

Penguin Random House is committed to a sustainable future
for our business, our readers and our planet. This book is made
from Forest Stewardship Council® certified paper.

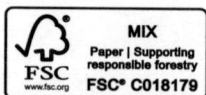

MIX
Paper | Supporting
responsible forestry
FSC
www.fsc.org   FSC® C018179

For Mark, my partner in crime

It's hard to think of myself back at home in our cottage that morning, having an ordinary day. It feels like another lifetime. In that lifetime, everything was normal: I'd seen a client, made a cup of tea, typed up my notes on my laptop in the kitchen, then gone upstairs. I was thinking about what we would have for dinner that evening. I was wondering whether we needed clean hand towels in the downstairs cloakroom. I was thinking normal thoughts, doing normal things, and then I went into the bedroom – and everything changed.

INTERPOL YELLOW NOTICE

Identity particulars

Family name	DUNSMORE-FARIS
Forename	SAMUEL
Family name at birth	DUNSMORE-FARIS
Gender	Male
Date of birth	14/2/22 (2 years, 3 months old)
Place of birth	WYEBRIDGE, UNITED KINGDOM
Nationality	UNITED KINGDOM
Place of disappearance	Chorley Common, UNITED KINGDOM
Date of disappearance	3rd JAN 23 (WHEN 11 MONTHS OLD)
Issuing country	UNITED KINGDOM

Details

Father's family name and forename	FARIS, ANDREW
Mother's family name and forename	DUNSMORE, HOPE

PART ONE

Now

1

Lauren

Mantilla de Mar, Spain

I can see the police car from my vantage point above the rooftops, overlooking the bay. It's dusk and they haven't yet turned on the municipal lights, but as I stand on the terrace, I can easily make out the white-and-royal-blue-chequered vehicle as it travels along the road below us, then winds around the bend and continues its path up the hill.

I step, barefoot, back through the terrace door and into the bedroom, where I pause, listening for the magical sound of Sam's breathing, my toes clenching and unclenching against the cool terracotta floor. I take another step and peer through the half-light, moving around my bed to the small one beside it. Sam is fast asleep, snuffling gently. I lean over to kiss him, pressing my mouth against his downy cheek and letting it linger there.

'What is it?' asks Gabe, looking up as I walk back into

the kitchen. I glance across at him. He's sitting at my table, drinking an espresso. I would be awake all night if I drank coffee at this hour, but it doesn't seem to bother him.

'Nothing,' I say, exhaling deeply and leaning against the worktop.

Gabe doesn't press me, even though he can tell there's something wrong. It's one of the reasons I like him. He lives three doors down. I met him soon after I moved into the apartment, when we were putting out the bins. A few days later, we bumped into each other in the supermarket in the old town and walked up the steps together, and before long he was here most evenings. We played cards while he taught me Catalan and I helped him to perfect his English, which was far better than my Spanish. He was gentle and kind and asked nothing of me – nothing at all – in fact, he asked very few questions, even though I knew he was curious about what had brought me to Spain, to this pretty fishing town.

Moments later, the kitchen is lit up by the glare of head-lights through the window. The stillness outside is broken by the sound of car doors slamming and male voices shout-ing, and I feel a deep, visceral fear in my gut. I sidestep the kitchen table and move quickly out into the hallway, where I fling open the front door to pre-empt any loud knocking. There are two uniformed policemen on my doorstep, both dressed in black – black stab vests, black trousers. They are armed with batons and guns, and I immediately feel both scared and grateful that Gabe is here.

'Señora Hopwood?' the first officer asks me. He's young, I notice. Slim. Good-looking. Olive skin, deep brown eyes and a goatee beard. I take a glimpse at his colleague, who is of a similar age and build.

'Yes,' I say, in English.

'I'm Officer Juan Alvarez of the Policía Local.' I look beyond him to the writing on the car, which confirms this. 'This is my colleague, Officer Rodriguez.'

'How can I help you?' I say, again in English.

'May we come in?'

I glance round at Gabe, who has followed me out and is standing in the kitchen doorway. He gives me a brief nod of the head and I step back to allow the officers to enter. My hallway immediately feels uncomfortably crowded with men and weapons. 'You'd better come through,' I say.

'You own this house?' Officer Alvarez asks me as we go into the kitchen. He looks around at the old-fashioned walnut units and white laminate worktop, at the pots and pans stacked on the slightly grubby gas cooker.

'I rent it,' I say. 'From the guy who owns La Roca.'

'The restaurant?'

'Yes. In Miramar.'

'How long have you been here?'

'Eighteen months.'

'You are working here?'

'Yes. At the restaurant.'

'You work at La Roca?'

'Yes. I wait tables.'

His eyes move to the door leading to the bedroom. 'And who else is in the house?'

'My son,' I say. 'I have a little boy.'

'Hold on,' Gabe interrupts in Catalan, eyeing the officers one by one, his voice cool and measured. 'What is all this about?'

Alvarez pauses and turns to look at Gabe. 'Who are you?' he asks.

'No,' says Gabe. 'First you need to tell us why you are here. It's the law.'

'He just means,' I say, jumping in quickly, 'that . . . you know . . . you haven't given us any information. But whatever it is, we'd like to help you, of course.'

'We've come about a missing child,' Alvarez informs me, still looking Gabe hard in the eye. 'An English child. A boy.'

Gabe looks confused. 'What are you talking about?'

Behind me, Rodriguez steps forward, peering around the door leading to the bedroom, which is slightly ajar.

'Wait,' I say. 'My son's asleep in there. Please don't wake him. Just tell me what it is you think I can help you with.'

'How old is he? Your son?' asks Alvarez.

'Two years and five months. Almost.'

'When is his date of birth?'

'Fourth of January 2022.'

The two officers exchange glances. Gabe looks perplexed.

'I don't know what it is you think I have done,' I say, gazing from one officer to the other, 'but I don't know anything about a missing child. The child in there is my son, and I can prove it. You want to see his birth certificate and passport?'

Alvarez narrows his eyes. 'You have them?'

'Of course,' I tell him.

'Then let us see the identity documents. And let us see the child.'

'The documents are in the bedroom where my son is sleeping. I'll put a night light on. I would just prefer you don't wake him if at all possible.'

'Lauren, we should call a lawyer,' Gabe warns me. 'They don't have any right to search your home.'

'No need for that,' I say, breezily. 'This is just a misunderstanding. We can sort it out.' I step around the table, squeezing awkwardly past Rodriguez, who is blocking my path. 'Come with me,' I say to the officers. 'Just . . . quietly, please.'

The two men follow me. My mouth is dry and my heart is beating its way out of my chest, but I can tell that they are less sure now of whatever it is they've been told. I creep into the bedroom, flick on Sam's night light and point them to his bed, then slide open the wardrobe door. My back is towards the officers as I rummage around in the bottom drawer of the creaky old chest that sits inside it, but I can hear Sam snuffling and turning over. I quickly slip my fingers inside the box where I keep the passports and the plastic wallet that holds Sam's birth certificate and slide them out.

'OK,' says Alvarez, straightening his back. 'We'll let the child sleep now.'

I let out a shaky breath and follow them into the hallway. Gabe is standing just outside the door, looking worried, and I give him a reassuring smile. Back in the kitchen, I place everything on the table. Alvarez leans down and picks up our passports, turning them in his hands. He looks at mine briefly before opening Sam's. I watch as he checks the information, then passes the passport to his colleague, who peers at the photograph.

'Your son was only just born when the passport was issued?'

'He was three weeks old.' I clear my throat. 'We came here on holiday a few years ago, his father and me. We were going to come back with Sam, just as soon as he was old enough to fly. I was on maternity leave and . . . well, we'd fallen in love with the place. We were planning to move out here for good.'

Rodriguez looks up at Gabe and frowns. 'But this is not his father?'

Alvarez also turns to look at Gabe, then at me.

'No.'

'So, where is the father?'

'In England.'

The officers wait for me to elaborate, but I take a breath. I realise I'm talking too much. Everything the police need to know about Sam is there on his passport and on his birth certificate, which should be proof enough that he belongs to me.

Alvarez unfolds the certificate and studies it, then picks up both passports again. 'Can I take photos of these?'

'Why do you need photos of her documents?' asks Gabe, coming to my defence again, as if he is a lawyer.

'A two-year-old boy has gone missing in England,' Alverez replies. 'And he has the same name as your son.'

'The exact same name?' I ask, narrowing my eyes.

'His Christian name is the same.'

'Samuel,' Gabe snorts. 'How many little boys named Samuel do you think there are in the world?'

Alvarez shoots him a hostile look, then turns back to me. 'The police in the UK were given your name by his parents, who say that fifteen months ago, you abducted their child from their home in England.'

'That's ridiculous!' I protest. 'That absolutely *did not* happen. Sam is *my* son. You saw my name on the birth certificate.'

'So, now I want to take photographs for evidence,' says Alvarez, taking out his phone.

'Go ahead,' I say.

'Who are these people?' Gabe asks as the officers busy themselves opening up the documents on the table and pointing their phones at them. 'These people who have made such a ridiculous allegation. What are their names?'

Alvarez takes out a notebook, skimming the pages. 'The people who made the complaint are called Faris.'

'Faris?' Gabe repeats.

'Yes. A husband and wife.'

I glance across at Gabe blankly and shrug my shoulders.

'Look here,' Gabe says to the officers in Catalan. 'It's a

scam. The world is full of weirdos. Trolls. You hear about them all the time. These childless people have found Lauren on the internet and have seen pictures of her and her son.'

I fall silent, waiting. 'Can you step out to the front of the house, please?' Alvarez says to me at last.

'What for?' I ask, feeling my breath catch in my throat as the ground beneath me begins to slip away. 'Are you placing me under arrest?'

'Just come with us.'

Gabe is as white as a sheet, but the officers are already moving out into the hallway. I feel a stab of confusion. Are they really going to arrest me and leave Sam behind?

'It's OK,' I say under my breath to Gabe. 'Just stay here. Please. With Sam. If I don't come back, call me a lawyer.'

Gabe nods.

I follow the officers out into the hallway and close the kitchen door.

Alvarez turns to me. 'Are you in a dispute with the father of your son? Is that what this is all about?'

I hesitate, then shake my head, my heart thumping its way out of my chest.

'Has there been violence in the relationship?'

'No,' I say. 'It's nothing like that. He's coming here as soon as he can. It's just taken longer than expected. He has to make arrangements.'

Alvarez and Rodriguez look at each other. 'So who is that guy in there? To you?'

I take a breath. 'He's no one special,' I say softly. 'He's

just a neighbour.' I feel disloyal as I say it. Gabe has been such a good friend.

But the officers seem to like this answer. Alvarez eyes me carefully, but Rodriguez is already on his radio, accepting another job.

'We'd like to talk to you some more,' Alvarez says. 'Can you come into the police station?'

'Yes. How about Friday afternoon?' I say. 'I'm working Friday lunchtime. I'll ask the babysitter to stay longer. I'll be finished by half past two.'

'Yes,' says Alvarez. 'Friday at half past two will be fine.'

When they have gone, I shut the front door and lean against it. This life, the life I've built, is over. This little bay has been an oasis; on the dark, rain-soaked evening I arrived here, it was quite literally a port in a storm. But everything has changed.

I take a long, deep breath, feeling my heart plummet at the thought of starting all over again. But it's no longer safe here. It's time for us to move on.

2

It's two weeks since I left Mantilla de Mar and when I turn my phone on, I see I've had twenty-two missed calls from Anna. Anna is my best friend in England and I'm afraid the police are tapping her phone, which is why I haven't answered her lately, although that may just be paranoia on my part. But I'm pretty sure she's the reason the Spanish police came knocking. Anna and my mum are the only ones who could have guessed where I was, and I'm pretty sure my mum would never have told the police. Besides, when I was on the coast, Anna and I spoke once a month and now she's calling every day, twice a day, even.

I was surprised I could even get a signal up here in the mountains, to be honest, although I've never skied or hiked or otherwise been high enough above ground level to think about this before now. But it's a relief that I can get updates from Gabe. He's been my only contact with the outside world for the past fortnight, and he's the only person I can now fully trust – Gabe, who came through for me in the most unexpected of ways. Back in Mantilla, after the police left, he'd taken one look at my stricken face and said, 'I'll help you. Whatever it is, whatever you need, I'll help you. Just tell me what it is that you need me to do.'

And so I told him. Within the hour, we'd packed up all of my belongings and lifted Sam out of bed and placed him, wrapped in duvets, into the rear footwell of Gabe's car. Within an hour and a half, we were on the road out of Mantilla, heading inland to the west. We took the back roads towards Lleida and Zaragoza, then turned north through oak and pine forests and through meadows and vineyards, towards the Pyrenees. The journey took over seven hours and the sun was coming up by the time we reached the cabin, a traditional rustic stone and slate chalet, two-storeys high, with a run-down wooden veranda above the terrace, looking down onto the valley. It used to be the home of Gabe's grandparents, Frederica and Josef, who are now both in a care home in France.

I don't know what I've done to deserve Gabe's unswerving loyalty, but I sense he understands my predicament, and that there's some kind of shadow in his own past connecting the two of us. I ponder this as I sit at the table in his grandparents' small kitchen, dipping bread into the stew I made two evenings ago. In the past few weeks, my affection for Gabe has grown exponentially. Gabe, with his dark, tousled hair, deep-set hazel eyes and the five o'clock shadow that grew denser as we drove along the road to the cabin in the early hours of the morning. Being seated next to him in the car all night had felt intimate and there was an energy between us. The tiredness in his eyes had tugged at my heart. I have long suspected that he has feelings for me that run deeper than friendship, but I can't risk finding out. I can't love him, not like that. I wish I could. I wish that so much.

Once I've eaten and checked that Sam is asleep, I take my herb tea out to the terrace, as I have done every evening since we arrived. I kick off my flip-flops and arrange myself – book, mug, bottled water, cushions – on the bench outside the door to the cabin. I never end up reading much, though. My mind is too full of the situation I'm in, and of the view too: the snow-capped peaks to my left, the dappled evening sunlight in the forest to my right, the meandering brook in the valley below. It's a small piece of heaven up here, not just on account of being so close to the clouds, or because of the intense beauty surrounding me, but because Sam and I are safe again, at least for now.

In the distance, I can see Blanca coming up the hill. Blanca Guzman Solana is an eighty-year-old shepherdess with skin like leather and legs that carry her on daily eight-hour hikes. As the sun sets, and when she has finished climbing up and down the mountains, grazing and milking her flock, she climbs up the escarpment to the cabin to bring us fresh linen, goat's milk, cheese and home-baked bread. She manages the cabin with pride and has already taken Sam and me under her wing.

Gabe warned me not to refuse her help. 'It will offend her and make her worry that she will be out of a job,' he'd said.

Not that I could have undertaken the fifteen-mile trip to the next town anyway, not with Sam and not without putting myself at risk of being seen. I am now entirely reliant on Blanca and Gabe for food and toiletries and – of course – for shelter. Gabe said we could stay as long as we needed, but he had a life back in Mantilla and had to work, so, on the same day we arrived and after just a few hours' sleep, he made the long journey back to the coast, leaving Sam and me alone with the occasional company of Blanca and Luna, the tabby cat. I can see Luna now, padding across the hot tiles of the terrace and slinking in between the legs of the chairs, scratching her back. After a moment, she comes over and jumps up onto the bench beside me. I reach out to stroke her and she only ducks her head very slightly. I think we're friends now. The question is: for how long?

My phone rings. I turn it over to look at it. It's Anna again. My stomach tightens and I realise that I'm getting anxious about what it is she's calling for. Anna is a lawyer – a family lawyer – and if the police have told her about me, she's probably a pretty good person to be talking to. So long as I can be sure she isn't going to betray me for a second time, that is.

I draw a deep breath and pick up my new burner phone. Gabe sent it in the post to a friend in the town nearby who delivered it to the cabin yesterday morning. I hold the two handsets side by side as I enter Anna's number into the burner and tap the call button.

'Anna,' I say, my voice low.

'Lauren? Is that you?'

'You'd better not have anyone with you,' I warn her.

'What are you talking about?'

'The police.'

'Lauren! I swear I'm on my own.'

'They could have tapped your phone.'

We fall silent. I'm listening for clicks on the line, but I can't hear anything.

'Nobody's tapping my phone, Lauren.' She sounds incredulous and in spite of everything I find myself believing her.

'Are you OK?' she asks me.

'I'm fine. Apart from the fact that you told the police where I was.'

I sound reproachful and she falls silent. Anna would never deliberately do anything to hurt me, I do know that. We've known each other since I was seventeen and used to babysit for her twin daughters. She's eleven years older and has been like a big sister to me ever since. She was there for me when I crashed and burned and had to take a year out of university; when I broke up with my ex-boyfriend, she was there for me, too. But she can't do anything illegal. She can't even do some things that are *not* illegal. As a lawyer, she has to uphold the public's confidence in her profession, which means she has to be a flagship for all that's good and right. *I could get struck off for that*, she was always fond of telling me. But she feels sorry for me, too, and wants the best for me, I know that.

'I didn't *tell* them anything, Lauren,' she says. 'They looked through your old Instagram account. They'd seen your holiday photos and they confronted me with them and asked what the place means to you, if you could have gone there, and when I didn't answer . . . well, I couldn't lie, and besides, they're saying you abducted a baby. I mean . . . for Christ's sake, Lauren. What the fuck?'

It's my turn to fall silent.

'So what are they talking about?' Anna presses me.

I heave a sigh.

'They're going to arrest you, Lauren. They're going to get a warrant. Your mum is out of her mind with worry.'

I hate it when Anna does this. I love my mum, but I love Sam too. I never wanted to have to choose between them. I never wanted it to be this way.

'So . . . do you have a child there with you? In Spain?'

A trickle of fear runs down my spine. How does she know I'm still in Spain?

'Or wherever you are,' she adds, reading my mind. There's a pause. When she speaks her tone is calmer. 'Look, Lori. I don't know where you are, and I don't *need* to know where you are. I just want to help you.'

'You can't help me, Anna. I don't expect that.'

'I'm talking about giving you some legal advice.'

'And then the police knock on your door again and you have to tell them what you said and where I am?'

'Not if you're my client I don't.'

'What do you mean?'

Anna begins explaining about client confidentiality, or *legal professional privilege* as she calls it, but I already get it. If there is a professional, legal relationship between us, she can't be considered complicit in anything I've done wrong. But can I trust her? That's the question. I look out over the valley and a shiver of incredulity runs through me. What the hell has happened to me? Anna's my best friend; she's the kindest of people. She's always looked out for me; she's always looked out for everyone. This is what all the pain and suffering has done to me. This is how cynical I've become.

Blanca has reached the top of the escarpment now and is making her way along the dusty track towards me, weighed down by her backpack full of groceries. I want to run down there and help her, but I promised Gabe I wouldn't do anything to make her feel redundant. Nonetheless, I realise how pathetic this makes me, that an eighty-year-old woman has to take care of me. I am completely and utterly dependent on her and Gabe and it's far from ideal. Whenever I see Blanca or Gabe or a friend of Gabe's going out of their way for me, it makes me feel bad because I shouldn't be putting them in this position. It reminds me that Sam and I can't stay here for ever. But I don't have any other plan.

'I have a friend,' Anna is saying. 'Well . . . she's a friend, but she's also a colleague, someone I used to work with. She's a criminal defence lawyer, and she's brilliant. The best. Her name is Sarah Kellerman. I can get her to make enquiries, find out what the police are planning – what they know and, more importantly, what they *don't*. Between us, we'll look after you, Lori. Whatever kind of trouble you're in, I'm not here to judge you. I'm here to help.'

'OK,' I whisper.

'So, I'm your lawyer, and you're my client. Agreed?'

'Yes,' I agree. 'So what have the police told you?'

She hesitates and I can tell she is composing herself, forcing herself to sound calm and professional. I can tell that – as my friend rather than my lawyer – she is still struggling to understand whatever it is she thinks I've done. 'They're saying you've abducted someone's baby,' she says, and we can both hear how crazy it sounds. 'A baby belonging to someone you met the summer before you left England. They're saying you took this baby out of his bedroom and ran away with him – that this is the real reason you left the UK.'

'What else?'

'They're saying that it's some kind of surrogacy agreement gone wrong,' she says, sounding baffled. 'That this person – this woman – was a surrogate for you and that you took the baby because she wouldn't hand him over.'

I listen in silence, my pulse racing. So that's the story.

'Which makes zero sense, of course,' Anna says.

I clear my throat. 'Anything else?'

'That's all I know. But I can find out more.'

'Yes,' I say. 'Find out what you can.'

'OK. I will.'

There's a pause. I'm finding it difficult to breathe.

'Lauren,' she says, her voice sounding choked. 'They said the missing child is called Sam.'

Another pause. 'He's *my* son, Anna,' I say at last.

'But . . . how?'

I force a smile and wave to Blanca, who is now walking up the path to the cabin. 'Someone's here,' I say. 'I'm going to have to go.'

'OK,' Anna says quickly. 'I'll ask Sarah to call you, shall I?'

'Sarah?'

'My lawyer friend. She'll be able to help you. She'll advise you on what to do next.'

3

It's Monday morning and Gabe has been up to visit us for a long weekend. Today he's going home. It's still early and we're drinking coffee on the terrace. I've taken to drinking mine black – the Spanish way – because the milk from Blanca's goats is unfortunately not to my taste. Gabe has his usual espresso and we are gazing out across the valley. The sun is coming up behind the mountains, an exquisite orange globe shimmering against a backdrop of pale blues, pinks and whites. The spectacle is breathtaking and we are both sitting in silence, taking it in. Gabe hasn't even left yet, but already I realise how much I'm going to miss him. A month ago, two weeks ago, even, I would have told myself that the tightness in my lungs is because of the altitude, but I know it's more than that. I know that when Gabe gets up, leaving a space between the cushions on the bench next to me, I will look at that space all week and I will imagine him still sitting there, and I will think about the incredible weekend we have just had.

When he arrived on Friday afternoon, he'd brought ice cream for Sam and seafood – lobster, clams and shrimp – for me, in a giant icebox packed with a ton of ice. We'd chatted and played board games with Sam outside on the patio. Later, when Sam had gone to bed, we'd eaten the seafood with spaghetti and cold glasses of Verdejo Rueda, the dry but fruity white wine that Gabe knows I have come to love. On Saturday morning, we'd lounged around in the sunshine again, watching Sam 'hunting' at the edge of the terrace – collecting small rocks and pulling up tufts of grass 'to make a bed for Luna'. We trekked up the hills a little in the afternoon. And then yesterday, we packed lemonade, sandwiches and coffee and drove the fifteen miles or so down into the valley to the Baño de Pinares, a beautiful swimming lake surrounded by pine trees and bordered by a stretch of stone and shingle and a small strip of soft white sand. The lake was stunning: a deep emerald green in the centre, with shades of turquoise and cobalt blue at the shallow edges. We'd paddled, Sam in the middle and Gabe and me either side of him, holding his hand. We'd swung him up in the air before splashing him down into the water and he'd squealed with excitement and begged us to do it again and again.

Gabe and I had then taken it in turns to swim out into deeper waters while the other one sat on the rippling shore with Sam. We'd placed a blanket over the hot stones and stretched out in the sunshine to drink our lemonade and eat our sandwiches. As we did so, I had taken Sam through the alphabet.

'A, B, C,' he'd begun and continued well. When we got to Q, he'd paused.

'What's after Q?' I'd asked him.

'Cumber,' he'd said, and Gabe and I had both laughed out loud. Sam had joined in, even though he didn't understand the joke, and we had all fallen about on the blanket, Gabe and I alternately hugging and tickling him.

Sam had refused to take a nap on the journey home, even though he was exhausted and his eyes kept closing. Gabe pointed out chamois, grouse and vultures and we swivelled our heads to gaze at these magnificent creatures as they stood stock-still like sentinels along the mountain path. Gabe and I had eventually fallen silent, grinning and exchanging knowing glances as we looked in the rear-view mirror at Sam, who was repeatedly nodding off in his car seat and then forcing himself awake a few seconds later, desperate not to miss a thing.

'It was a lovely day yesterday,' says Gabe now, reading my thoughts. 'It was a lovely weekend. I will treasure it.'

'Me too,' I say. There is emotion in my voice, and he hears it and glances at me sideways. I clear my throat. 'Sam had such a lovely time,' I add. 'It was so good for him to have you there. He's so fond of you.'

Gabe nods and says gently, 'And I of him.' He continues to look at me and I know something bad is coming. 'Lauren, I didn't want to tell you this,' he says. 'I didn't want to spoil the weekend. But I need to let you know that there have been people in our street this past week asking questions about you.'

I feel my heartbeat quicken, but I try not to show it. 'What people?'

'Two men in a car.'

'The police?'

'The police have been back too, yes, making inquiries. But I think these men are private investigators. One just sits in the car watching, watching, always watching.' He shakes his head ruefully. 'And the other one has been knocking on the doors of all the houses along Carrer Mirador del Codolar. I think they have also been to La Roca, asking questions of the manager there and probably the other servers too.'

'Are these people Spanish?'

He nods. 'From Barcelona, I think.' He looks at me awkwardly. 'They've talked to everyone in the street, me included. I didn't want to refuse in case it looked suspicious. The other man came on Thursday to my apartment.'

'And what did you tell him.'

'Nothing. I said nothing. I said I didn't know where you were, of course. But I don't think he believed me. Several of the neighbours noticed that we were friends, and so they have been interrogating me too.'

I sigh. 'And if these men have been to La Roca, no doubt Javi will have told them I left in a hurry without asking for my wages or giving notice on the apartment.'

'I expect so,' he says, looking sorry. 'I had to be very

careful to make sure I wasn't being followed when I left to come here on Friday morning.'

My heart skips a beat. 'Are you sure you weren't?'

'I'm sure.' He smiles at me reassuringly. 'Don't worry. Nobody knows about the cabin. I think you know that I only moved to Mantilla from Huesca two years ago and, like you, I have pretty much kept myself to myself. I don't talk about my family to strangers and nobody in Mantilla knows my grandparents.'

'You didn't tell me about the cabin either,' I agree.

'I think you would say that I talk about it on a "need-to-know basis".' His eyes twinkle as he says this and we share a smile. This was one of the first phrases I ever taught him.

'Thank you, Gabe,' I say. 'Thank you for helping me.'

He shrugs. 'It's nothing.'

I shake my head. 'It's definitely not nothing.'

Gabe looks pensive for a moment and then gazes down into his lap as he says, 'I did it for selfish reasons. I knew I was never going to see you again.'

I feel my pulse quicken. I glance sideways at him, but he doesn't look up. We fall into silence. I think about all the things I could say to put a stop to the direction this conversation has taken. *Look at the sky. The clouds are pink. Isn't that beautiful? It's time I went to check on Sam. You've got a long journey ahead – would you like some more coffee?* But I don't say anything.

Gabe continues to look into his lap, his fingers laced

loosely around his coffee cup. 'As soon as the police left your apartment that night, I knew you had already decided that you had to leave Mantilla. I heard you telling them that you would come into the police station to talk to them, but I knew you wouldn't.' He stops and swallows hard. 'I didn't know if there was any truth to what they were saying – what they were accusing you of – but I know, too, that you are a good person. I've watched Sam growing from a baby into a perfect little boy and I know what an amazing mother you are to him. I wanted to help you. But I did it for myself too, because I can't lose you.'

My eyes swim with tears and I blink them away.

'I had a son,' he continues. 'He was beautiful. So gentle and kind and funny. He was just like Sam. But he had cancer. *De la sangre*.'

'Leukaemia,' I say.

'Yes. Leukaemia. I lost him when he was just one year old.'

'Gabe,' I say, reaching out and taking his hand in mine. 'I'm so, so sorry.'

He smiles and grips my fingers, his eyes shimmering. 'He was the same age as Sam was when I first met him, you know? But it was too much heartbreak for my wife and me. It tore my marriage apart. She left and . . .' He hesitates. 'And I know that in some way, through you and Sam, I am probably trying to get back what I lost. I'm not so blind that I can't see that.' He turns his wet eyes to meet mine. 'But when we met, I also felt this . . . this *connection* between us.' He pulls his hand from mine, places his empty coffee cup on the bench beside him and taps his chest with his fist. 'It's as if – without words – you knew my pain. And I knew yours. And we offered each other comfort. Without words, you know?'

I nod. 'I know.'

'That's how it felt to me. And Lauren, you still don't have to tell me anything. I promise. I'm not asking for that. But if you want to. If you ever feel you want to talk—'

'I went through something similar,' I interrupt him, blurting it out before I have time to stop myself. 'I think that's why we connected.'

Gabe waits for me to continue. When I don't, he speaks for me. 'But you still love Sam's father, don't you?'

I can't answer him. Instead, I look up at him and ask, 'Do you still love your wife?'

'I did. Until I met you,' he says simply.

Again, I find myself unable to say anything.

'It's OK. I understand. I don't expect anything from you, Lauren.'

I sigh. 'It's just that—'

'It's OK,' he interrupts me gently, reassuringly. 'I told you, you don't have to explain. I've had a perfect weekend. I couldn't ask for more. I'm not asking for more.' He smiles. 'And now, we must leave it like that.'

After he has driven away, I stand outside on the gravel path, feeling the wave of emotion flooding through me, just as I knew it would. I go inside and creep into the bedroom, where Sam is still sleeping soundly, peacefully. He loves it here in the mountains with Blanca and Luna and I can't bear the thought of disrupting him yet again, but he needs to be around other people, to play with other children, to have a normal life. A shiver of guilt runs through me as I think: *He needs to be near doctors and hospitals*. I also know that I can't continue to put Gabe at risk like this. I don't know anything about Spanish law, but harbouring an offender must be a serious crime.

I lean down and kiss Sam on his sweet, damp forehead, stroking back locks of his golden hair, then I go into the kitchen, where I close the door and reach for my phone. I sit down at the table and scroll down through my recent contacts. There aren't many, of course.

She picks up on the second ring. 'Sarah Kellerman speaking.'

'Hi, Sarah. It's Lauren Hopwood. We spoke last week.'

'Lauren. Good to hear from you.' Her voice is low and reassuring.

'We agreed I would have a think about my situation and that you would then make a few enquiries.'

'Yes, I remember.'

'Well, I've thought about it and I'd like you to make those enquiries.'

She hesitates. 'OK. But, as I mentioned, it will start the ball rolling. I'd have to tell the police we've spoken, that you've asked me to represent you and that you are looking to hand yourself in.'

I take a long, deep breath. 'Yes. I'm aware of that.'

'OK,' she says. 'If you're sure that you're ready to do this.'

I shrug. 'Not really. But I don't think I have any choice, do I?'

There's a pause on the line, and then she says, 'We always have a choice, Lauren. But, for what it's worth, I think this is the right one.'

4

The thunderstorm breaks at around two in the afternoon.

It's July and hot, even in the mountains, and Sam and I have been feeling languid and lazy. We are sitting at the window of our cabin, watching the downpour. The relief from the heat is welcome, but I'm thinking about Gabe, who is on his way to us today, the rain pelting down on his car. I hope the journey is not too treacherous. Maybe he will be forced to stop in Lleida or Huesca and wait for it to pass.

There is a crackle of lightning followed by a loud explosion like gunfire from behind the mountains.

'Thunder, Mummy,' Sam says, his face lighting up with pleasure. 'That's thunder.'

'It is, Sam,' I say, smiling. 'Isn't it incredible that the sky can do that?'

'The sky is . . . bang, bang, bang,' he says, clapping his hands together in excitement, and it pleases me that he has had the experience of living so close to nature like this. He isn't a bit afraid.

The storm passes and we are still sitting at the window when my phone rings. I snatch it up quickly, expecting it to be Gabe, hoping he's OK. But instead it's Sarah Kellerman. My stomach twists a little. It's the other call I've been expecting. I give Sam a hug and get up, picking up his colouring book and helping him climb into his seat at the kitchen table. I push some crayons towards him and pick up my phone, pushing back the slider.

'Hello?'

'Hi, Lauren,' Sarah says. 'Are you able to talk?'

'Yes. Definitely.' I glance at Sam and then move out of the kitchen and onto the terrace. I stand in the doorway, out of Sam's earshot, eyeing the puddles of rainwater that have pooled on the patio underneath the cracks in the veranda above. I suck in my breath, preparing myself for what's coming next.

'So, I've talked to a detective from the Child Protection team at Wyebridge Police Station,' Sarah informs me, 'and they said the case has been handed over to the Major Crime Unit. They won't confirm or deny this, but I suspect they have an arrest warrant for you. If they do, it means they have enough evidence to charge you with an offence. Again, they haven't said what the charges might be, but I've managed to get a little more information from the detective at the MCU.'

I take a deep breath. 'OK.'

'The child was reported missing by his mother in early January of 2023. It seems the police have made inquiries

35

with both the birth registry and the maternity unit at the Woodley Ridge Hospital in Wyebridge, and they are confident that she gave birth there to a baby boy called Samuel on the fourteenth of February 2022. Valentine's Day.'

She pauses and I close my eyes. 'Go on,' I say.

'The records at the maternity unit show that the baby was given the surname Dunsmore-Faris, and this is also the name registered on the birth certificate, along with the names of both Hope Dunsmore and Andrew Faris, who are registered as his parents. The police are now looking into the authenticity of the birth certificate you showed to the Spanish police. I understand this related to a male child also named Samuel but with your surname – Hopwood – and a different date of birth. The date of birth was six weeks earlier, which means that if the certificate is genuine, Samuel Hopwood would be six weeks older than Samuel Dunsmore-Faris.' She pauses again, giving me a chance to confirm or deny this. Again, I wait.

'The police are looking into the claim made by the Dunsmore-Farises that there was a surrogacy agreement between the three of you, because they don't see how – if you only met Hope Dunsmore in May of 2022, as she told them – there would have been sufficient time for that to have happened. They are saying that you would have had to have met her at least a year before then for her pregnancy to have been a surrogacy. So, they want to know how you really met and what the agreement really was between you.'

'So why don't the police ask them?'

'They have done. So far, the Farises have been vague about

everything. The police now believe that something more worrying went on between you all and that the Farises are trying to hide it. The police seem to think you may have met them in the neonatal intensive care unit at the Woodley Ridge Hospital and that an arrangement was made there, *after* he was born, in which they agreed to sell you their baby. They haven't told me this directly, but I get the impression they think the Farises were in some kind of financial difficulty.'

My heart flutters. 'So they could get arrested and interviewed too?'

'It's possible. Giving your child away after birth to anyone but family is basically adoption. However, it's illegal if it isn't done through a regulated adoption agency. The police are confident that no adoption or parental order was made by a court. So, whatever the agreement between the three of you, it seems the Farises remain the legal parents, which means that if you have their child, there has been an abduction. And so their primary focus is on finding the missing child. You are the named suspect for this and you are therefore the focus of their investigation, but . . .' Sarah hesitates. 'They are also worried about the potential for this to be a wider adoption fraud or scam. Anna and I have been looking into this together. There has been an increasing prevalence of "predatory" adoptions, both in the UK and abroad.'

I feel my gut twist. 'You mean . . .?'

'Pregnant women being kidnapped, coerced or forced into giving away their babies.'

I grab hold of the door frame to stop myself from falling.

'Either way, the penalties are severe,' she says.

My heart is thumping. 'How severe?'

She hesitates. 'We're talking up to seven years in prison for child abduction. More for trafficking.'

'Trafficking!' I cry out. 'Human trafficking?'

'I'm sorry, Lauren,' she says. 'I don't want to alarm you. I'm just looking at all the scenarios that could play out. Children are increasingly being trafficked and sold for adoption. The police may not be going down this route, but they are definitely holding something back. That's what they do,' she says. 'We'll find out at court or at the police station. And that's where I come in. I'm used to dealing with them. I can help you. When you and I are sitting in the same room together and I have had disclosure of everything they are willing to give me, then we can talk.'

I close my eyes. 'So how does it work, then, me handing myself in?'

'Well, if they have an arrest warrant – it's called a TaCA warrant – this means that the Spanish police can arrest you if they find you or if you turn up at the police station there. But unless you agree to it, they won't be able to formally extradite you to the UK. Your case would have to go to court first, and in the meantime you would, in all likelihood, be held in a Spanish prison and Sam would go into foster care. You could be held there for months. The other option – the better option – is that you come back to the UK voluntarily. I can represent you here.'

I feel my heart flutter. 'And if I bring Sam back with me?'

She hesitates. 'At this point it's hard to say, especially if the Farises are also under suspicion. Social services will have been contacted for sure, and there will be a safeguarding and child protection plan in place. He could go back to his parents, or a family member if there is someone suitable, but equally he may go into foster care.'

I force myself to breathe deeply, then step back into the kitchen to check on Sam. He's still sitting at the kitchen table, humming to himself and clutching a crayon, his head bent over a picture of Bob the Builder, who is covered in purple scribbles. I step back out through the open door onto the terrace and lower my voice. 'If I get a flight back to the UK, will the Spanish police find out and try to stop me?'

'They could, but they won't. If you make it as far as the airport, they're not going to bother. Both forces will know it's easiest if you get back to the UK under your own steam, because as soon you land back on British soil the whole problem of extraditing you goes away and the usual British rules of arrest apply. As you go through advance passenger information at the airport in Spain, it will trigger a notification to the UK police and they'll come to the airport. You'll be arrested on your arrival. If you come into Heathrow or Luton, they'll take you to the police station there. If you let me know when you're flying and which airport you're flying into, I can be ready too.'

After the call ends, I go back and sit at the window in the kitchen. Mercifully, Sam carries on colouring at the table and doesn't notice that I'm pressing my palms into my eye sockets to quell the tears that are threatening to spill out. As I squeeze my eyes shut, I can hear him singing softly to himself: *'Bob the Builder! Can we fix it? Yes, we can!'* As I listen to his sweet, lispy little voice, a few tears escape and I'm overcome with relief when we hear the sound of a car engine outside.

'Gabe!' cries Sam, dropping his crayon, then sliding off his chair and racing to the door. I jump up and run after him. Outside, Gabe pulls up, gets out of the car and waves before going to the boot and opening it.

'Ice cream! Yeah?' Sam asks him, and Gabe and I laugh.

It's getting dark when I bring up the subject of my impending arrest with Gabe. Sam is asleep and we are out on the patio, Gabe with his espresso, me with my herb tea. The sweet scent of wild flowers lingers in the air, intensified by the earlier rain. As we sit in companiable silence, I consider how much I need to tell him. I still don't want to involve him in what I've done; for a year and a half I've tried so hard not to involve him. I've tried so hard to pretend to myself that I can recreate the life I lost – Gabe isn't the only one who's done that. But now I have an important decision to make, and I need his help.

'I need to go back to England,' I say finally.

Gabe turns to face me. Even without looking, I know his expression is one of surprise and sadness. He asks, 'For good?'

I sigh. 'I don't know. I really hope not. But the British police are looking for me and . . .' My voice cracks, but I force myself to go on. 'I need to go back and face the music.'

He nods. 'When you say "face the music", you're not talking about going dancing, are you?'

'No, I'm not,' I say. 'It's an expression. It means—'

'It's OK. I get it.' A flicker of a smile crosses his face and I realise he was just trying to lighten the situation. 'So, when will you go?' he asks, sombre now.

'As soon as possible. As soon as I can get a flight. I need to get to Girona airport.'

'And Sam?'

I take a deep breath. 'Well. This is the thing . . .'

Gabe stiffens beside me.

'I don't want to take him with me,' I say. 'I'll get arrested at the airport in England and I don't want him to see that. It will be traumatising for him, and besides, they'll take him from me. The police.' I feel my throat tighten. 'They'll take him away and put him in a room on his own with people he doesn't know, and then social services will come and he'll be put into foster care.'

'No. That can't happen,' Gabe says abruptly.

'But I don't know what else to do.' I hesitate. I need to be honest, or as close to honest as I can be. I need to give Gabe the full picture so that he will know the right thing to do. 'It may not be foster care,' I admit. 'There is a chance he will be placed with . . .' I pause again as I try to find the words. 'With a family who knows him. Who loves him.'

'What family?' Gabe sounds confused.

I hesitate, then drop my head in my palms. The lump in my throat tightens as I say, 'His mother. His birth mother. And his father.'

I don't want to look up. I don't want to witness Gabe's reaction, because if I see it reflected back at me, then it will be true.

Gabe is silent as he takes this in. Finally, he asks, 'Do they have a legal right to him?'

'Yes,' I whisper. I press my palms into my eye sockets until my vision goes blurry. Only then can I look up at him. 'Legally, yes, they have a right to him. But they have also done something very wrong. The police may not give him back to them. They may not let any of us have him. They may just put him into foster care with a family that doesn't know him, and he doesn't know them, and it will be a strange country that he won't remember, because all he's ever known is Spain. At least, that's all he will remember, and . . .'

I pause. My heart feels as though it will burst with sorrow, not just at the thought of being wrenched apart from Sam and how much I will miss him, but at the prospect of the sweet, kind, loving little boy who is sleeping inside being thrust into strange company with strange routines and strange people looking after him. I know he will be so frightened.

'I am the only person he knows well, the only person he is close to,' I continue.

'Apart from me.'

I wipe my tears away and gaze into his eyes. Gabe's expression is earnest.

He taps his chest. 'He knows *me*. He is close to *me*.'

'But, Gabe . . .'

Gabe frowns. 'You don't think he would be happy with me?'

I almost laugh. 'Of course he would be happy with you. But how can you look after him? You have your job and your life in Mantilla, and you can't go back there with him. How can you?'

'I have no life in Mantilla,' Gabe says. He looks at me, as though he is about to say something, then appears to change his mind. 'My life there is nothing,' he insists. 'It means nothing. I'll take some time off from my job and go to Huesca. I have family there – my sister and my aunt. They will love Sam. They will be glad to have him, I guarantee it. Between us, we will look after him until you can come back for him.'

I shake my head. 'But, Gabe, the police are looking for him. They will still be looking for him. You will be in trouble if they catch you – and so will your family.'

'Well, then, I will make quite sure they don't catch me. And as for my sister and my aunt, I will not tell them about Sam's parents or what you will do. They can't get in trouble for something they don't know.'

I continue to look at Gabe for a moment, my breath halted in my chest. It's dark now, and I can barely see his face. I can only see his outline next to me. I say, 'Think about it, Gabe. Think about what might happen to you if you're caught.'

He shrugs and says, 'I don't need to think about it.'

I let out the breath I've been holding in. 'You'd really do that? For me?'

'For you – and for Sam.' He hesitates, then adds, 'And for Deniel.'

Fresh tears spring to my eyes. 'Is that the name of your little boy?'

'Yes,' Gabe says, then adds, simply, 'He wants this.'

The lump in my throat is back. 'It's a beautiful name.'

'It's a variation of Daniel,' he says. 'It means "God is my judge".'

We fall silent again. Eventually, I reach out and my hand finds his. He pulls me closer and puts an arm round my shoulder. 'Don't worry, Lauren,' he says. 'I will look after Sam. Everything will be OK.'

And then before I know what's happening, I'm in his arms and I'm kissing him and it's suddenly everything I needed but didn't know I needed. I thought I would feel nothing but guilt if this ever happened between us, but I don't. All I feel is an intense, burning need to be close to him, as close as it's humanly possible to be to another person. He kisses my eyes and my neck and my mouth and I feel consumed with desire for him. 'Let's go inside,' I say.

'Lauren, are you sure this is what you want?' he asks softly.

My answer is to take him by the hand and lead the way.

5

I booked an early flight for the Monday. Gabe had wanted me to wait a week, but once I'd made up my mind, I had to go quickly. After what Sarah had told me, I wasn't going to wait for the police or anyone else to find me. I couldn't risk being locked up in Spain and Sam being handed over to strangers, nor could I bear to prolong the agony of playing with him and being his mummy and sleeping in Gabe's bed with him at night, not knowing how this was all going to end.

We set off at dawn on the Saturday morning and drove to Huesca, once again taking everything we owned. To Sam's delight, Gabe said that Luna the cat could come with us. She sat, meowing gently, in her cat box in the back of the car next to Sam while he reassured her.

'Be OK, Luna,' he said repeatedly. 'Be good cat. Yeah?'

Gabe's aunt – Lucía – and his sister – Marta – were welcoming. They lived together in a rural stone farmhouse on

the outskirts of the town. The house was clean and comfortable and there was a pretty garden with a yard backing onto
fields for Sam to run around in. I was intrigued to see how
alike Marta and Gabe were – they had the same dark curls
and sombre hazel eyes, and the same arched eyebrows and
mischievous expression when they were surprised or curious. They had the same warm smile, too, and I knew instantly
that Sam was going to be loved at this house. Gabe introduced me as a work colleague named Felicity Scott and said
that Sam and I were from Hong Kong. He'd told his aunt
and sister that I had to go back there to care for my elderly
mother who had a terminal illness and needed round-the-
clock care. I didn't want to take my son with me, he said. It
would be too tough for him.

Marta and Lucía didn't seem to care much about my reasons. They immediately fell for Sam, taking him for a tour
around the yard and showing him how to feed the chickens.
They crouched down with him, showing him how to let the
cat out of her box gently, explaining that they all needed to
keep her safely shut in the kitchen until she'd become accus-
tomed to her new home. Lucía didn't speak any English,
but Sam didn't seem to notice. He'd been around Spanish
children at the babysitter's house in Mantilla and seemed to
understand what she said.

On Sunday evening, after dinner, I told Sam that I was
leaving for a while. We got him ready for bed and then Gabe
and I sat with him in his new bedroom in the eaves, overlooking the farmyard. Sam listened distractedly as he moved

around the room in his pyjamas, picking up and playing with the books and toys Gabe's sister had owned as a child.

'Why going, Mummy?' he asked, even though I'd just told him. Sam liked to ask 'Why?' – it was his favourite word. It allowed a conversation to develop, even if he didn't have all the vocabulary he needed. He liked to keep us engaged. I tried to picture what kind of conversation I'd be having with him the next time I saw him, but I couldn't. It was impossible to imagine that I wouldn't see him tomorrow morning and the next day, and the day after that.

'Because I have to sort some things out,' I told him again, swallowing and blinking back tears. 'But Gabe is going to be here to look after you. And you'll have Lucía and Ana too.'

'And Luna!' he said happily.

'And Luna,' I smiled.

'And chickens,' he said.

'Yes, and the chickens. And when I come back, I'm going to bring you a present.'

His eyes widened. 'Why?'

'Because I love you.'

'Oh,' he said happily. 'I love . . .' He paused, thinking through his options. 'Presents,' he said, finally.

Gabe and I both laughed.

I left Huesca at midnight. Gabe had arranged for his friend Mani to lend us his car. The plan was for me to drive myself to Lleida, where I'd leave the car for Mani and Gabe to collect after dark the following night. From Lleida, I'd get the bus to the airport. We'd decided it was better this way – it would be safer not to have Gabe with me in case he was followed, and nicer for Sam that Gabe would be there when he woke up.

We said goodbye on the steps of the farmhouse. The moon was bright and cast a shard of light through the olive trees. I pressed my face into Gabe's shoulder and he put an arm around me, drawing me close.

'I love presents too,' he whispered softly, and I looked up to see his hazel eyes shining.

'I'll be sure to bring you one back,' I smiled, even though I knew what he'd meant.

'You don't need to worry about Sam,' he said. 'He will be happy and he will be safe here.'

I nodded. 'I know.' And then I got into the car and drove away.

And now here I am on the flight back to England. We've left the Pyrenees far behind, we've crossed France and the English Channel and it won't be long before we are circling over London, preparing to land at Heathrow. My face is numb against the cabin window, my entire body cold. I wonder who they will send, what the cops from the Major Crime Unit will look like. Will I get through security first? More likely, they'll be right there waiting for me as I step off the plane. Maybe they'll even come onto the plane. My stomach jolts at the thought. There will be an announcement and everyone will be prevented from leaving their seats while the police make their way down the aisles, looking from left to right and back again until they see me. I gaze around the cabin at my fellow travellers – all dozing, or reading, or politely standing up in the aisle to let the person in the middle seat next to them get up to go to the bathroom – and I imagine the shock and surprise on their faces as they watch me being handcuffed and escorted off the aeroplane, as they wonder what kind of a person they have been sitting in a locked cabin with, what terrible thing it is that I have done.

I can imagine it now, but I never imagined it before because I hadn't thought about it when I left England. I hadn't thought about how it would feel to be brought back and locked up and to have Sam taken away from me. It had been like a dream sequence, all of it: packing our bags and passports, locking up my house, carrying Sam, putting him in his car seat and driving straight to the airport. Holding him in my arms on the flight out to Spain and pressing my face against his milky, sleepy cheek.

'His dad's coming out to join us,' I'd said confidently to the woman in the seat next to me when she'd struck up a conversation. 'We're going out first to set things up, and then he'll join us when he has sorted out everything at home.'

I didn't think about anything else, really, except getting to Mantilla and finding a home for us, somewhere up high, overlooking the bay, somewhere just like 'our' place – the place we'd stayed the last time, the time when I'd found out

I was pregnant. We'd been so happy. So very happy. All I wanted was to go ahead with our plans.

But now . . . now it's time to stop pretending – although it's hard to do that when I barely even recognise the person I used to be. All I see when I look back is my empty house, my empty driveway and the winding road leading to *that* village – and a distant spectre of myself, stumbling around like a kid in a game of blind man's bluff as I tried to make sense of what had happened to me.

PART TWO

One Year Earlier

Transcript of 101 call to Thames Valley Police from Jessica Brierley on 8th July 2023

CRIS no: 1 76498266 77

Original Investigation: Child abduction

Original report date: 3rd January 2023

Times	Person speaking	Text
		File name: 7073993-T111860.848371.mp3 *Call duration: 8 minutes and 19 seconds*
10:07	Operator	Thames Valley Police. How can I help?
	JB	Hi. Erm. I'm calling about a missing baby.
	Operator	OK. And is it your baby that's missing?
	JB	No, no. It's my next-door neighbour's. (Pause.) I'm a bit worried about calling you, to be honest. I don't want to cause problems for them, but . . .
	Operator	OK. But you think their baby has gone missing?
	JB	He has. They already reported it. I just think it's . . . well, something's not right.
	Operator	OK, so when did the baby go missing?
	JB	Well. That's the thing. They reported him missing in January, but . . .
	Operator	January this year?
	JB	Yes. But I haven't seen him since last September, and neither of us . . . my husband (inaudible) . . . seen him since September. Last September.

	Operator	OK, and what's the baby's name?
	JB	Sam. Samuel.
	Operator	And what's his last name?
	JB	Dunsmore-Faris.
10:08	Operator	Can you spell it for me, please?
	JB	D-u-n-s-m-o-r-e (pause) hyphen F-a-r-i-s.
	Operator	Thank you. Bear with me for one moment. OK. First name, Sam?
	JB	Yes. Samuel.
	Operator	And how old is Samuel?
	JB	Well, he was born in . . . erm . . . February. Last year. So he would be . . . erm (muffled sound) seventeen months old now?
	Operator	And you're calling because . . .
	JB	Because I'm worried. Something strange has been going on next door and . . . and I just felt I should tell you.
	Operator	OK, and is this the first time you've called us about this?
	JB	Yes. The police spoke to me on the night he went missing. Well, the night Hope said he went missing. She said she went into the bedroom and his cot was empty. So, the police did, like . . . house-to-house inquiries in the village and so they spoke to us then.
10:09	Operator	OK, so the baby's not in any immediate danger?
	JB	No. Well. (Pause.) I don't know, do I?
	Operator	OK, but you haven't seen him since . . .
	JB	Since last September.
	Operator	OK. I just need to take a few details, please? What's your name?
	JB	Jess. Jessica. Brierley.
	Operator	Can you spell that for me, please?

	JB	B-R-I-E-R-L-E-Y
	Operator	We've got a mobile number ending in 6375 which is the one you're calling from.
	JB	Yes.
	Operator	And can I take your address?
	JB	It's Rook Cottage, Chorley Common.
	Operator	Is there a house number?
	JB	No. It's . . . there are only four houses on our road.
	Operator	And your neighbours live next door, you say?
	JB	Yes. To our right. Their cottage is . . . Flint. (Clears throat.) Flint Cottage.
	Operator	OK. And what are your neighbours' names?
10:10	JB	Hope. Hope Dunsmore.
	Operator	And she's the baby's mother?
	JB	Yes. Well. (Pause.) Yes.
	Operator	And who else lives there?
	JB	Drew. Her husband. His name's Andrew, but everyone calls him Drew.
	Operator	And is he the baby's father?
	JB	Yes.
	Operator	And what's his surname?
	JB	Faris. F-a-r-i-s.
	Operator	Anyone else living there?
	JB	No.
	Operator	And you mentioned your husband? What's his name?

	JB	Erm. (Pause.) It's Nick. Brierley. (Pause.) Look . . . does this have to go on record? Nick didn't want me to call you. Hope and Drew are our friends. Well, they were. It's all been a bit . . . strained since this happened. But we live right next to them and I don't want to get anyone into any trouble. It's just that they told us . . . well, they said some things that don't really fit.
	Operator	OK. What did they tell you?
10:11	JB	Well, like I said, we didn't see their baby . . . Sam . . . for quite a while. I used to look after him for Hope whenever she had a client . . . she's a psychotherapist and I'm an osteopath and so we both (inaudible) . . . and I looked after Sam for her when she was working. And then I saw him in, I think, September, and then I never saw him again after that. When I saw her outside, she never had him with her. And when I asked her where he was, she told me . . . well (pause), what she told me didn't make any sense. First of all she said he was back in hospital. He was premature, and he was in hospital after he was born, in the NICU (inaudible) heart problems . . . and so I believed her at first . . .
	Operator	That he was in hospital?
	JB	Yes, but then it was like . . . well, it was like they were avoiding us and . . . and then on Boxing Day . . . we always used to get together on Boxing Day for drinks, that was kind of our . . . tradition, I don't know. But this Christmas – the one just gone – it was their turn and they didn't invite us. I thought Sam was in hospital because that's what Hope told me, but . . . but then I saw Hope outside her house. On Boxing Day. She looked . . . distraught. Completely . . . devastated. And I honestly thought . . . well, I thought Sam had died.
10:12	Operator	You thought he had died?

	JB	Well, yes. That was the first thought that crossed my mind. I mean, she looked so completely . . . broken. You know? Drew's car wasn't there, and so I grabbed a bottle of brandy from my cupboard and I went over and knocked on the door and I insisted that she talk to me, and so we went into the kitchen and I poured her a drink and Hope broke down in tears and told me that Sam wasn't her baby. She said she'd been a surrogate for another woman and that she had handed Sam over and . . . and I couldn't believe what I was hearing, because . . . Hope has wanted to be a mother for such a long time and so I couldn't believe she would agree to be a surrogate for someone else. It just didn't make any sense.
	Operator	Did you ask her to explain?
10:13	JB	Yes, but she just insisted that was what had happened, so I didn't really have any choice but to believe her. But I didn't, not really, and then in January she reported him missing. And so it just doesn't add up. How can he have gone missing suddenly in January if she had already given him away?
	Operator	OK. Well, I think I need to get someone from Child Protection round to see you, Jess. Is that OK?
	JB	(Sighs.) I'm not sure. (Long pause.)
	Operator	Jess? Are you still there?
	JB	(More sighing.) I'm sorry. No. Please tell them not to come round. Hope will see their car. Look, Hope's my friend and even though things are awkward between us I really care about her. I don't want to make a statement. I don't want to get her into any trouble.
	Operator	Why do you think she would be in trouble?
	JB	I don't know. I just don't want to say anything that could hurt her. I'm just worried about her. And about Sam.
	Operator	OK.

	JB	(Pause.) Look, I really shouldn't tell you this, and please, can this not go on record, but . . . there's something else.
10:14	Operator	OK. Go on.
	JB	Well, Hope says it was a woman called Lauren who took Sam and that she was being stalked by her. And that's true, but . . .
	Operator	OK. OK. So . . .
	JB	Well, I can't actually prove it, but this all started after Drew had an affair.
	Operator	He had an affair?
	JB	Yes.
	Operator	With Lauren?
	JB	I think so, yes. Although she said her name was Anna.
	Operator	Anna?
	JB	Yes. Anna Wall.
	Operator	Wall?
	JB	Yes. As in a brick wall.
	Operator	OK, that's fine, Jess. I've made a note of all this and I'm going to liaise with the Child Protection Unit and I will provide them with all the details and I'm going to request that they give you a call. Is that OK?
	JB	(Pause.) OK.
	Operator	Just a call so you can tell them what you told me. Is that OK?
	JB	(Pause.) OK.
10:15	Operator	Listen. Thanks ever so much for ringing in.
	JB	No problem.
		Call ends.

6

Hope

I'm coming down the stairs when I hear the knock at the front door. Drew appears in the kitchen doorway, looking pale and flustered. He makes a frightened face at me, then steps forward resolutely and slides back the latch. I see them straight away: Jazmin and Sally, the two detectives from the Child Protection team in Wyebridge who were assigned to Sam's case after I reported him missing in January. Initially they were in and out of our house regularly, gathering information and giving us updates, but we've heard nothing for ages. I pause on the step and grab the banister.

'Hello, Hope.' Jazmin speaks first, her eyes landing on mine.

'Is it Sam?' I ask immediately, my voice coming out high-pitched and breathless. 'Have you found him?'

'Can we come inside?' says Sally soothingly, and I know straight away that they haven't – or that if they have, it isn't going to be good news. I start to cry. I'm not sure I can take it, whatever it is they've come to tell us.

'Hope . . .'

'Have you found him?' I cry out again.

Drew stiffens at the foot of the stairs and shoots me a look that tells me I need to get a grip.

I clutch the banister tighter. My legs have turned to mush and so I stay where I am while Drew ushers the officers inside, closes the front door and leads them the few short steps into the living room. He comes back for me then, and says, under his breath, 'You need to stay calm.' I allow him to take my hand and lead me into the front room, where Sally and Jazmin are seated in our wingback armchairs. Drew and I take the sofa.

'Have you found him?' I ask for a third time.

'I'm sorry, no,' says Jazmin. 'We don't think he's in the UK.'

The room spins. 'What do you mean?'

'We think Lauren has left the country. We're going to liaise with Interpol and ask for an international alert to be issued.'

'No!' I cry out. 'She's taken him abroad? How could she even do that? He doesn't have a passport!'

Jazmin and Sally exchange glances.

'He's vulnerable. He has a heart condition,' I remind them, trying not to cry again. 'He spent the first three months of his life in intensive care.'

Jazmin looks interested. 'Let's talk about that, shall we?'

'So this was the neonatal intensive care unit at the Wood-ley Ridge Hospital? Is that right?' asks Sally.

'Yes. He was born prematurely. He was tiny. Only three pounds and two ounces. They had to intubate him. He had a hole in his heart because it hadn't finished developing. He nearly died.'

I pause, feeling Drew's foot pressing against mine. I look back and forth from Jazmin to Sally, who are exchanging glances again.

'What?' I ask. 'What is it?'

I can hear an edge in Jazmin's voice as she asks, 'And is that where you first met Lauren? At the hospital? At Woodley Ridge?'

My stomach seizes.

'Hang on,' says Drew. 'Is Hope in some kind of trouble here? Do we need a lawyer?'

'No,' says Jazmin. 'It's nothing like that. We're just trying to bottom a few things out.'

I take a breath. 'I already told you,' I say. 'I'm a therapist. Lauren came to me for counselling because she'd lost a baby. Her marriage had broken down and . . . you can ask Jess,' I say eagerly. 'My next-door neighbour. She met Lauren first. She was the one who asked me to take her on as a client.' I pause as Drew's foot presses harder up against mine and I shoot him a face that tells him to stop.

There is a pause. Sally has a pen poised over a notebook. Jazmin leans forward. 'Actually, we *have* spoken to Jess.'

My heart bumps. 'When?'

She doesn't answer my question. Instead, she sits there in silence for a moment or two, looking a little sorry for me, as if she wishes she didn't have to say what she is about to say. 'Jess told us that the last time she saw Sam was in early September 2022, almost four months before you reported him missing.'

The room falls silent. I feel Drew's hand take hold of mine and squeeze it. He looks at me with a tight expression. I know what it means. It means: 'Watch what you say'.

'Like I said, he had a heart condition,' I say. 'He was back in hospital.' But my own heart is thumping now.

Drew is sitting very still on the couch next to me. Sally is still, too, pen poised over her notebook. The clock in the hall-way chimes four and a kite screams from the back garden. Jazmin turns her head towards the window, letting it rest there for a moment, and then shoots me a pitying half-smile.

'OK,' she continues. 'Well, we can check the hospital records, of course.'

Drew shifts beside me. 'You said this wasn't an investigation.'

'And it doesn't need to be,' Jazmin says. 'We're not here to try and trip you up. But we do want to understand why you didn't report your son missing immediately.'

She looks me hard in the eye, but I feel Drew put his hand over mine again, warning me not to speak.

Jazmin waits for a beat, watching our faces. 'Jess saw you at Christmas, Hope. You told her that you didn't have Sam any longer, that you'd been a surrogate for another woman and had handed him over, but that you now bitterly regretted it and wanted him back. Is that true?'

The room falls silent again. I am furious with Jess. I am

ready to tell the officers that she's got it wrong, that I'd made it all up, but before I can say anything, Drew jumps in.

'Yes,' he says. 'Hope's sorry for lying to you. We're both sorry. Hope *was* a surrogate for Lauren.'

'So Hope carried a baby for Lauren?'

'Yes.'

'And who is the biological mother?'

Her question floors me. I open my mouth to answer, but I'm too slow. Drew gets there first. 'Lauren.'

'And who is the biological father?'

'Me. My sperm. Her egg.' Drew pauses, halted by my expression as I turn to face him. For a split second, I think I'm going to be sick. I want to say something to stop him, to stop the way this conversation is going, but my heart, my mind . . . everything is in turmoil. How could he? How could he tell them this?

'So, you used a fertility clinic? To implant the embryo? Yours and Lauren's embryo?'

Drew hesitates. 'Yes.'

Jazmin nods. 'And after he was born, you changed your minds about handing him over?'

'Yes.'

'So Lauren came and took him? Is that what you're saying?'

'Yes,' Drew says again.

'OK. So why wait to report him missing?' Jazmin presses him.

Drew hesitates and I have the chance to say something, but my mind has frozen.

Jazmin is talking. 'Look, as I'm sure you know, surrogacy isn't illegal in this country, and although it's against the law to advertise, or for a third party to profit financially, it's not actually illegal for money to change hands between the surrogate and the intended parents. That's a common misconception. It's just something the family court will take into account when making a parental order. So that's not what we're here for. We just want to understand the true situation. Because unless there was a parental order made by the court—'

'There wasn't,' Drew cuts in.

'Then, legally, you're still his parents. No matter whose child he is biologically, the law in this country says that the baby belongs to the surrogate unless and until a parental order is made. We're just trying to establish the exact circumstances behind his disappearance, and that means understanding what kind of arrangement was made between yourselves and Lauren, and why the baby wasn't handed over at birth.'

Drew takes a deep breath. 'Like Hope said, he was ill and then by the time he left hospital we'd bonded with him.'

'So why not tell us the truth about when he went missing?'

'He hadn't gone missing,' Drew says. 'Not exactly. Lauren had him, but we were trying to reason with her.'

'So you handed him over and then changed your mind, is that it?'

'No,' I say angrily. 'That's not what happened! She took him. She took him from our house and refused to give him back. And that's abduction, right?'

Sally looks at me kindly. 'But why didn't you tell us all this the first time, Hope?'

'Because I was afraid you wouldn't take it seriously,' I say. 'That you wouldn't look for them hard enough. Sam's *my* baby.' A sob rips through me and tears spill out of my eyes and stream down my cheeks. 'He's mine!' I let out a low groan as I wipe a stream of snot from my nose. 'I *love* him!' I sob. 'And I need him back!'

Drew's hand is on mine again, but I yank it away. Jazmin's expression has softened. Sally, too, looks distressed. 'Hope, we understand,' she says, leaning forward, 'and we are going to do everything we can to find him. Like you said, Sam lived with you, and now he's not here, and in the absence of a parental order, *you* are his legal parents. But we need you to be straight with us from now on. OK? And we are going to need to ask you more questions about the surrogacy arrangement, how you met Lauren, the fertility clinic you used, things like that. Don't worry, we're not interested in the legality of the arrangement itself,' she adds. 'We're interested in finding Sam. But we have to ask the questions. So you might want to speak to a lawyer for that.'

After they've gone, Drew comes back and sits down beside me. Neither of us speaks. A moment later, he gets up again and leaves the room. I can hear him moving around in the kitchen and I know he is pulling the stopper out of the wine bottle on the worktop and pouring us each a glass.

'Here,' he says, coming back in and handing me mine. I

take it. I am so angry. I need to be numb. Drew sets his glass down on the coffee table and sinks down onto his knees on the floor beside me. 'It's going to be OK,' he says gently, reaching a hand out towards me.

'Don't touch me!' I scream at him, and he recoils quickly. 'How could you?' I snap. 'How could you tell them I'm not Sam's natural mother?'

'Because Lauren's going to talk, Hope! Because they're going to find her—'

'Good!' I cry out. 'I *want* them to find her!'

'Do you?' he asks. 'Do you really? Because when they do, and they've backed her into a corner and taken Sam into their custody, she's going to *talk*.'

I shake my head, a sob catching in my throat again. 'I don't care! I just want my baby back.'

Drew inhales deeply and his eyes pierce mine. 'But, Hope, don't you realise what's going to happen . . .'

'I don't care!' I swing an arm at him.

He grabs hold of my wrist. 'Hope . . .'

I yank hard and he lets me go.

I mimic him. '*When they come back, let me do the talking.*'

'Because you *lied* to them, Hope. When you spoke to those two cops about what happened that day . . . the day Sam was born . . .' He swallows hard. 'You lied to them, and I told you it was going to come back to bite us. I told you to let me find her, not the police.'

'But you didn't find her, did you?' I scream at him. 'You were nowhere near finding her!'

'My PI—'

'Your PI?' I sneer, taking a large gulp of wine. 'Your PI is completely useless!'

'That's not exactly true. He had leads.'

'Leads!' I snort. 'She's managed to leave the country, Drew! With our baby!'

Drew sighs. 'Even so, Hope. You lied to the police and it tripped us up.'

'You're putting all this on me?'

'Of course not. I'm just explaining why I told them what I did, because—'

I slam my glass down against the tabletop. 'You're the one to blame here, Drew! *You're* the one who brought all this upon us.'

He turns his eyes up to meet mine. I can see the hurt there. 'Hope, I was only trying to look after you. To protect you. You know that!'

I shake my head vehemently. 'I'm talking about *before* that. You brought all this upon us the day you decided I wasn't enough for you, the day you decided to sneak around and sleep with another woman.'

'Hope,' Drew begs, a tear rolling down his cheek, 'how many times can I say I'm sorry? It's you I love; you know that. You and Sam. And we're going to find him. We're going to get him back.'

7

I turn over on my pillow and open my eyes, then reach out and look at the digital clock on the bedside table. It's eight o'clock. I must have turned my alarm off. Or did I even set it? I can't remember. I climb out of bed and peer out of the window. The driveway below is empty, the street beyond silent. Drew has left for work. I must have been sleeping really deeply not to hear the car. This road is so quiet that the only sounds you ever hear are the screams of the kites and foxes or the bark of a muntjac from the fields behind us, or the very occasional growl of a car engine – usually when one of us or one of our three sets of neighbours arrives home. The familiar knot of guilt and shame twists its way through my stomach as I glance across at the house next door. For months, I've avoided my next-door neighbour, Jess. Now, it seems, she's avoiding me too.

We live in Chorley Common, a small village in the Chiltern Hills in Buckinghamshire, about six miles north-west of

Wyebridge, the nearest town, and a few miles from the border with Oxfordshire. The village has just two roads in and out which meet at a crossroads, with a third that turns into a bridleway leading uphill to a farm. There's a church and a village hall and a riding stables and a smattering of around twenty houses – not enough inhabitants to sustain a pub or a school. Without the church and the village hall, it would be a hamlet, a mere settlement on the roadside.

I never thought I'd ever live anywhere this quiet, but when Drew and I first saw the cottage – on a foggy October day, looking all misty and mystical like something straight out of *Midsomer Murders* – we fell straight under its spell. We were under pressure to find somewhere to buy, having sold our house in St Albans and moved to Wyebridge when Drew got a fantastic new job opportunity as head of planning for one of the district councils in Oxfordshire. Our lease was up on our rental and we didn't want to renew it and be stuck there for another year. We came across the house by complete chance. We were on our way from Wyebridge to Oxford when we took a wrong turn. We passed the 'For Sale' sign and looked at each other, then Drew pulled over into a lay-by and we got out and walked back along the road to peer into the front garden at the pretty brick and stone cottage. ('Flint,' Drew said. 'From the Chiltern limestone. Unique to this part of the world.') There was no car on the driveway. Drew nudged me and I nudged him back. He laughed, opened the gate and we walked in.

'It's beautiful,' I said. 'How old do you think it is?'

'Mid-nineteenth century, I'd say. Let's knock,' said Drew.

'We can't do that,' I protested.

'What harm can it do?'

I shrugged. 'None, I suppose.'

We knocked. No one answered. So we stepped to the side of the porch and peered through the leaded windows into the living room.

'Ooooh. There's an inglenook fireplace,' I cooed happily. 'It's so gorgeous. And look at the doors!'

'Ledge and brace,' said Drew.

'Is that what they're called?'

'That's what they're called. I wonder if it's listed. Look, though,' Drew said, 'they've put an extension on the back. That's a pretty cool dining area. Bifold doors, by the look of things.'

'Imagine. Imagine eating there, looking out onto that garden.'

Drew gave me a sideways look, grinning. 'You're in love.' He stretched out the word.

'I am. I do love it,' I said. 'Do you?'

'It's got a lot of character.' Drew stepped to the side of the building, looking up and down, appraising the grounds and the plot behind. 'It's got a garage. And a good-sized rear garden. Three bedrooms, at a guess. And it's close enough to Oxford.' He pulled out his phone and did a quick search. It was well within our budget and when we phoned the estate agent we were told it was still for sale.

It was ours just two months later. We moved in just in

time for Christmas. We hung a holly wreath on the door and cooked a goose from the local farm in the range cooker and invited our new neighbours in for sherry on Boxing Day. And then we went upstairs and made a baby, our first baby, who we lost at three months.

And then we made our second baby, and then our third.

Sam was our fourth and it was a miracle when I kept him.

But then the nightmare started and we lost him too.

I know Drew and I are not the only ones to have suffered. I am profoundly alert to the agony Lauren must have lived through. Ironically, it was our shared experience that motivated me to help her; I just didn't know the true extent of what we'd shared at the time. I was winding down my practice and I wasn't taking on any new clients, but when our neighbour Jess told me about Lauren, I made an exception. Maybe on some unconscious level I thought that by saving her I could save us both. But, as a therapist, I should have known better; I was the last person on this planet who should have been counselling her, and I should have known that.

For over a year, we have survived, Drew and I, but it can't be called living. Drew went to work because he welcomed the distraction and because someone had to, but I could barely function. I closed down my practice and hung about the house all day in my pyjamas. I took pills and lay back on our big blue sofa, gazing up at the exposed oak beams on the ceiling as I waited for the desperation to leave me, for the sharp, jagged edges of what had happened to us to be sanded down and smoothed away. Drew and I stayed together, or at least we carried on living alongside each other. But the life we have been living has barely resembled a normal life, and maybe it never will again.

The thought grips my lungs so forcefully that I can't breathe for a moment. I grab hold of the windowsill and force myself to inhale and exhale deeply and steadily as I realise it's been there all along, lurking in the darkest corner of my mind: the truth that Drew has been trying to get me to confront. We have to find Lauren. We have to find her ourselves. Because there's a very good chance that unless we find her before the police do, we may never see Sam again.

I pull on my dressing gown and go downstairs into the kitchen. As I wait for the kettle to boil, I gaze out of the kitchen window at the empty branches of the apple tree in the front garden, the one we always used to hang the Christmas lights on, and I feel an urgent, intense tsunami of emotion so strong that it almost knocks me over. It's November already. If I go out, the shops will be full of tinsel and Santa-shaped chocolates. If I stay home, there will be reindeer pulling sleds and the sound of jingle bells on every advert on TV.

I can't go through another Christmas like the last one, with nothing to look forward to, nothing to live for.

I need to find Lauren. *We* need to find Lauren.

I need to do my homework, just as she did hers, about me.

I make tea, then sit down at the kitchen table with

my laptop and open up my therapy notes. There must be something she said, something she did, some clue to her whereabouts. I need to look back on everything that happened that summer. I need to remember every single thing I ever knew about her. There can be no more numbing of my pain with medication. It's time for me to remember.

PART THREE

Eighteen Months Earlier

8

Lauren

I found her online: Hope Dunsmore. Licensed practitioner and member of the UK Council for Psychotherapy. There was a photo, too, of an attractive, blonde-haired woman in her late thirties or early forties, a similar age to me. She had a full, pretty face with even features, big blue eyes and a welcoming smile. She looked like someone I could talk to.

Now, I'm in my car with the engine running. It's hot and I've switched on the air con and am waiting for it to kick in. I don't want to roll down the windows in case Joy, my next-door neighbour, comes out and talks to me, which will throw me completely. My palms are slippery with sweat against the steering wheel and I'm sick with fear, as though I'm about to drive off a cliff, but I want to do this. I *need* to do this. I need to drive to Chorley Common to see my therapist. Well . . . to see if she's home. To see if she'll be my therapist. She didn't pick up the phone.

My car engine revs a little as I accidentally nudge the accelerator. I look up to see that Joy has pulled back the net curtain and is peering out of the window. She looks about to say something and I pretend I haven't seen her, but it's the incentive I need. I put the car into gear, release the clutch, look over my shoulder and slowly, jerkily pull away. I'm shaking a little, but the air con has cooled the car and it's helping. I turn the corner and go at a slow twenty to the end of the road, before turning west onto the high street. Within minutes, I'm heading out of Stow and into the countryside on the Old Chiltern Road.

This is the hardest part, going through the jagged hills, seeing the trees jutting across the road, the hedgerows, the fields and, beyond them, the edge of the woodland. My heart begins to pound again, faster and faster. I want to slam on the brakes and pull over, but it's a country road and there's nowhere to stop. Besides, if I stop now, I'll never do this and I am desperate to do this. I need to take action.

Luckily, the turning for Chorley Common is not far up ahead and once I'm on the B-road my panic subsides a little. I drive along a narrow road, past a clump of houses, until I come to a crossroads. My satnav loses signal and so I make a guess and turn left, passing the village hall and ending up on a small lane that leads uphill. There's nothing beyond, so I turn round in the middle of the lane and go back towards the crossroads, then decide to pull over into the village hall car park, where I get out and continue along the road on foot. The sun is warm on my skin and the air is filled with the sweet scent of cowslips. I take deep breaths, feeling calmer. A dog walker gives me directions and a few minutes later I find myself on a narrow verge next to the road, looking into the front garden of a beautiful period cottage. *Flint Cottage* says the sign on the fence, and I realise this is it. I'm in the right place.

I hesitate by the entrance. The gate is wide open and there's no car on the driveway. There's a garage, I notice, but not many people park their cars in those these days, so the chances are there's no one home. I am hovering on the narrow verge, wondering whether to go in and knock anyway, when a woman emerges from the house next door and goes through another gate that sits between the two properties. She crosses the path towards the back garden.

'Hello!' I call out.

The woman stops and turns to face me. I can see straight away that she's not Hope Dunsmore. She is tall and slim and has long, straight red hair.

'I'm looking for Hope,' I call out again, conscious of the way this sounds, as if Hope Dunsmore and I are friends.

The woman turns and walks towards me. In spite of the heat, she's dressed for the countryside in a gilet, jeans and olive-green wellington boots. She lifts a hand and shades her eyes from the sun. 'She's at the hospital,' she says, in a tone of voice that tells me I should know this.

'The hospital,' I repeat, trying to sound as if I *do* know this. 'Of course.'

The woman walks towards me, smiling. 'I'm Jess. I'm just bringing her washing in. Glorious weather, isn't it? It's only been out an hour and it's dry already.'

'It's lovely,' I agree.

'Are you . . .?' she tails off, looking me in the eye. 'Sorry. Who are you? To Hope, I mean.'

I take a breath, thinking fast. She'll google me later, of course. 'Anna,' I lie. I glance at the drystone wall that borders the cottage. 'Wall,' I add.

'Oh.' She puts down her basket. 'Do you live in the village?' She glances out to the road, looking for my car.

'Er. No. I just . . .' I take a breath. 'OK. This is a little embarrassing,' I confess, 'but I'm looking for a therapist. Hope was recommended by a friend.' The last part is an afterthought, which I hope will make me seem a little less like a stalker. 'I couldn't get an answer on the phone, and . . . and I was actually just passing through. My friend lives in Water Oak,' I add quickly, realising that Chorley Common doesn't lead to anywhere except the next village. I brace myself, hoping she doesn't ask me who my friend is, but it doesn't look as though she's going to. She seems a little regretful, though.

'I don't think she's taking on any new clients at the moment,' she says.

'Really?' A tear clouds my eye and I quickly wipe it away. 'Oh, God. I'm so sorry,' I say. 'I didn't mean to get emotional.' And then, genuinely, my lower back goes into spasm. I gasp and keel forward, grabbing hold of the top of the wall in front of me and leaning against it. The pain is intense and I close my eyes.

'Are you OK?' I can hear her asking.

I nod, slowly, waiting for the pain to subside. I let out a few deep breaths and straighten up again, clutching my waist.

Jess steps forward. 'Should I call someone?'

'It's fine,' I murmur. 'I'll be OK.'

'You don't look OK.'

'Honestly.' I close my eyes and try not to make any sudden movements. 'I just need a second.'

Jess waits for a beat. 'Do you want to come inside? Sit down for a minute?'

The muscle spasm has passed, but it's left me feeling a little faint. I take a long, deep breath. 'Maybe just for a minute, if you don't mind?'

Jess steps closer, reaches out a hand and places it under my elbow. 'Come on. I'll get you some water.'

'I don't want to trouble you,' I say, meaning it. She seems so nice.

'It's no trouble.'

She leads me across the garden and through the gate into her own front yard. Her cottage is old and full of character, like Hope Dunsmore's. There are two cars on the drive, which I check out. One's a navy-blue Golf and the other's a white Mercedes.

'I work from home,' she says, following my gaze, 'and my husband's also home today.'

'What do you do?' I ask.

'I'm an osteopath.'

'Really?'

She nods.

I take this in. I could do with an osteopath. Maybe I need an osteopath *and* a psychotherapist. Even though I've been signed off work, Mike, my boss, is still paying my wages. Maybe this is fate. Maybe this is meant to be?

We go along a path to the rear of the house and through the back door into a lobby, where Jess steps out of her wellington boots. I slip off my trainers, then follow her into the kitchen, which is a stunning combination of contemporary glossy and traditional. There's an Aga along one exposed brick wall, and in the far corner next to the lobby, looking out onto the back garden, is a desk with an open laptop, which I'm guessing is someone's workspace. I hover next to Jess for a moment as she takes a glass out of a cabinet and turns on the tap.

'Please,' she says, over her shoulder. 'Have a seat.'

I pull out a chair and sit down. She places the glass of water in front of me, then sits down opposite. There's a small yellow vase of wild daisies in the centre of the table, which is otherwise clear. In fact, the room is spotless. It doesn't look as though Jess and her husband have any children.

'How are you feeling?' she asks.

'Much better.' I shoot her a weak smile. 'It's just an old sports injury that flares up a bit.'

She nods sympathetically. 'You should maybe think about seeing someone for that. I'm not suggesting it has to be me, but—'

'Could it?' I ask. 'Could it be you?'

'Well, maybe you ought to have a look online, consider your options?'

I want *her*, though. I already know I want her. 'I lost a baby,' I say, the words tumbling out quickly. 'It was a couple of months ago and . . . well, my back has been hurting ever since.'

'I'm so sorry.' Her eyes seek out mine. 'I really am. Was it a miscarriage?'

I hesitate as the ball of pain in my abdomen tightens. 'A late one. It's . . . it's still a bit hard to . . . to talk about. And my husband . . .' I stop, swallowing back tears, unable to continue.

'You're not together any more?' she asks gently.

I squeeze my eyes shut and shake my head.

She frowns sympathetically. 'A lot of marriages struggle after a woman loses a baby.'

I open my eyes and gaze back at her for a moment, not knowing how to talk about what happened to me, and so I ask instead, 'Has it happened to you?'

'Not to me. My husband and I never wanted children. It was a decision we made before we married. Luckily we both felt the same.' She hesitates. 'But I know people it's happened to. It can be hard on a relationship.'

She pauses. I know she's giving me room to talk about

my loss if I want to, but it's all I can do to hold my glass of water and bring it to my lips. My fingers are trembling and she sees this.

'You should talk to Hope,' she says decisively. 'She'd be a good person. I mustn't say too much, but I guarantee she's the best person you could talk to, and she's brilliant at what she does.'

'You said she wasn't taking on any new clients?'

'Well, she's not meant to be.' Jess purses her lips, then smiles. 'But let me see what I can do.'

'Really? You'd ask her?'

She nods. 'Sure. I'll see what she says. I'm not really taking on many new patients either, but if you do decide you want to come and see me for an initial session or two, I'm sure I can squeeze you in.'

'Really?'

'Yes,' she says. 'We often store pain and tension in our body and most professionals agree it's a good idea to treat both sets of symptoms simultaneously.'

By the time I've drunk my water, we've swapped numbers and Jess has booked me in for an appointment the following week.

'I'll ask Hope if she can see you either before or afterwards,' she says. 'How does that sound?'

'It sounds great,' I agree.

Jess holds out a small, bird-like hand and I shake it. She doesn't seem strong enough to be an osteopath, but I'm happy to give it a go. In fact, I'm more than pleased to have met her and to have had the opportunity to make her acquaintance. Visiting her for treatment can only be a good thing.

Back outside on the verge, something makes me turn left, up the hill, instead of right, back down into the village. There's no pavement and I have to walk in the road, but the air is still and silent. It doesn't seem as though many cars come this way. I walk a couple of hundred yards until I come to a lay-by. I step into it, then up onto the kerb, where I squeeze into the bracken so that I am concealed by the woodland, and then I wait. I wait for just over two hours. I'm hungry and I'm tired and my back aches. I drank the last of my water ages ago, but I can't bring myself to leave. I realised as I left Jess's house that what she had told me about Hope Dunsmore being at the hospital had been hovering at the edge of my consciousness, and that a dark, strange semblance of a thought has been forming ever since.

At just after three o'clock, my patience is rewarded by the sound of a car engine in the distance, getting louder and louder. I push back the branches in my eyeline and watch as it comes up the hill. It slows as it draws closer and my heart leaps as I recognise the vehicle: it's an SUV, a Range Rover Sport, dark grey with black tinted windows. It pauses outside Flint Cottage and swings into the driveway.

Hardly daring to breathe, I step out of the bracken and walk quickly back down the road. As I get closer, I can see them on the gravel driveway: Hope Dunsmore is standing still, straightening her back, while he – and I can see clearly, now, that it's him – takes a baby's car seat out through the open front passenger door. They have their backs to me, so I move closer, stepping back when I reach Jess's house and peering round the hedge.

Hope Dunsmore is at the front door now with the baby in the car seat on the ground next to her. She pushes a key into the lock and reaches down for the handle, turning the seat slightly as she lifts it so that I catch a glimpse of a small, sleeping baby covered in a light-blue blanket. The front door swings open and she takes the baby inside. I shift my focus back to the man, who is lifting the boot and taking out a bag and a small travel case. As I watch, there's the sudden sound of an animal screeching somewhere in the field behind me. The man pauses and raises his eyes towards it, and for a split second I think he's looking straight at me. But then he lowers the boot, points the remote at the car and as it clunks, turns and walks into the house with the bags, closing the front door behind him.

I let out a gasp of air and of relief. He didn't see me.

But I saw him.

9

A week has passed and I arrive just before two o'clock for the first of my two appointments, the osteopathy one with Jess. This time I drive right up to the house and park on the drive, in front of Jess's Golf and next to her husband Nick's Mercedes. It feels almost surreal to be here like this – legitimately here – and I feel a twinge of anticipation as my tyres crunch over the gravel and I pull on the handbrake. The journey here was easier this time, because all I was able to think about is that now I'm getting somewhere. I barely slept last night thinking about it, but I must be running on adrenaline because I don't even feel tired, at least no more than usual. I haven't had any enthusiasm for anything for ages, but when Hope called to say she was happy to see me, I felt better than I had in a while.

That was last Wednesday. She called late in the day, just as I was putting a ready meal into the microwave for dinner. We chatted for a bit and she told me that she was 'person-centred' and explained that therapy with her was all about going at my pace and talking only about the things I wanted to talk about.

I was intrigued. 'Anything?' I asked. 'Anything at all?'

'Of course.' She said it straight away, sounding sure, and it spurred me on.

'Jess said that you would be a good person to talk to,' I said, clearing my throat. 'I was wondering why she said that.'

She hesitated. 'I've lost three babies. I've had three miscarriages. That's probably what she meant.'

'I'm sorry,' I said.

'Thank you.' She paused. 'I don't mind talking about my own experiences if you think it will help you, but I'm not going to say I automatically know what you're going through.'

She said she'd managed to find a way through the pain each time and wanted the same for me, but that each person's pain and grief was unique and personal to them, and that there were no rules about loss, nor was there any magic end date to get over something like this. She said I would probably never truly get over it, nor would I want to, but there were things that could help to make some days feel a little brighter and easier to get through.

She seemed smart and I liked her and we fixed the appointment for three o'clock today. I still don't know what I am going to tell her about myself, but I figure I'll find something. A trickle of optimism runs through me as I wonder if it might even be possible to be completely open with her, but I quickly dismiss this.

At some point, perhaps – but not yet.

There's a tap on the car window. It's Jess. I didn't hear her coming, and I jump. Then I turn off the engine and take off my driving glasses.

'Hi, Anna,' she says.

It takes me a second to realise she's talking to me. This is going to take some getting used to, mainly because *Anna* is Anna and I'm used to *saying* Anna, not *being* her. I shouldn't have used my best friend's name, I know; it was stupid of me. But then I really only have to be Anna when I'm in Chorley Common, and it's not as if anyone is going to see us here together or call out my real name. Anna's surname is Finch, so it's not like I used her *entire* name. And as far as the Anna Walls of this world are concerned, I'm a non-existent fish in a very big pool. I googled myself when I got home last week – it was the first thing I did – and luckily for me Anna Wall is a little bit famous. She's a DJ and a musician and there are pages and pages on the internet about her achievements. After eleven or twelve of them, I got bored of scrolling without finding a single thing about anyone else, so hopefully Jess and Hope got bored of it too.

That's if they even tried. Maybe they're not allowed to. The thought is encouraging.

Jess takes me in through the front door this time, then up the stairs to her treatment room, a spare bedroom at the back of the house smelling of lavender and eucalyptus. She tells me to sit on the edge of the couch while she stands behind me and gets me to lift my arms and put pressure against her hands, then turn my head from side to side and raise my legs. She sits down at a desk and asks me a series of questions about my medical history. I answer truthfully until we get to the day I lost my baby. I tell her I'm not ready to talk about this yet and she says she understands and asks me to lie down. The treatment is not as painful as I expected. She is really good at what she does – and surprisingly strong. Afterwards, I follow her downstairs into the kitchen and wait while she goes to fetch her card machine. I slide my credit card into the reader, enter the wrong PIN, then fake surprise when the transaction is declined. I tell Jess that it's fine, I have enough cash. As I'm opening my purse and handing her the money, we are interrupted by the sound of the back door opening and shutting and then a woman walks into the kitchen holding a carrycot. My heart lurches. It's Hope Dunsmore. She, too, looks surprised and a little awkward when she sees me, but quickly composes herself and puts her finger to her lips.

'Put him down there,' Jess whispers, pointing to a corner of the kitchen near the back window.

Hope steps forward and lowers the carrycot to the ground. As she does so, I have a clear, unobstructed view of the baby. It's a boy, I can tell. There's a stirring in my womb, and a familiar ache fills my chest as I take in the delicate slope of his head through the soft layer of hair that covers it. I marvel at his little eyelids, the sombre nose and bow-shaped mouth. I can't stop looking at him. He's so very small and so very *knowing* and so very beautiful. Every feature is a perfectly formed miniature of the face he will have when he's older. I imagine picking him up and holding him against me, and the ache in my chest intensifies.

'Anna?' Jess is speaking and I realise she has just introduced me to Hope.

'I'm sorry,' I whisper as I shake my head and roll my eyes at my own rudeness.

Hope shoots me an apologetic look. 'No, *I'm* sorry,' she whispers. 'It wasn't meant to happen like this. It's just that . . . well, this arrangement is all a little new.'

'That's OK,' I say softly, still trying not to give away how completely I've been thrown off balance. I glance at the carrycot and make an *aww!* face. 'He's so gorgeous,' I mouth.

Hope looks uncomfortable but pleased. 'Well . . .' she begins.

'I'll wait out the front, shall I?' I ask them both quickly. 'I'll sit in my car for five minutes. I could do with a moment anyway to grab a snack.'

Jess shows me out to the front porch and I hope she doesn't notice how much I'm trembling. When I try to unlock the car, I drop the keys twice and have to bend down and scoop them up. I'm conscious that Jess is still there on the doorstep and that I must look ultra clumsy, but as I open the car door, she calls out, 'We made good progress today,

Anna, but make sure you do the exercises I gave you. I'll see you next week.'

Once inside the car, it takes me several moments to compose myself and get my breathing back to normal, but I wonder now if I've maybe passed some kind of test because, on reflection, I seem to have handled the situation well.

Hope Dunsmore's therapy room is at the back of the house and we have to walk down a path at the side of the cottage to reach it. As I follow my new therapist, I'm able to take in her appearance. She's average height and has strawberry-blonde hair – an enviable jumble of pretty curls, which she wears tied back in an elegant yet messy knot. She is wearing flip-flops and cream leggings under a loose red-and-white floral shirt dress that floats around her as she walks. I can tell she still has some baby weight to lose. Maybe she's always been on the heavier side, but I like it. It suits her. She's curvy and pretty and feminine, and as we round the corner onto a small patio and she opens the bifold doors to the extension, I feel gaunt and insubstantial beside her. I didn't choose to be this thin.

We step inside and Hope offers me a seat on a comfy cream couch facing the garden while she sits down in a leather swivel chair opposite me. Next to us is the dining table – solid oak, expensive – with a set of four upholstered chairs around it. There's a pair of frosted Shaker-style folding French doors beyond, which screen off the rest of the house. As I glance towards them, Hope explains that no one else is home and we can open the screen doors if I prefer. I tell her I do, and she gets up and pulls them back. I am now granted a view of her sitting room, of her inglenook fireplace, her flat-screen TV, her wingback armchairs and saggy big blue sofa. I can see that the wooden floorboards are originals, as are the doors. The rug in front of the fireplace looks like a genuine Ersari, which I recognise from a holiday I once took to Turkey. Someone has good taste.

'You have a beautiful house,' I say.

'Thank you.'

'How long have you lived here?'

'Two years – and a bit.'

I turn my gaze towards the garden, which is equally impressive – it's as wide as it is long and is lightly landscaped, appearing at once rugged and cared for. As I gaze into the distance, an animal darts out from behind a shed and slides under a low picket fence that backs onto the fields beyond. 'Wow,' I say. 'Was that a fox?'

'Yes. They're pretty friendly. We get a lot of wildlife in the garden, as you'd imagine.'

'Who's the gardener?' I say, then add, 'If you don't mind me asking?'

Hope smiles and says, 'I'm happy to answer, but I'm curious as to why you'd like to know.'

'No reason. Sorry.' I bite my lip. 'It's just that I've never done this before. It feels a bit weird not to ask the usual questions you would ask when you meet someone for the first time.'

'Hmm. I get that.' Hope gives me a gentle smile. She thinks for a moment, then says, 'My husband and I are both pretty good gardeners, but I probably do most of it. I planted all the flowers.'

'They're beautiful.'

'Thank you.'

I cast around, trying to think of something else to talk about, but I can't. We sit in silence for several minutes and all the while, Hope just sits there, looking at me, smiling, waiting, saying nothing. Presumably this is what 'person-centred' means, but I'm not sure I like it.

'Don't know what to say,' I confess eventually. My hands are clammy and I wipe them on my jeans.

Hope takes pity on me. 'Maybe we should begin by talking about what just happened?'

I frown, not understanding.

'Next door. When we bumped into each other. I wonder how you felt when you saw I had a baby.'

The familiar ache fills my chest, but I don't want her to think I can't be around children. 'It was fine,' I say, smiling. 'Really. I liked seeing him.'

I decide I need to give her something else to work with and so I tell her I find it hard to sleep and that I am angry a lot of the time.

'I know I'm pushing the people around me away,' I say. 'My best friend—' I stop short, realising I was about to say

Anna's name. 'My mum,' I continue. 'Anyone who tries to help me, really. But I can't seem to stop myself.'

'Anger is one of the first stages of grief,' Hope explains. 'It's completely normal to feel this way.'

'But what if I don't want to move on to the next stage?' I find myself asking her. 'What if I want to stay angry?'

She blinks. 'Why do you think you might want to stay angry?'

This is a very good question. 'I don't know,' I say.

She pauses for a beat, waiting to see if I am able to find my own answer. 'Maybe,' she suggests, 'you feel that if you move through all the stages of grief and come out the other side, it will mean leaving your husband and baby behind. It will mean moving on without them.'

I nod. This *is* how I feel. I've spent the past three months curled up in bed feeling this way. Not wanting to move on.

But I know there's more to it than this. I don't actually want to stay angry. I don't like being angry, in fact I hate it; it's burning a great big hole inside me.

But before you can stop feeling angry, you have to know who you're angry with.

When the session is over, Hope asks if I'd like to come back on Friday, and I tell her I would. As I leave, I ask to use the toilet. She shows me to the downstairs cloakroom, which is through the lounge and the front hall and then through the kitchen, which is just as pretty and full of character as the rest of the house. Inside, I shut the door and stand there for a moment, my head spinning. I don't actually need the toilet, so I flush it and squirt some soap out of the dispenser on the washbasin and turn on the tap. I let the warm water run over my fingers while I try to get my thoughts straight, then dry my hands, unzip my handbag and take out my AirPods. I pause for a moment, gazing around the tiny cloakroom, thinking, and then I open the case, take out one of the AirPods and tuck it behind the toilet, on the floor, out of sight.

Hope is in the kitchen when I come back in. She's wiping plates and putting them away in the dresser. 'OK?' she asks me.

'Yes. Thank you.'

She says goodbye and I walk out of the front gate, go next door and get into my car. As I reverse towards the road, I notice Hope appear from the back of the house and cross the garden to the gate that sits between the two properties. She's gone to collect the baby. I wonder what he is called, and then I realise I could have asked her. She was ready to talk about him and I stopped her. I could have asked her then, and I didn't. I want to kick myself. Why didn't I?

As I drive towards the village, the ache in my heart overwhelms me again. I take a right at the crossroads and drive along the road towards the village hall. I glance into the car park, but it's too open there, too exposed, and so I continue up the lane towards the farm at the top of the village, relieved when I notice how quiet it is. There's no one around. I park up on a grass verge behind a cowshed and turn off the engine, then lower the window and lean back against the headrest and sit still for a long time, breathing in the warm air with its strong farm smells of sun-baked cow-pats and hay bales.

Hiding the AirPod in the bathroom was a spur-of-the-moment decision and I'm not even sure why I did it, but after an hour has passed and I've drunk some water from the bottle in my cup holder, I start to think that maybe I do know why I did it after all.

10

Hope

It's Thursday evening and I'm downstairs with Drew, wishing I wasn't going out. Jess has persuaded me to join a fitness class with her, something called Core Conditioning – a combination of yoga, Pilates and strength training – which has just started up at the village hall. It's five thirty now. The class starts at six and lasts an hour, so I won't get home until gone seven. I'm exhausted and, quite frankly, I can think of better ways to spend an hour of my free time, although these alternatives involve either lying down or sitting down and putting food and wine into my mouth. I haven't done any proper exercise since I became pregnant with Sam and I'll lose all my muscle tone if I don't do something about it.

But I am also feeling guilty and a little anxious at the prospect of leaving my baby, who is now asleep in Drew's arms. I run through my list of instructions one last time and ask him to message me with regular updates.

'You'll be gone an hour and a half, tops,' he says, smiling. 'Just go off and have a good time.'

'I won't have a good time if I don't hear from you,' I say. 'I'll just be worrying.'

'Hope, it's the village hall. It's not the Outer Hebrides,' he says. 'Of course I'll message you if there's a problem, and if you take the car, you can be home again in a flash.'

He's right, obviously, but it's such a big thing, leaving my precious baby who has only been out of hospital for nine days, and if I'm honest with myself, it's because I still don't entirely trust my husband to be there for me. For us. Will he *really* watch Sam as closely as I would? Or will he open a beer and get lost in a box set on the telly? Even the village hall feels too far. It's not the same as Sam being twenty yards away next door with Jess.

On Saturday, she and Nick came round with a bottle of wine 'to wet the baby's head', as Nick put it. While he and Drew went off to look at Nick's new golf clubs, Jess and I sat in the kitchen and I poured us each a glass. Jess picked up Sam and cooed over him and we caught up with each other's lives. It felt really good to hear all her gossip. I didn't mention Drew's affair – or at least, I didn't tell her that it had started up again after I told her it had ended. The truth is, I just didn't want to give it any more air time. I've chosen to believe Drew when he says it meant nothing and that it's definitely over this time. It's been a rocky few months, but we've got through it, just as we've got through so much else together, and I don't want to dwell on the pain.

Instead, I remind myself of all the things we have together, all the things we share. We have our cottage. We *love* our cottage – our brick and flint haven! (*'Brick and flint,'* we say in unison, smiling at each other, every time we pass another building that's made from the same materials.) It's *our* thing, just as the bone-china dinner plates in the dresser and the antique clock in the hallway and the Afghan Ersari rug by the fireplace are *our* things. They're the trinkets that tell the story of our shared life, of where we've been together, of how *long* we've been together. There are the matching valentine cards, framed, side by side in the bedroom like a set of paintings. (We laughed out loud when we opened them and found we'd bought the same one!) There's the yellow plastic clock that we bought for the kitchen in our first flat together, which now hangs in the kitchen here and is referred to jokingly by Drew as the family heirloom. We can't bring ourselves to throw it away.

There are the things we do. We go to auctions in the countryside at weekends and forage for hidden treasures. We buy nice wine. We are soppy about the wildlife in the back garden, about rescuing hedgehogs from the road and filling the bird feeder outside the front porch. We have our in-jokes: on a Thursday, when Drew gets home from work and while we prepare dinner together, we seek out each other's eyes, smirking as we wait to see who will be the first to announce that our no-drinking-on-a-weekday rule is about to be broken. (We don't have a dishwasher and the one who gives in first has to do the washing-up!) We fall into a companionable silence, our eyes misting up, when-ever 'Golden Slumbers' comes on the radio. These are *our things*.

Whatever *they* had together, it's not the same as having built a life together, having loved each other enough to marry, to commit to a future together. It's not the same as having lost three babies together, having grieved and cried and healed together. People talk about having a *happy marriage* as if it's this elusive state of pain-free living reserved for those superior beings who were clever enough to meet and marry the right partner at the right time and make all the right choices, but what if you meet the right person and then life throws a series of bombs at you? I've learned something that my psychology degree could never have taught me: that being able to go through pain and loss and hardship together is the truest indicator of the strength of a marriage. The grief that came with each of our losses has fused us together in a way that a few months of office foreplay and illicit sex will never, ever touch.

Not that I forgave him easily, of course. It hurt, what he did. It dented the trust I thought we had, that I thought we were built on. It dented *our thing*. But now, here is the baby that will mend us. (Yes, yes . . . it's true that you can't mend a broken relationship with a baby, but our relationship isn't broken; it's just been chipped and needs restoring.) Maybe I worry that Jess won't approve of my decision, that she will think I'm weak, but actually this isn't about weakness or strength. I still love Drew, but most importantly, I don't want to be a single parent and I don't want Sam to grow up in two different homes. That's the crux of it.

As a therapist, I've learned that we don't have to follow our 'life script' – as we call it in my profession – the one we create for ourselves in childhood, which is then rein-forced by our parents and which (unless we become aware of it) we will spend the rest of our lives finding evidence to support. *Men always leave me* or *I'm never good enough* are common ones. *I'm a waste of space. I'll never amount to anything.* As the only child of a narcissistic mother and a father who adored her, my life script is to feel left out. I always knew that my father loved my mother far more than he loved me. I was the third wheel in their relationship – I could never break into that bond. At school, I didn't fit in, and I always felt on the fringe of things at university. My go-to response to being cheated on would therefore be to feel excluded, especially if it was with someone Drew worked with – someone with whom he has building design and town planning in common, things that have nothing to do with me. My *scripted* position would be to feel crushingly unimportant (with all the weight of my original childhood pain); I'd conclude that there must be some-thing fundamentally flawed in me to cause Drew to seek out someone new. I'd conclude that this person must be more compelling, more lovable, more *interesting* than me.

But, no. I've made a conscious decision not to see things the way my five-year-old self would and to instead see them as they *really* are: that most men think with their dicks and are biologically hardwired to want to have sex with pretty much every woman they meet.

So rather than take his fling personally, I've chosen to see it for what it is – or who *Drew* is. He's fallible. He's weaker than I thought, but he's *human*, too. I've chosen to make the most of the situation, to take him up on his pledge to make it up to me, and what better time to let him show me exactly how sorry he is than when there are night-time feeds to wake up for, shitty nappies to change and a colicky baby who needs bouncing around and singing to by one parent so that the other one can eat a hot meal with both hands in front of the TV at a time of their choosing? (That's me, by the way, eating the hot TV dinner!)

And so, yes, I've forgiven him.

Now I cuddle Sam one last time and hand him back to Drew. Most of the women in the village will be at the class, and after living here for more than two years, it will be good to get to know them a little better.

More importantly, I haven't yet had a chance to speak to Jess about Anna Wall, who I have mixed feelings about. I can usually get a feel for a client – whether they're likely to make progress, whether they'll keep coming, whether they're really ready to do the work, that sort of thing. But these aren't the kinds of things I'm wondering about with Anna. I don't like to be negative about people, and I really do feel for her, what with everything she's been through, but I'm worried she doesn't seem to be respecting the boundaries between us. There's something about her behaviour that's not quite right.

Yesterday evening, just as Drew got home from work, she turned up in the driveway. She was literally standing there, waiting for him, as he was getting out of the car. I had just put Sam down when I heard him pull up, and so I looked out of the bedroom window, which was already open. She appeared to be on foot, or at least I couldn't see her car. I heard her telling Drew she'd lost an AirPod and wanted to check our cloakroom to see if it was there. This immediately made me wary. I'd left my phone downstairs in the living room, but I was pretty certain she hadn't called me. I also heard her say she was on the way to the gym and that she couldn't run without music, but she wasn't dressed for the gym; she was wearing jeans and a T-shirt – in fact, the same clothes she'd been wearing when she came earlier in the day for her session with me.

I ran downstairs to open the front door and as I did so, I heard her say to Drew, 'Nice car. Is it new?' Drew looked really uncomfortable, and I was cross with her. I wasn't sure if she realised how inappropriate it was for her to be here, uninvited, talking to a member of my family like this. All the same, I let her in and waited outside the cloakroom while she went in and looked for the AirPod. She came out a moment later, saying she'd found it. The light in the lobby was bright and I could see her face more clearly now. Even though she was smiling, trying to look happy, I could tell she'd been crying. I felt sorry for her when I saw that. My intention had been to tell her that in future she needed to call to check if it was OK before she came to my house, but I decided to wait until the next session and broach it with her then.

All the same, I was unsettled. I was tempted to google her, but my professional ethics held me back. I expect there are some therapists who do this, but a client should be able to trust that you are a safe space for them to disclose whatever they feel comfortable disclosing without being prejudged. Besides, there's also the thorny issue of what you would then do if they told you something different from something you'd already found out about them online. It would be more than awkward – it would be professionally embarrassing. I don't mind clients lying to me – it's up to them what they want to tell me, and besides, they may need time to be able to fully trust me. But in order to work with them, I need to at least be able to believe that what they are saying *could* be true.

Anyway, I must have already made up my mind to keep on seeing Anna, because I didn't look her up. But I now really want to know Jess's viewpoint on this. I smile to myself as I watch Jess close her back door and stride towards me in her trainers. It's the kind of conversation Jess loves to have: both gossipy and intellectual in one hit.

'You're looking sporty, Dunsmore,' she smiles as she points her key fob at her Golf and unlocks it.

I glance down at my shorts and oversized T-shirt. 'Don't worry,' I smile. 'I'll never be as thin as you.'

I don't know why I said this, and I can tell she doesn't

either because her expression changes. 'You're beautiful,' she tells me, frowning. 'Stop body-shaming yourself. Your postnatal curves are as sexy as hell. Drew loves you the way you are.'

I smile, feeling awkward at the oblique reference to the condition of my marriage. Jess never actually comes out and voices her disapproval of Drew, but I'm pretty sure what she *really* means is that he *should* love me the way I am. Maybe I'm imagining this, but if I'm not, I can't really blame her for judging him when I keep on reminding her of the damage his affair has done to my self-esteem. As my friend, I suppose it's hard for her to forgive him for that.

I suppose, if I'm honest with myself, I have been feeling very slightly insecure today. Drew was really quiet all of yesterday evening after Anna came to the house. When I tried to discuss it with him, he told me it was nothing, he was just tired. I know it's probably the old paranoia creeping back, and obviously it's going to take time for me to fully trust him again and not to find a hidden meaning whenever he's a little withdrawn, but I suppose, if I'm even *more* honest with myself, seeing Anna behaving in such a familiar way with him was a trigger for me. It made me wonder about her, about whether they know each other.

But I need to be more rational. After all, Drew gave me the PIN to his phone (which we both knew I'd already guessed, because that's how I found out about his affair) and he told me I could check it whenever I wanted. He leaves the phone lying around all the time, and although I don't want to look at it – I don't *need* to look at it – I like that he's willing to do anything to get me to trust him. And as for last night, it was probably exactly as he said. He probably *was* just tired from work – and maybe even a little pissed off at having one of my clients turn up and behave weirdly, asking him questions.

'What do you think of Anna Wall?' I ask Jess now, as we get into the car.

Jess starts the engine and reverses in a wide arc, then swings out of the drive and heads down the lane towards the crossroads. 'You mean . . . do I like her?'

'I mean, do you think she's . . . creepy?' I add, 'For want of a better word.'

Jess laughs. 'Yes, that's not very professional, Dunsmore.'

I tell her about Anna turning up on the doorstep last night.

'Hmm,' says Jess. 'She ought to have called first.'

'Exactly,' I say.

'That *is* a bit weird,' Jess agrees. She gives me a sidelong glance. 'She's painfully thin, isn't she?' she adds.

I initially feel another burst of insecurity, then quickly reprimand myself. Anna *is* painfully thin – *too* thin – and I don't think it's a fashion statement. She had been dressed to hide it, if anything. This makes me feel sorry for her again. 'Well, she's probably not taking very good care of herself.' I hesitate, then say, 'Would you google her? I mean . . . ethically, what's your position on that?'

Jess frowns, then checks the rear-view mirror and indicates

right. 'If I was really worried I would, but I'd have to be really worried. Wouldn't you?'

I nod. 'Yes. That's what I was thinking.'

Jess gives me another sideways glance. '*Are* you really worried?'

'No,' I say. 'And maybe it was my fault for bringing Sam into your kitchen before she'd left. That wasn't very professional either. Maybe it was me that blurred the boundaries between us.'

Jess thinks about this, then says firmly, 'She's just a bit lost and a bit lonely. It's probably nothing. Just tell her she needs to call you first next time.' She hesitates. 'I wonder who her friend is? I might know her.'

'Which friend?'

'The one who lives in Water Oak. The one who recommended you to her.'

I immediately feel unsettled again. 'Is that what she said?'

'The first time she came, remember? I told you. She said she had a friend who lived in Water Oak.'

'Yes. You told me that,' I say. 'But you didn't tell me the friend had recommended me.'

'I'm sure I did,' Jess frowns.

'No, Jess. You didn't,' I protest. 'Because if you had, I'd know who it was, wouldn't I? And I'd have questioned you on it. I've never had a client who lives in Water Oak.'

'Well, maybe it was just word of mouth, then.'

This seems unlikely. I never really built my practice back up after Drew and I left St Albans. We were hoping to get pregnant and I was content with the handful of Hertford-shire clients who had wanted to stay with me after I moved away. I run through them in my head. There was a couple who were having marital issues and who I still occasionally see online. There was a young woman who lived west of the city, near the Buckinghamshire border. She had an eating disorder – she couldn't eat in front of anyone – and wanted to try and get better in time for her wedding last year. I have one client who still travels from Dunstable to see me, which is flattering because it's twenty-seven miles each way and a two-hour round trip. He's a man in his fifties who used to be a train driver and was on duty when a young girl threw her-self in front of his cabin. Unsurprisingly he has PTSD and I am helping him find ways to deal with the flashbacks.

Maybe Jess is right. Maybe Anna's friend in Water Oak is someone who knows one of them.

Jess turns into the village hall car park, pulls into a space and switches off the engine. Several women in yoga pants and vest tops are standing around outside the entrance to the hall. One of them, who I recognise to say hello to, turns to wave at Jess and shoots me a friendly smile. I sigh inwardly. I'm really not feeling up to this, but it's too late to back out now. Jess is already out of the car, so I get out too, and as it's a beautiful evening and we are fifteen minutes early, we join the group and stand around in the sunshine. Jess intro-duces me to a woman named Penny who owns the riding stables nearby, to a pretty British Indian woman named Kiren who works in IT, and to a blonde-haired woman called

Nikki who is a full-time mum. They all have children and are excited to hear there is a new baby in the village. Nikki insists that I show them the photos I have of Sam on my phone. There is a lot of oohing and aahing, followed by questions about the birth and stories of long labours and difficult deliveries.

We go into the class and the soft transcendental music starts. Victoria, the teacher, positions herself at the front of the room and tells us how to breathe and how to switch off our minds. I try to follow her instructions and lose myself in the flow of each movement, but while my body is doing almost everything it's supposed to be doing, I just can't get my brain to relax. I can't stop thinking about Anna. Who is she?

11

Lauren

Sam. Hope's baby is called Sam. I could hardly believe it when I found out. I thought I was going to faint, but somehow I managed to keep smiling and nodding and said, 'That's so sweet.' I don't know how I made it back to my car. I don't remember any of it, not the walk up to the farm or the drive home or what I did for the rest of the evening. I only remember that I was in a lot of pain by the time I got home, and I must have taken quite a few painkillers because this morning I can see the packets on the floor next to the bed. The silver foil blisters look emptier than I remember.

But I wasn't sick and I'm still here, so I must be OK.

I ease myself up onto my elbows and tug at the pillow next to me, pulling it under my head and propping myself up a little. I reach out to the bedside table for my phone and check the time and date, then cast my mind back to the previous evening, running through what happened. Did I give the women at the fitness class anything to be suspicious about?

I don't think I did. In fact, I think it all happened completely naturally – well, almost.

I'd been looking online for pictures of the baby. I knew I couldn't ask Hope anything about him, not after what happened on Wednesday. I could tell she thought it was completely inappropriate of me to turn up at her house and talk to her husband, and I don't think she believed my story about the AirPod either. Not that she said anything. She didn't have to. All day yesterday I was fully expecting her to phone to give me a telling-off, and I thought I might as well get it over with, so I stayed in bed with my laptop, my phone next to me on the bedside table, for most of the day.

I wasn't really expecting to find anything new online. I'd already done extensive searches for 'Hope Dunsmore' and 'Andrew Faris' and 'Hope Dunsmore-Faris', and I knew everything there was to know about them both, which wasn't much. Neither has a Facebook account, or if they do, I haven't been able to find it, and anyway, it makes sense that they would keep a low profile. As head of planning at Wallingford District Council, he is in the public eye locally, if not nationally, and as a psychotherapist, she isn't going to want her clients to know about her personal life. So, aside from all the professional stuff – and there are pages and pages of those about him – I knew I wouldn't find much.

But then I had an idea. I went back onto Facebook and did a search for 'Chorley Common, Buckinghamshire' and up popped the village group page, with its 1.1k members. I was surprised there were so many. My intention had been to create a fake profile, join the group and see if I could find out anything useful, but then I realised the visibility was set to 'Public' and that I could see everything anyway. My eye was immediately drawn to a prettily designed advert on the 'Recent Media' page. It was an offer of babysitting posted by a teenager called Hollie Parsons. I clicked on it and scrolled through the other photos. There was one of a cat climbing through a window and, underneath, another one of a bunch of chickens who appeared to be selling their own eggs. And then I struck lucky. My eyes landed on a notice about a fitness class that had just started up in the village hall on Thursdays. I immediately froze: today was Thursday. As my eyes flipped down, I saw that the class was due to start in just over an hour's time.

I got out of bed, brushed my teeth and changed quickly into a T-shirt and a pair of leggings, then grabbed my water bottle from the kitchen. Luckily, in the shed, I also had an old yoga mat. I was ready in fifteen minutes and suitably dressed – well, I was a bit scruffy and my legs looked way too thin, but at least I looked like I was about to do some exercise this time. I managed to get there early, parking in the lane behind the farm, the same place I'd parked the evening before. I walked down into the village, keeping my distance and watching from behind a big white van on the opposite side of the road as a series of cars pulled into the car park and a group of women gathered near the entrance. My heart fluttered and I stepped back further when I saw Jess's blue Golf pull in. I knew I couldn't go across the road then – not that I was intending to join the class anyway – so I walked back up to the farm and got into my car and waited.

At five to seven, I headed back down to the village hall, timing it so that I'd arrive at five past. Jess's Golf had gone and so, as the last few women filtered out, I strode across the road and into the car park. 'Oh no. Is the class over?' I called out, shading my eyes from the sun.

'Yes,' said a woman in navy-blue leopard-print running tights. 'It's just finished.'

'It was six till seven,' said the woman with her, and they both looked sorry for me.

'Damn,' I said. 'I thought it was seven till eight. I must have misread it. And I was hoping to catch a friend, too.'

'Which friend?' A dark-haired woman stepped forward.

'Hope Dunsmore.'

'Oh, yes,' said a woman with fair hair tied up into a top-knot. 'She was here. She just left.'

'What a shame.' I sighed, then smiled brightly and asked, 'Has she had her baby yet?'

'Yes!' The fair-haired woman smiled back. 'Didn't you know?'

'No,' I said. 'What did she have?'

'A boy. He's . . . what, three months old now?'

'You're kidding! I didn't think he was due until . . .' I pause, as if trying to remember.

'He came early,' said the woman in the navy tights.

'Ah,' I said, wistfully. 'I wonder what she called him?'

'Sam,' they all said at once, and someone added, 'Samuel.'

That was when my mind froze. But then someone laughed and said, 'They should have called him Valentine.'

'No, they shouldn't,' argued someone else. 'That's dreadful.'

'Why?' I asked, already half understanding but not quite believing what I was about to hear. 'Why Valentine?'

'He was born on Valentine's Day,' said the fair-haired woman.

I stood there in a daze. 'How sweet,' I murmured, more than once I think, and then I asked where he'd been born, and although I could tell she was a little curious as to why I wanted to know this, the fair-haired woman told me, 'Woodley Ridge.' I thanked them all, saying I'd have to pop over and see him, and then I stumbled back up to the farm, feeling sick. I got into my car and sat there for ages. I could barely drive home and last night was a blur. I couldn't think straight.

But now, this morning, there's no doubt in my mind that this is significant. Something has definitely happened to me, something involving Andrew Faris and Hope Dunsmore, even though I can't fully understand or remember yet.

I push back the duvet and get out of bed, the ball of my foot crushing one of the empty painkiller packets. I glance down and gaze at it, realising I need to be more careful. I need to write down what I've taken or get one of those pill dispenser boxes. Or, better still, stop taking them. I really need to stop taking them. No matter how much pain I'm in, no matter how lost and lonely and angry and hopeless I feel, I don't actually want to die. Maybe I did at first. I know that's what my mum and Anna (the real Anna – my friend Anna) were thinking. It's why they watched me round the clock from the day I left hospital until several weeks afterwards. They didn't leave me alone at all in the beginning, not even to go to the toilet.

After a while, I insisted they both go back to London where they have jobs and lives, and in Anna's case, a family. My mum tried to persuade me to go with her, but I couldn't bear the thought of moving back to the home I grew up in. I wanted to stay in my own house, at least until I had worked out what kind of a future I would have, or could have. Most days, I couldn't imagine one at all. Most days, when I woke up, I would open my eyes and see where I was and that the bed next to me was empty, and that the room was empty, and I would think to myself, *But I'm still here. Why?* Most days, I just wanted to take a pill and sleep some more and make everything go away.

But not every day.

Hope's right about one thing. Some days are better than others. There are some days when you find something to live for, and today is one of those days. I haven't worked it all out yet, but my gut instinct tells me that it's too much of a coincidence that Hope Dunsmore was giving birth to *her* baby while I was losing *my* baby, in the exact same hospital on the exact same day.

12

Hope

Until yesterday, I'd been in two minds as to whether to say something to Anna about the night she came back for the AirPod. I thought she probably knew at the time that I wasn't happy about it and that she shouldn't have come, because she phoned to cancel her next session, saying her car had broken down, which I was pretty sure was an excuse. She said she'd book another session when she'd got it repaired. Drew was back to his old self and everything had returned to normal – in fact, things had been *really* good between us. On Saturday, we put Sam into the baby sling and went for a long walk in the forest, then on Sunday we went to an auction at Stoke End and for another long walk along Ashcombe Ridge. Yesterday, Drew cooked steak for dinner, which he announced would come with 'all the fixings', a phrase he'd borrowed from *Frasier*, our favourite nineties TV show – we'd been watching it on catch-up – and which he knew would make me smile. We were eating in the kitchen, with

Sam in his bouncer on the floor beside us, when Drew suddenly suggested a holiday.

I immediately felt a little panicked at the thought of all the organisation this would involve, of being away from home with Sam without access to our hospital consultant or GP. 'When?' I asked him.

'Soon. Why not?' Drew turned to look at Sam. 'You want to go to the seaside, don't you, little fella? Make a sandcastle and eat an ice cream? Hmmm. Ice cream,' he said, making a clown face and rubbing his tummy in an exaggerated circle.

Sam rewarded him with a gummy giggle and my heart melted. He had been chuckling like this for a few weeks now. It was adorable, and still got to me every time.

'There you go,' Drew said triumphantly, turning back to me. 'The boys want to go on holiday – and it will be the perfect thing for Mummy. A nice rest and a bit of sea air. Just what she needs.'

'Where were you thinking?' I put down my knife and fork, trying to quell my anxiety. I didn't want to fly, not yet. It was too soon for a baby who had gone through heart surgery just thirteen weeks ago and had been on a ventilator for eight weeks after that.

Drew put his own knife and fork down and reached across the table to take my hand. 'Hey. I'm just talking about booking an Airbnb in Wales or something.'

'Wales,' I said, breathing out. We could go to the Gower Peninsula. I knew the hospital in Swansea and it was a

good one. I'd done some work for the NHS there a few
years back.

'You don't need to worry about money, Hope. We're
doing fine.' Drew paused for a second, then picked up his
knife and fork again and said, 'In fact, why don't you tell
your clients you're taking some maternity leave? We can
have a nice few days away, and then you can take a break
for a while.'

My heart dropped as I watched him cutting his steak and
putting a piece into his mouth, all the while not meeting my
gaze. I knew immediately that it was because of Anna, that
she was the reason he was saying this. I looked him in the
eye and said, 'Drew, do you know her?'

'Who?' he asked through a mouthful of food, but he isn't
a good actor and he still couldn't look at me. Instead, he
turned his attention to Sam, putting his foot on the bouncer
and bobbing him up and down repeatedly. I could see sick
starting to come out of Sam's mouth and I had to tell Drew
to stop.

'What's going on here?' I asked him.

'Nothing's going on,' he said. 'I just thought it would be
good for you to have some time with Sam, that's all.'

'Drew,' I said sharply, feeling my stomach twist. 'Tell me
how you know her.'

'Who?' he asked.

'My new client,' I said. 'The one who came here. The one
who was waiting for you on the drive when you got home.'

Drew sighed, lowering his eyes for a moment and staring

at the plate of food on the table in front of him, then he looked up at me again. 'I don't know her,' he said. 'I've never seen her before in my life.'

'So, why . . .?'

'I just don't like her,' he said.

I hesitated, blinking. 'Because she came to the house?'

Drew bit his lip. 'It wasn't just that time. She was here again at the weekend, snooping around and peering in through the garage window.'

'She was here? Anna?'

'If that's her name – then, yes.'

I swallowed. 'How do you know she was here?'

'Nick saw her. He went outside to put away his golf clubs and he heard the bushes rustling in our garden, and then he looked up and there she was. She was standing on tiptoes, looking into the garage through the side window.'

'And when was this?'

He hesitated. 'Sunday, I think. He said it was either Saturday or Sunday. When we were out.'

He looked up at me. I could see that his neck was pink under his collar.

'There's more, isn't there?' I asked him.

He sighed, pushed his plate to one side and put his elbows on the table. 'I didn't want to worry you.'

'You're worrying me now,' I said.

'It was probably nothing.'

'But . . .?'

'But I got followed.'

THE DAY I LOST YOU

'When?'

'A few weeks ago. When Sam was still in hospital. It was the day I went to the showroom in West Wyebridge to test-drive the Range Rover. I might have been imagining it. I *thought* I was imagining it, at first, but I think they followed me from the hospital.'

'Who? Who followed you?'

'Someone in a taxi. They followed me from the hospital to the showroom and then they waited at the showroom while I test-drove the Range Rover and then they followed me home. Well, they tried to. I lost them on the Old Chiltern Road.'

I tried to make sense of what he was telling me. 'And you think it was Anna?'

'It could have been,' he said. 'I don't really know.'

'But why would someone follow you from the hospital?'

He shrugged and looked into my eyes as if he was begging me to understand, but I didn't. Did Anna have some kind of obsession with me, or my husband, or his car? My heart fluttered. Or my baby? But . . . why? 'Is she someone from work?' I asked.

Drew gave me a perplexed look.

'Where then?' I asked. 'Where do you know her from?'

'I don't know her, Hope. I told you. I've never met her before. But I'm worried she might be . . . you know?'

'Mentally unwell?'

Drew nodded slowly.

I sighed. 'Well, I think that's a given, isn't it? Anyway,

I'm going to have to confront her with all of this. I'll have to tell her that if she doesn't stop, I'm going to call the police.'

'No!' Drew said abruptly. 'Don't do that. I mean . . . maybe I imagined it, being followed? Or maybe it was just some angry taxi driver or something, trying to get past me?'

'OK, but . . .'

'Just get rid of her. Stop seeing her,' he said, and made a begging face. 'Please?'

I mulled it over for the rest of the evening and didn't sleep well. In all the years I'd been practising, nothing like this had ever happened to me before and I hadn't really considered how I would handle it. But I did have deep concerns about Anna Wall. Coming to our house and knocking on the door when we were home was one thing, but if she'd been here, looking through our windows and doing God knows what else when we were out – then this was serious. I contemplated calling my supervisor, but I didn't want to disturb her during the evening, besides which, I was certain she'd say it was a good enough reason to end our professional relationship, and that I was right to want to put my family first.

This morning, I called Jess, who came straight round. She made us both coffee while I sat at the kitchen table and fed Sam. She agreed with me that it *was* serious, that I should call time on my professional relationship with Anna, and said she would do the same.

'Even if she wasn't the one who followed him home from the hospital,' she said, 'the rest of it is still stalking.'

'The rest of it?' I eyed her, playing devil's advocate. 'You mean, two visits to the house, one of which was to collect something she'd forgotten, and then a peek through the garage window?'

Jess placed the two mugs of coffee on the table, then turned and gazed out through the window into the front garden and said, 'Your akebia's doing well.'

'Jess,' I said, in a warning tone of voice.

'OK,' she said, sitting down opposite me and pulling her chair in closer to the table. 'I didn't want to worry you . . .'

I sighed. 'Why does everyone keep saying that, right before they tell me something that's going to worry me?'

'Because they care about you, Hope, and you've been through so much.'

'So,' I asked, 'what is it?'

She picked up her coffee mug and took a sip, peering at me over the rim. 'Penny from the stables said her car is up at the farm a lot.'

I frowned. 'Anna's?'

She nodded. 'Penny was out riding with Fiona. They were in the field next to the lane and she looked over the hedge and saw Anna sitting in her car. It was parked on the grass verge near the cowsheds and she was looking to see if it was definitely her, and then Fiona said, "Oh, that car is *always* there."'

'Wait. How does Penny know Anna?' I asked, confused.

'She turned up after Core Conditioning, apparently. That first time we went. It was just after we left. Penny said she turned up late and told them she knew you, and then started asking questions about Sam.'

I felt my stomach turn. Sam was wriggling in my lap and had stopped sucking, so I lifted him up and held him against me. 'What did she ask?'

'I don't think it was much. Just whether you'd had him yet, and what you'd called him.'

I frowned. 'She knows I've had him. Why would she ask that?'

Jess shrugged. 'I don't know. I told Penny that.'

'Well, I'm going to have to confront her with all of this and get some answers. She's obviously *not* able to deal with the fact that I have a baby. Or maybe that's the reason she's here – *because* I have a baby. Maybe she's come for therapy with me . . . with *us*,' I corrected myself and Jess gave a vigorous nod, 'because she's already obsessed with Sam.' I hesitated. 'Or Drew.'

A shadow crossed Jess's face and I instantly knew where her money was.

'I'll ask her what's going on and see what she says,' I continued. 'And then I'll tell her that if she doesn't stop, I'll call the police. Drew doesn't want me to do that, but . . .' I tailed off, losing my thread. Jess's face was impassive, but I knew what she was thinking, because I was thinking it too. If Drew had never seen Anna Wall before in his life, why didn't he want me to call the police?

Jess nodded. 'I'll tell her the same. I mean, I did already tell her I was booked up and that it might only be a couple of sessions, so maybe I'll just tell her I don't have any more space.'

I hugged my baby to my chest and breathed deeply, closing my eyes as I rubbed his back in little circles and pressed my cheek against his hair.

'Do you think . . .' Jess ventured.

'It's not *her*,' I said. 'I mean . . . it's not the same woman. I mean . . . it *could* be. They're both skinny, tall, dark-haired . . .' I let out a derisive snort. 'The complete opposite of me.' Jess looked upset when I said this and I paused and forced a smile. 'But it's not her,' I continued. 'I know what she looks like. I looked her up at the time.'

'Yeah. So did I,' Jess said, then added, 'I couldn't see the attraction myself.'

I smiled again, appreciating her loyalty. A thought occurred to me. 'Did you look Anna up?' But I knew as I asked the question that she would have done.

'There's nothing,' Jess said. 'I don't think it's her real name. I mean, it's hard to tell, because there's another Anna Wall online and there's a lot of stuff about her, but . . .'

I took a long breath. Maybe Drew had rejected her. Maybe it was just a crush. But maybe it wasn't. 'I'm going to find out the truth from her before I speak to Drew again,' I said. 'But I won't see her for therapy any more, and she'll need to stay away from us. I'll be telling her that.'

Jess nodded, firmly. 'Agreed.'

Sam's head had started to flop against my shoulder, so I stroked his hair, gave him a kiss and told Jess it was time to put him down. I stood up and carried him across the kitchen to the hallway, pausing in the doorway, trying to think of something to say to Jess to alleviate the shame I felt. I couldn't help it. I'd been banging on to her for weeks about how wonderful Drew had been since Sam was born, how much he'd been trying, how he'd been the perfect husband and father, and now . . .

As I turned back to face her, Jess flashed a weak smile, then stared down into her coffee mug and I knew exactly what she was thinking. She was thinking that if my husband had been having an affair with Anna Wall – or whatever her real name was – and had ended it, and she hadn't been happy and had followed him in a taxi, then found out where we lived and what I did for a living, and had deliberately sought me out for therapy . . . then *of course* he would be behaving like an angel. He would be doing everything in his power to make it up to me.

13

We're on our way back from the seaside. Drew is frustrated at the amount of traffic on the motorway, but there's nothing I can do and Sam is asleep, so I close my eyes and lean against the headrest, letting the warm sun toast my face through the windscreen. I may as well pretend I'm back on Rotherslade beach, lying on a towel and listening to the waves. We made a mistake picking a Friday to come home, even though we set off early, and even though we waited to go away until half-term was over. We picked the right week, though. The weather couldn't have been more perfect. The sun was out almost every day – hot but not too hot. The week passed in a haze of warm air and sea spray, breakfasts at the pier and lunches at one of the cafés at either Langland or Caswell, then walks along the clifftops or afternoons on the beach. We stayed in a pretty seafront cottage in the Mumbles, which was a bit noisy in the evenings, but we had a ton of restaurants on our doorstep and an incredible view across the bay.

Anna Wall wasn't mentioned, and I was pleased. I realised I was happy, that Drew and I could be happy, and that if I wanted it enough, she could, in time and with practice, fade from my memory. Whoever she had been to my husband (if anything – and it could well have been a crush or an unrequited obsession on her part), it was clearly over for him, otherwise why had she tracked me down and come to me for therapy? I assumed it was to check me out, to come face to face with me, to see what I was like and probably – at some point – to tell me who she was and to confront me with the terrible truth about my husband. In fact, at our final session, she had the look of someone who wanted to unburden themselves but had chickened out.

Anyway, she had promised she wouldn't come back, and I think she meant it. Jess and I hadn't managed to find out who she really was, but I had a strong sense that she had decided she wasn't going to hurt me, and that *not* telling me the truth was her way of saying that it was over. All of it. And this was all I needed to know. I'm not one to dwell on what might have been; I'm one to look forward. I want to think about the future, not the past. This might seem a strange stance for a therapist, but it's who I am. Having hope goes hand in hand with emotional healing for me.

And after all, how could I be anything other than hopeful? My name was a gift from my hippy parents, or, more specifically, my mother, my *life script* handed down through at least three generations of female Dunsmores, a glowing torch of optimism passed from my mother's mother to my mother and then to me. I was taught to make the best of things, to make lemonade from lemons, to see silver linings, and to generally march through life singing like a von Trapp on a mountainside – and I'm glad, because it's a stance that has served me well. Some may call it magical thinking, but my life has been so much more joyful for having been able to tell myself that things might have turned out the way they were meant to and that – even though I didn't yet know the reason – no doubt the universe was unfolding as it should.

So, as far as I'm concerned, it's time to move on. Drew said he didn't know her, and what's the point in going over old ground? Whatever it was – if anything – it must have happened before Sam was born; there is just no way in the world Drew would have cheated on me after that. The thought is actually ludicrous after everything we went through that day and during the days that followed, and after all the time it took me to forgive him. We have Sam now and he is our new beginning, and this holiday has been perfect.

Our new start.

The traffic has just begun to move again when Drew's phone bleeps from the console between us. I yawn sleepily and open one eye.

'Could you get that, love?' Drew says, indicating right and swinging out into the fast lane. I know he's worried about the work that's been piling up for him all week and the planning meetings he's missed about the Crowthorpe development. *Crowthorpe.* The name still makes me cringe. It has bad associations for me. It feels good, though, that he's asking me to check his phone.

'It's Jim,' I say, picking it up and reading the name on the screen.

'Which Jim? Atkins?'

'I don't know,' I say. 'It just says Jim.'

'Jim Key.' Drew sighs. 'I bet I know what that is.'

I peer at the notification. 'It says "Green light".' I glance up at Drew.

'Seriously?' His face falls.

'Do you want me to read it out to you?'

'Yes. Please.'

I click on the message and open it, then read, ' "Green light. Back on-site tomorrow. How quick can you get here?" '

'Oh God,' Drew says, sighing.

'What is it?' I ask.

'It's Crowthorpe. The contractors are back on-site. What time is it?'

'Twelve fifteen.'

Drew glances at the satnav. 'Can you tell him I'll be there by . . .' He pauses and glances at me. 'What do you think?'

I pull out my phone and check Google Maps, which has live traffic updates. 'There's another build-up ahead. A ten-minute delay, it's saying. But there's a faster route if you come off at the next junction. Do you want to take it?'

Drew is already indicating left and edging back over into the middle lane and then into the slow lane, ready to come off the motorway. I get us home twenty minutes ahead of our original estimate and I can tell Drew is impressed. We get out and he unstraps Sam, taking out his car seat and putting it down by the front door. I remind him that I will need Sam's changing bag and he says he will bring the rest of the luggage in later, then gets back into the car again and prepares to pull away. I turn to put my key in the lock, but I hear him call my name and as I look round, he says, 'I love you.' I smile and say that I love him too and he winks and says, 'Put some champagne in the fridge. I will be as quick as I can, and then let's finish our holiday off properly, shall we? I'll grab some pizza on my way home.'

As he drives away, I feel elated, not just at what this past week in the sun appears to have done for our relationship, but also at the way Drew so casually asked me to look at his phone and read and answer his message. If he had anything to hide from me, he would never have done this, or at least he would have to be a *really* scheming and premeditative person to organise something so elaborate in order to meet a woman, and I know he's not that scheming. He's not that good an actor, either. I smile to myself at the thought. He would have to be pretty stupid, too. I know Jim Key. He is a senior planning officer at the council. Drew knows that I know him. I could easily ask him if he sent Drew a text message to say that Crowthorpe was back up and running. Not that I would do this. I would never embarrass Drew like that, and anyway, I don't believe for one minute that it was anything but genuine.

I open the front door, thinking how a glass of ice-cold champagne and a slice of pizza will be the perfect end to the perfect week. But as the door swings back and I reach for Sam and step into the porch, I realise that the glorious week of sea and sunshine and our plans for the evening are about to be eclipsed by a dark shadow, because it looks as though we've had a visit from the police, who have left their card on the mat.

14

Lauren

I've been sacked. Not by my boss – by my therapist, and not only that, by my osteopath, too. It happened almost two weeks ago, but it's been on my mind ever since. It was humiliating, especially when Hope threatened to call the police. I knew I'd crossed a line by going back to their house again, and I should have guessed that the village busybodies wouldn't be able to resist a little more gossip. I should have been more careful, but I don't regret going to the fitness class that day and asking what I did; I'd never have got this close to finding out the truth if I hadn't. Anyway, in the end, it gave me the idea to call the police myself.

I'd fully intended to confront her first, though, to ask her to explain how she'd come to name her baby Sam, and what she thought about the fact that he was born and mine had died at Woodley Ridge Hospital on the exact same day. On the Saturday morning, I felt courageous and it was playing on my mind so much that the next day, I drove out there. I knew she'd have a go at me for turning up without calling again, but I didn't want to give her any time to come up with an excuse. I knew exactly how I was going to bring it up and so I just went. I was really disappointed when I saw she wasn't at home. Her Honda Civic was on the driveway, but the Range Rover was gone and so was she.

I decided it was probably for the best and I booked a session with her. I got myself all geared up for it again, but when it came to it, Hope ended up confronting *me* instead, asking me who I was and why I was there, putting me entirely on the back foot. I could have got answers to so many questions. I could have told her who I really was and what I'd come for, but instead I just ended up mumbling a load of nonsense about how I felt lost and how I was unable to structure my days after being signed off from work. I ended up telling her that my boss, Mike, is still paying me and has left my job open for me – which is true. I said I was wondering if I should maybe go back to work, if it would help, perhaps. I thought this would please her, but then she asked where I worked and because I hadn't yet told her who I really was, I lied and said I was an accountant and gave her the name of a fake company, which I knew she would look up.

After I said all this, we both sat there for a moment and I could see she was trying to decide whether or not to believe me, but before I could get my mouth open to say anything else, she asked me what my connection was to her husband, and why I had waited until he was home before coming back for the AirPod that evening. I stuck to my story and told her I had only just realised it was missing and that I'd needed it for the gym. I said that when I got to her house, I'd guessed she would be busy with the baby and hadn't wanted to disturb her, but then I saw the Range Rover coming down the road and turning into the drive, so I decided to wait for her husband to let me in.

'Where was your car?' she asked.

'In the lay-by up the road,' I told her.

'You didn't look like you were going to the gym,' she said, frowning. 'You were wearing jeans.'

'My gym clothes were in my bag in the car,' I said.

She gazed at me for a moment, looking uncertain. I hadn't realised until this point that she actually thought there might be something going on between me and her husband. I wanted to tell her she'd got it all wrong, but something stopped me.

The funny thing is that I *do* like him – or I would do, I think. We work in the same industry and so we do have quite a lot in common. I know this because of my online searches. When you search for Andrew Faris, his LinkedIn profile with his impressive list of credentials is the first thing you find, and after that there is a long string of local newspaper articles reporting on his involvement in the county's planning decisions. They'd be boring to most people, but I found them interesting and I have read pretty much all of them. They are all along the same lines: 'Mr Faris said the ecological impact of the planning application was not in the public interest,' or 'Mr Faris said the council couldn't approve the kind of loss of biodiversity that would result if the project went ahead.' I liked his ecological ethos and commitment to the preservation of the countryside.

And I do think about him, it's true. I think about him a lot. I think about them both. I imagine them watching Netflix together on that big blue sofa, having a regular, normal kind of life, like the one I used to have. I used to love curling up on our old orange sofas and watching a good period drama. I miss those sofas. I don't know why we got rid of them and replaced them with the new ones, which aren't nearly as comfortable. My living room doesn't feel the same any more, and I spend most of my time in bed. I used to love it, though. I used to love this house. I remember the day we found it and how we fell in love with its pretty arched brick doorway and its perfect nursery overlooking the park. I loved the original Victorian features: the cornicing, the wooden floorboards. I remember the paint we chose: pale beige, cream and butter yellow. I think about how happy we were and how much we were looking forward to having our baby.

And then I think about how it was all snatched away from me.

'I think it would be best if you find a new therapist,' Hope had said. 'I don't think we can continue to work together in these circumstances.'

I nodded and said I was sorry and promised not to come back, ever again. She said she appreciated that and then she said she would show me out and I got up and left.

Afterwards, I kept thinking about all the things Hope had said to me, the way she must have turned Jess against me, how humiliated I'd felt and how I hadn't stood up for myself. All I could think was: *How dare she? How dare she threaten to call the police on me, when it should be the other way round?*

So I picked up the phone and called. I asked for PC Jenkins. I had his number on a card in my bedside table, from the time before. But when he and PC Walsh came and I started to explain why I had called them, I was too melodramatic, too emotional, too one-sided. I sounded unconvincing, even to myself.

It took a week for them to come, which I guess was the first sign that they weren't going to take me seriously. As they sat sipping tea on the new sofas in my living room, they must have remembered how many times they'd sat there previously while I told them I couldn't remember one single thing about that day. They'd been so supportive before, so keen to remind me that if I remembered anything at all, I should contact them, but now that I had, it was like they wished I hadn't.

'I'm afraid gut instinct isn't going to stand up in a court of law,' PC Jenkins said, but he agreed they'd look into it, and then he and PC Walsh stood up and left.

It's Saturday today and Anna is here – my best friend. The real Anna. It's been a hot day and it is still gloriously warm outside, but we're sitting at the table in the kitchen instead of being in the garden because I'm worried the police might just turn up and knock on the door and we could miss them.

I've told Anna that I want her help with some paperwork, but she knows me. She knows we're inside because I'm waiting for the police to arrive.

She puts down her pen and looks up at me now and shakes her head. 'Don't get your hopes up, Lori,' she says. 'It might not come to anything.'

I frown and pretend I don't know what she's talking about.

'I'm talking about the police,' she says.

I sigh. 'Why are you so against the idea of them following it up?'

'I'm not against it,' she says. 'But . . .' She fixes her big brown eyes on mine and says, 'Lauren, there's not enough evidence, and you need solid evidence to make a complaint against someone. Besides, you've already told them you couldn't remember anything.'

She sees my reaction and reaches for my hand across the table, but I snatch it away.

'I'm sorry, Lori,' she said. 'I don't mean to sound heartless. It's the lawyer in me. I'm too blunt, I know.'

I wipe my eyes and look up at her. 'You're supposed to be on my side,' I say.

'I *am* on your side,' she insists. 'I just don't want you to get your hopes up, that's all.'

'Why does everyone keep saying that?' I sob, my voice rising. 'Why can't I have hope? It's the only thing keeping me going!'

She sighs, gets up and comes round the table to hug me, but I push her away.

15

Hope

Sam is rolling over now and can almost sit up. I know it won't be long before he's crawling and pulling himself up onto furniture, and then I'm going to have to keep my eyes and ears permanently open. For now, though, it's so peaceful lying on the grass beside him in our back garden. It's something both Sam and I love to do. There's so much for him to watch.

Jess sits with us for a while, but she has a patient soon. She takes a deep breath and I know she's about to say something.

'Go on,' I say, smiling. 'Out with it.'

'I just wondered what the police wanted when you came back from holiday? Was it about . . .' she hesitates '. . . you know who?'

I nod, propping myself up on one elbow and giving Sam a tickle on his tummy.

'Oh God. Really?' She frowns. 'What has she done now?'

'Nothing,' I say. 'It was nothing new. Just . . . old stuff. Just the same old stuff that happened before we went to Wales. It's all sorted.' I hesitate. 'Look, do you mind if we don't talk about it?'

'Sure.' She nods vehemently.

'I don't want to think about her any more,' I explain.

'Got it.' Jess nods firmly, then raises her eyebrows theatrically and says, 'Anna who?'

I shoot her a wry smile.

'Well, I'd better be going,' she says, pushing herself up onto her feet.

'Thanks again,' I say. 'I'm winding things down, so I may not see any clients again for a while. But we'll see you soon.'

'Of course you will. Aunty Jess is going to be right next door, isn't she?' Jess says to Sam. 'Or is she?' she says mysteriously, putting her hands over her eyes.

'Where's she gone,' I ask Sam, smiling. 'Where's Aunty Jess gone?'

I watch in delight as Sam kicks his legs and tenses up, his gummy smile widening in anticipation.

'Boo!' Jess says loudly, removing her hands.

Sam bursts into peals of laughter. This is his favourite game at the moment, and it never gets old for me either. Not when I can hear him laugh like that.

'Better go,' says Jess. She stretches her arms up behind her head and yawns, then heads off towards the gate. I take a deep breath and lie back down beside Sam, holding out a finger. He grabs it and we bask together in the sunshine for a while.

I suddenly feel exhausted and close my eyes, just for a beat, knowing Sam's there right beside me, feeling his chubby fist gripping mine. I take a deep breath and think back to the day we got home from Wales, the day I found the card from the police on my mat, of the fear that had risen up inside me, how I'd grabbed the handle of Sam's car seat and run straight out of the house again and through the back gate to Jess.

She'd been in the kitchen and had seen me coming and immediately opened the door. 'I told them,' she said straight away. 'I told them you were away and I asked if it was about Anna, and I told them what she'd been doing, and that she'd been a complete nuisance.'

'But why were they here?' I asked. 'Who called them?'

She looked puzzled then. 'I don't know,' she said. 'I just saw the police car on your drive, so I went over. I assumed they'd come about her.'

I asked Jess not to mention this to Nick or to Drew. I went home and phoned the mobile number on the card and got a PC Jenkins, who said there had been a complaint from a woman named Lauren Hopwood, who was accusing Drew and me of something he said he needed to talk to us about. He didn't seem to want to discuss it on the phone, but told me not to worry. They just needed to have a chat with us, he said, to clear up a few things.

I made the appointment for a Tuesday when I knew

Drew wouldn't be home, and then went into autopilot, forcing myself to shut Anna out of my mind. I knew she was the one who had called them and made the complaint, but I made myself forget about it and switched the whole thing off. I wasn't going to let it spoil our evening, and so I put the champagne in the fridge and after Drew came home with the pizza and Sam was in bed, we snuggled up together on the sofa and watched a box set. Drew told me how lucky he was to have me and I said, 'You're not lucky. You deserve me,' which sounded as though I thought rather a lot of myself and made us both laugh.

I asked Jess to have Sam for me while the police were here and made her promise not to come over and interrupt, which she couldn't do easily anyway, not with Sam in tow. I told her that I would send them round to speak to her if they needed to.

I'd allowed an hour, but in the end they only took forty minutes of my time. I apologised that Drew wasn't home but told them I could explain everything. They listened and nodded a lot, and I could tell they were on my side. They apologised for bothering me, saying they were already aware that 'Ms Hopwood' had been making problems for me and my family. It was odd hearing her real name, but they didn't bat an eyelid when I kept referring to her as Anna. They'd already heard from 'other sources' that she had lied to me about who she was and that she'd been a bit of a nuisance, which they said they would warn her about.

When they left, they said they were completely satisfied

with everything I had told them and would be closing the investigation. So that's all over with now, which is a bit of a relief. It's a glorious day and everything in the garden is rosy – quite literally! – and my husband has promised to make steak with all the fixings again for dinner this evening and we're going to watch another episode of our box set and get a much-needed early night.

The sun is high in the sky and I'm feeling deliciously relaxed. I'd like to lie here for a bit longer, but it's actually starting to feel a little too hot now and Sam is starting to wriggle and whimper. I yawn and push myself up onto my knees, then lift his T-shirt and blow a huge raspberry on his belly, which makes him laugh. I do it again, or pretend I'm about to, and he opens his mouth wide and smiles into my eyes, seeking them out. As I pick him up, I think about the perfect life Drew and I have created with our perfect little boy and feel a surge of happiness as I carry him inside.

16

Lauren

I waited almost five weeks for the police to come back and say they couldn't do anything. They barely even explained their reasons to me, just that there was 'insufficient evidence' and it was going to be an 'NFA', as they kept calling it, until I asked what that was and PC Jenkins said it meant there would be 'no further action'. The words hit me like a ton of bricks and I wished I hadn't asked.

Anna was right, of course – Anna is always right. They thought I was deluded and that I was just trying to find someone to blame for my own misfortune. They even warned me away from Chorley Common and said that even though this wasn't an official harassment warning because there hadn't been an official complaint, I would be wise to listen to them and stay away from Hope Dunsmore and her family.

When Anna phoned to ask if the police had responded yet, I pretended I didn't care. I told her instead that I had found a new therapist; I knew this would please her, and I didn't want her to start going on about antidepressants again. If I agreed to those, the doctor might insist I stop taking the painkillers, which I knew I needed to do, but they helped me zone out. They made me feel sleepy and although I knew I was sleeping too much again, it passed the time.

Then, on a Friday around three weeks ago, my boss, Mike, called and asked if I was ready to go back to work yet. I felt under pressure and I knew I sounded flustered when I told him I wasn't sure. He was really sweet, but I could tell he was under pressure too. 'I don't mean to rush you, Lauren,' he said, 'but it's been six months now and I could really do with a decision either way.' I told him I'd think about it and call him back really soon, but as soon as the call ended, I immediately knew I wasn't going back to Egan & Meyer.

And then it hit me. I wasn't going to go backwards, I was going to move forward. I knew exactly what I was going to do.

I can't say the thought hadn't crossed my mind before, because it had – many times. But I had been too mired in grief to think about it properly; I couldn't think about anything properly. I couldn't even deal with everyday things like letters, emails and my bank account – Anna had been helping with all of that. I hadn't wanted to leave behind this house and everything Charlie and I had built up together. But suddenly it all made sense. Instead of reliving the memories we had already made, I would go ahead and create the new ones we had been *going* to make.

Relief is the only word to describe the way I felt at that moment. It was like the sun coming out from behind a cloud. Anna came that evening and she could see the difference in me straight away. She cooked spaghetti bolognese and we ate it together at the kitchen table, then I picked a romcom for us to watch on TV. The next day – a Saturday – we went clothes shopping in Wyebridge. In the car, she kept looking at me sideways and smiling when I caught her eye, which made me smile back. On Sunday, before she left, she said I seemed a million times better and suggested that maybe it was because I had let go of 'certain things' that were pinning me to the past. It was the perfect moment for me to tell her she was right. We were drinking wine in the back garden and I was sitting on the swing, as usual, while she was in the chair next to me. I told her I wanted to move on with my life and that I was going to put my house up for rent, sell my car and book a flight. I was going to just take off somewhere.

'On your own?' She looked horrified.

'Yes.'

She continue to look uncertain, but she could also see that I was feeling genuinely happy for the first time in a very long while. 'You're glowing,' she observed, peering at me with a combination of concern and amusement, and I wanted to hug her for understanding straight away, so I did.

'There's nothing here for me,' I told her. 'I love you, and I love my mum, but it's like there's the "before" and the "after" – and you and my mum are part of the before and the immediate after. And please don't take this the wrong way, Anna, but every time I see either of you, it reminds me of what I lost. It's keeping me trapped in trauma.'

Anna nodded, almost looking pleased. 'Is this what your new therapist said?'

'Kind of,' I lied. 'But actually, it's mostly something I worked out for myself. I hope that over time, and with a bit of distance, this will change, but for now it's how I feel. I hope you understand.'

She nodded again, blinking. 'Where will you go?'

I shrugged. 'Not sure. Maybe Australia. My mum's sister lives there. I've always fancied Canada, actually. Or the States. I'll figure it out. I may go backpacking in Asia.'

'Isn't that a bit dangerous,' she said, frowning. 'For a woman on her own?'

'Anna,' I said, in a warning tone of voice. But I was smiling.

'Sounds exciting,' she said, and she looked as if she was about to say, 'Can I come?' but had thought better of it, even as a joke.

I called Mike first thing on Monday morning and told him I wouldn't be coming back to work. I apologised for keeping him hanging on and thanked him for everything he'd done for me. When I told him my plans, he said he had someone new starting who had relocated with his family from Blackburn and that they were looking for a rental. He asked if I would be at all interested in talking to them. I said I would, and he gave me the phone number. I called the same day and spoke to a man called Colin Johnson. We had a very positive conversation and I arranged to show him the house in two days' time. He came with his family and they all seemed really excited. As they left, he turned to me and said they definitely wanted it, and I told him it was theirs. I said I wasn't sure exactly when I would be leaving, but that if I left before he was ready to move in, I would leave the house keys with my mum.

I sailed through the next couple of weeks on autopilot, mostly just mulling everything over, looking at flights and arranging to sell my car. A private buyer came quickly and took it off my hands before I was really ready, but luckily Anna's daughter Joni said she would lend me her old Fiat Punto to tide me over until I left.

My mum was sad but, like Anna, understood that I needed time to myself somewhere new, somewhere away from my painful memories, and she didn't try to dissuade me. I wasn't completely sure if she had guessed where I was going, but if she had, she didn't ask. My mum has always been the most discreet of people and I knew it wasn't in her nature to ask a question when it was clear the other person didn't want her to ask it.

But all the same, I have often wondered if she knew what was in the two envelopes that had arrived for me while I was still in hospital, and which she had tucked away in the kitchen drawer, out of sight.

17

Hope

It's not yet five thirty, but Sam is tired and ready for sleep, and so I tell Drew I'll put him down.

'I can do it,' Drew says, looking up from the stove, where he's heating soup for himself. 'You'll be late for your class.'

'It won't take long,' I tell him. 'Have your food in peace.'

I take Sam upstairs and lie him on our bed while I slip into my yoga clothes, turning to look at myself in the mirror. I haven't lost much weight, but I've built muscle and I feel stronger and thinner, which has given me confidence. I now really look forward to the Core Conditioning class and also to the female companionship I get from it. There's always a bit of a huddle and a chat outside afterwards, and last week there was talk of going back to Penny's house for a drink tonight, which Drew has encouraged me to do.

'But I want a last cuddle with my lovely boy before I go, don't I?' I say to Sam, picking him up again and taking him into his bedroom, where I change his nappy and put on a clean Babygro. I pop his dummy into his mouth and hold him against me, giving him a gentle bounce as I look past his shoulder and out of the back window. It's not yet dark, but the solar lights in the garden have started to come on. With Sam still in my arms, I turn on his owl night light and switch off the main light, then walk across and turn on the hallway light outside the door. I give him one last kiss and lay him down in his cot, hesitating before I leave. But he's sucking away on his dummy and already has the spaced-out look he gets when he's about to drift off.

It was hard leaving him to settle himself at first, and he would cry for me to begin with, but Drew insisted that a bit of sleep training was needed and that I should just go off to my class and let him be the one to settle Sam. It broke my heart to go down the stairs and out of the front door while my baby was crying, and not to be the one to go in and comfort him, but I had to admit that Sam soon began to sleep much better at night, and for longer. I guess Drew didn't smell of breast milk and didn't have the female curves Sam wanted to snuggle up to.

Drew smiled when I mentioned this and said, 'Well, he gets to cuddle up to you all day. It's my turn at night.'

I laughed and told him, 'Only if you play your cards right.' There was an awkward moment between us then. It didn't last long, but it hurt that I couldn't say something off the cuff like that any more without us both remembering that he *hadn't* played things right in the past and it had nearly destroyed us. I even felt sorry for him, the way his face flushed and his neck turned pink, and so I reached out and stroked his arm.

But there was still enough love there between us, and I was right when I said that Sam would help bring us back together. He really has done that. This life I'm living is the one I always wanted, and I need to remember that and count my blessings every day.

This is what I'm thinking about as I go downstairs and say goodbye to Drew, then put on my trainers and go out the back way and through the gate into Jess's garden. As I walk with her to her car, Jess tells me about some stupid thing Nick has done, and we are soon laughing about that. This, in turn, reminds me that, actually, there *is* no perfect marriage because we are human beings and human beings are imperfect, but that, with practice, we can train ourselves to think differently about the things that bother us. Our thoughts are the only things we actually have any control over, after all. It's what Viktor Frankl became famous for saying, and there are neuroscientific studies to support it. It's what cognitive behavioural therapy is, basically. I'm not a CBT therapist, but I use a bit of everything in my approach because different methods work for different people and, as I sometimes have to remind my clients, I, too, am one of those people. I make mistakes, just like everyone else, and I definitely don't have all the answers.

I *do* know my stuff, though – and I'm interested in that stuff, which makes me strive harder for those answers.

'You're solutions oriented,' Jess said to me the other day.

Now, as she pulls out of the driveway, I'm thinking this is true and that I already have the solution to my problem; I just need more practice. It's like how I didn't really enjoy Core Conditioning until I'd done it often enough to get good at it and for it to become entrenched in my life. I've heard runners and weightlifters say they really miss it if they stop, and this has to be the same. After all, if I can train my baby to go to sleep by himself, and if I can train myself to want healthier food and to burn fat instead of muscle, then surely I can train my mind not to think about the things I'd like to forget?

18

Lauren

I've found the perfect place to park the Fiat Punto. A few weeks ago, I discovered that if you pass Flint Cottage on your left and continue on up the hill, past the lay-by, and go just a couple of hundred yards further along the road, there is a left-hand turn into a small cul-de-sac with just a handful of run-down council houses. There's a piece of scrappy wasteland at the bottom on which there is a concrete water tower, and behind that there is a small gravel clearing – the perfect size for a Fiat Punto. Next to the clearing there is a wire fence with a gaping hole (made by kids, I expect – thank you, kids) and behind the wire fence is a field, and beyond that field there is another field backing directly onto the Dunsmore-Farises' garden.

Better still, if you come into the village from the opposite direction, via Ashcombe Ridge, you can reach the cul-de-sac before you get to the lay-by, without passing any other houses save for the council houses, which seem pretty desolate. There isn't a single car outside. They're possibly not even occupied, and if there is anyone living in any of them, I haven't seen them, not in the past couple of weeks I've been parking here. All I see is rabbits – tons of them. They're cute little things, always shooting out of the bushes and zigzagging around as I approach, or scurrying like wildfire across the grass.

Of course, the field I hang out in is the same one that backs onto Jess and Nick's garden, and I've had to be careful, but the evenings are drawing in now and the light has started to fade earlier. It's usually dark by six thirty. For weeks now, I've crouched here every single evening, watching both sets of neighbours pulling in and out of their driveways, watching their routines. Weekends are unpredictable. Weekdays are better. Nick often gets home from work late, sometimes not until eight or nine. Drew is usually home by seven, but sometimes he's back a bit later with a load of supermarket bags or a takeaway. Jess and Nick tend to go for a home delivery – Sainsbury's, mostly. Jess and Hope sometimes go in and out of each other's back gardens, one or the other carrying a bottle of wine. I watch them from my hideout behind the Dunsmore-Farises' shed, which, conveniently, is right in the middle between the two properties. Both gardens are well maintained and wide enough to see all the way to the front of the house.

There are a few occasions when Hope has been out in the car on her own, but I can't predict what will happen when she does, and so I'm biding my time. She could forget something and come back. I knew there probably wouldn't be the perfect time, but there will be the optimal time, and as I expected from the start, that day is a Thursday. Today, in fact. Today is the day I've been building up towards, the one I've been aiming for, and funnily enough, I'm completely calm. It's a weird feeling. It's like I'm not inside my body any more.

It's not yet dark, so I stay perfectly still and watch from behind the shed as Hope exits through the bifold door, shuts it behind her and walks across the grass, disappearing through the back gate into Jess's garden. When she's gone, I tiptoe along behind the shed and peek round, watching her emerge on the other side. Jess comes out to greet her and they walk towards the Golf together. Jess says something funny and Hope lets out a burst of laughter as they get into the car. The engine starts and the Golf pulls out, and they're gone a moment later, but I'm going to wait a little longer. It will be dark in half an hour, and if they're not back by six thirty, it means no one's changed their mind, so I can pretty much guarantee they won't be back until gone seven. It's best to wait. There will be enough time.

I creep back and forth between the two properties for a while, watching Nick's house first, then creeping back to check on Drew. The lights are dimmed in the living room, but he's in there watching TV. He's always in there watching TV in the evenings, once Sam is down. Sam's nursery is at the back of the house. I've seen them in there, putting him to bed. He's usually down by six thirty, around about the time it gets dark, but tonight he's down already. I can tell by the way the main light went off and the night light and the light in the hallway came on.

I move back behind the shed and pull my phone out of my pocket. It's six twenty-five and it's dark enough now. I put my phone away again, then move across and take one last glance at Nick and Jess's house, which is silent. Nick's still at work and even if he came home early, he wouldn't go round to see Drew, not on a weekday. He always eats in the kitchen during the week, then goes straight to bed and watches TV in there. I can tell by the way the light flickers bright one minute and dim the next.

I move back across to the Dunsmore-Farises' garden and swing a leg over the picket fence, stepping in and quickly flattening myself against the side of the shed before sprinting across the grass. When I get to the bifold doors, I peer inside. I can see Drew sitting on the couch, gaping up at the flatscreen. He's snacking on something or other that's on the sofa next to him, bringing his hand back and forth to his mouth.

I take my tennis-ball-and-stocking arrangement out of my coat pocket, then raise my arm and give the window a good, sound whack, immediately ducking back behind the log store that extends out from the downstairs cloakroom wall. As expected, I see the bifold door open and hear Drew step out. I peek out and watch as he gazes around in the darkness for a moment, then walks over and looks around the wall at the corner of the house. A moment later, he has disappeared out of sight.

I quickly dart out of my hiding place and slip through the open door, moving so fast that I surprise myself. I'm through the dining room, across the lounge and through the door to the hallway within seconds, and a moment later I'm upstairs. I pause on the landing. Sam's bedroom door is open and I can see the edge of the cot in the yellow glow from the night light beside it. I tiptoe in and lean down, and there he is. My baby. My angel. My darling Sam. I gently slip one arm underneath his sleepy body and the other under his head, lifting him up and holding him against me as I slide him into the baby carrier that I'm already wearing underneath my coat. He snuffles and whimpers a little as I struggle to get his legs through the holes in the carrier while also stabilising his body, then he opens his eyes and starts to cry. I quickly soothe him, saying, 'Shh . . . shh,' and stroking his hair, but he's still crying. I glance into the cot and spot his dummy. I snatch it up, holding it against his lip. His mouth opens like a baby bird's, and to my relief he accepts it. I smile to myself at the sensation of it moving in and out against my chest. He's like that baby on *The Simpsons*. It's adorable. I wrap my coat around him, and we head downstairs.

I manage to get across the lounge and into the dining room before Drew stops me. He appears in the open doorway in his socks, putting one foot inside, onto the carpet, and lifting the other to remove a piece of gravel. When he sees me standing in front of him, facing him, his eyes widen, first in shock and horror, then in recognition. They move to the bundle against my chest.

'No,' he says softly, shaking his head. 'No. No no no no no.'

'I've come to collect him,' I say.

'Oh my God,' he says breathlessly, putting up his hands in a 'Stop' motion. 'You can't be serious?'

He reaches out to grab for the baby carrier.

I step back and swing away from him.

'What do you want?' he asks, his voice trembling.

'Just Sam,' I say.

'You've got to be kidding.' He shakes his head in bewilderment. 'I'll call the police.'

'No, Drew,' I say. 'You won't. You know you won't, because if you call the police, they'll find out what you did.'

He swallows, puts one hand on his hip and scratches his head with the other. His cheeks are flushed, his neck pink. 'Have you spoken to them?' he asks shakily.

I frown. 'Didn't Hope tell you?'

He looks baffled. 'No.'

'Oh dear. She should have told you,' I say.

'Do they know?' He looks terrified.

I shake my head. 'No. And they won't – if you let me go.'

He hesitates. I seize my moment and move past him. He spins round, open-mouthed, and watches as I hug Sam towards me, pulling my coat around us both, and then step out through the bifold door and onto the patio.

There's a three-quarter moon up above, which, along

with the solar lights along the path, is casting a glow over the garden. I smile to myself. The moon and the sun, lighting our way. It feels magical. It was meant to be. The air is fresh and cool and the grass smells good as I cross the lawn, my baby's body pressed up against mine. His head is right there in front of me and I press my lips against it. He smells like a small piece of heaven and I can't quite believe this is happening. Me and Sam, together again.

Drew is there a moment later, following me across the garden, trailing a few steps behind me. He's still in his socks and I can hear him swearing as he treads on something that has hurt his foot. 'Please,' he says, sounding tearful. 'Don't do this. It will destroy Hope. It will kill her.'

I ignore him and hug Sam close to me as I step over the fence into the field, pulling my phone out of my pocket, swiping the on-screen display and tapping on the torch. I stride along the boundary of this field towards the next. It's the same route I've walked every evening for the past three weeks. I know it well.

I can hear Drew behind me. I can tell he's struggling to keep up with me as he pads in his socks after me over the uneven ground. 'This is *not* the answer!' he calls after me.

'So what *is* the answer, then?' I say, not looking round. 'That you get to live happily ever after in your lovely cottage in your lovely village, with Sam and your lovely wife, while I'm left with nothing?'

He doesn't answer. He's trodden on something hard, again, and I can hear him curse. I carry on walking fast and

Sam and I are soon in the next field. I can see my car up ahead. I'm nearly there. Drew, meanwhile, is losing pace. The field we are in now is freshly ploughed and the ground is still rugged and damp from last week's rain, and although he's not far behind me again, he's struggling to walk on the uneven surface.

'Please, Lauren,' he begs me.

I stop and swing round to face him, momentarily pleased that he's acknowledged who I am at last, that he's had the courtesy to recognise that I'm a real person with real feelings.

'Please, Lauren,' he says again. Unlike me, he doesn't have a torch and I can only just about see him in the darkness. I hear him yell out as he trips and stumbles to the ground. 'Let's talk. Please. We can sort this out.'

'There's nothing to sort out,' I say, and I turn and walk away, leaving him on his knees in the dirt.

'Bring him back. I won't tell anyone!' he begs, and I can hear that he's crying.

'No,' I say firmly, and then I turn and look at him one more time. 'I'm sorry.' I'm not completely devoid of feeling towards him. I do care that I'm hurting him. I'm not that cold.

But I have what I need now and it's time to go.

Minutes later, I'm at the fence. My car's just on the other side, only a few yards away. I pull out my car keys, pointing the fob. The car clunks open and the internal lights come on. I open the passenger door, take Sam out of the carrier and settle him in his car seat, then walk round to the driver's side, which is closest to the field. I reversed in, of course, and the car is pointing away, ready to make a quick exit.

'Please,' I can hear Drew calling after me in the darkness, his voice shaking with desperation. 'I'll give you anything you want. Money. I can give you money.'

I ignore him.

'Please. Give him back!' he calls out plaintively.

'No,' I say, for the final time. 'He's mine. He belongs to me.'

19

Hope

Something has happened. I know this straight away, before we've even pulled into the driveway. The outside lights are on in the garden at the back, and I can see Drew hovering behind the living-room window, looking out.

I say goodnight to Jess and walk quickly away from her house and towards mine. Drew is now in the porch, at the open front door. As I approach, I can see straight away that all the colour has drained from his face.

'What's wrong?' I ask, noticing that the knees of his jeans are muddy and he has bare feet, both of which look as though they've been bleeding.

He waits until I'm inside and he has closed the door behind me before he speaks. 'Hope,' he says, his voice quivering, 'you have to promise me not to panic.'

I push past him into the hallway and race up the stairs and into Sam's bedroom. The main light is on and the cot is empty. I suddenly can't feel my legs.

'Where is he, Drew?' I scream, going back out onto the landing as all the possibilities flash through my mind. He's downstairs in the bouncer. He's been sick. Drew has been trying to deal with it. He's been taken to hospital. He's in the lounge.

But I know none of this is true.

Drew appears at the bottom of the stairs. His eyes are glossy.

'Where is he?'

'She's taken him,' he says shakily, and my entire body goes cold.

'Who?' I say. But I know who. 'When? When did this happen?'

'Not long. Half an hour ago.'

'Well, she won't have got far,' I say. 'You've called the police, right?'

Drew flushes. 'No.'

'You *are* kidding?'

'She threatened me,' he says, taking a step up towards me, tears shining in his eyes. 'Us. I tried to stop her, but . . .'

'You mean . . . you saw it happen?' I ask in astonishment, gaping at him. 'You spoke to her? You watched her take him?'

Drew continues up the stairs. 'Hope,' he pleads. 'She said if I called the police, she'd tell them everything.'

'Oh my God, Drew!' I say in disbelief, and burst into tears. Drew gets to the top of the stairs and reaches out to comfort me, but I push him back and he has to grab hold of the banister to stop himself from falling. 'What have you done?' I scream at him. 'What have you done?'

'Hope, listen to me—' Drew begins.

'This is our baby!' I sob. 'We have to call the police, right now!' My phone is inside my handbag, which is strapped across my body. I pull the bag over my head, open the flap and begin to rummage through it for my phone.

Drew reaches out and snatches my bag out of my hands, throwing it behind him. I hear it thud down the stairs. 'We're not calling the police, Hope,' he says angrily. 'Not until you tell me what you said to them. She said you already spoke to them. What the fuck did you say?'

I feel sick suddenly. Is this all *my* fault? Is that why she's done this? Because of what I told the police? I drop to my knees on the landing carpet, my legs unable to bear my weight any longer. 'She doesn't know anything, Drew,' I protest. 'She called them and she told them what she *thought* happened, but she didn't know anything for sure. She can't remember anything!'

'But what did you say to them?' Drew persists.

'What?' I close my eyes, thinking about where Anna . . . Lauren . . . might be at this very moment. *With my baby.* A sob rips through me, but I gulp it back. I need to think. I need to think straight. 'Which way did she take him?' I ask. 'Was she in her car?'

Drew closes his eyes and slumps down onto the stairs. 'She went out the back way, across the fields. Her car was in that cul-de-sac up at the top, past the lay-by.'

'I know the reg,' I say, thinking quickly. 'Penny wrote it down and gave it to me.'

'Good,' Drew says, opening his eyes and sitting upright. 'Let's go. Let's find her.'

'Are you stupid?' I snap. 'How the hell are we going to find her? I'm talking about the police! We need to give it to the police!'

'No,' Drew says. 'You have to listen to me, Hope. Find her phone number. Call her. We have to reason with her. She'll wake up tomorrow—'

'Tomorrow?' Has he lost his mind?

'—and she'll realise this isn't the answer. We'll tell her that she's not in any trouble and that we understand and we want to listen to her.'

'And if she doesn't answer?'

'Then we call again. We keep calling her, and if she still doesn't answer – or she doesn't listen – we find her. We find Sam. But we do *not* call the police.'

I think about this for a minute. Maybe he's right. You hear about hostage situations going wrong, about desperate people doing desperate things when the police turn up, when they're under pressure. Besides which, I have no idea where she really lives or where she might have gone – and what if she's driving a different car?

'She's been planning this for weeks,' Drew says. 'This isn't some spur-of-the-moment decision.'

I put my head in my hands and start to cry.

'Hope,' Drew says gently. I feel his hand on mine and I

slap it away. He waits for a beat, then says, 'Hope, did you sign anything?'

I look up. 'When?'

'When you talked to the police.'

I think about this for a moment, then nod.

He closes his eyes again, takes a deep breath and says, 'Hope, if you made a statement to the police which isn't true, we could *both* be in serious trouble – you do understand that, don't you? If you call the police and report Sam missing and they get to her before we do, there could be consequences for *both of us*. Serious ones.'

I look up at my husband and he looks back at me as if he's begging me to understand. I do, kind of. But I'm torn in two. A part of me knows what he is saying is true, and that he is saying this to protect me as well as himself, but a bigger part of me just wants my baby back.

The first part of me knows he's right, that although those uniformed cops I spoke to couldn't be bothered to investigate the case properly, a clever detective might do. Jess and Nick will also wonder why Lauren might think she has a right to take Sam from us. Jess will have her own theory, of course, but she'd be wrong.

Or would she?

And then I start to think about all the other reasons why Drew might not want me to call the police. As I look up at him and see his weary, scared, beautiful eyes gazing back at me, I can't help but wonder if maybe he *is* that clever, that good an actor. And then it hits me in one sudden, horrible, gut-wrenching second that I may have been a complete fool. Maybe I have completely underestimated my husband. Maybe he helped her? After all, it was he who encouraged me to go to the fitness class in the first place and to go back to Penny's this evening, even though we decided not to go in the end. Maybe they thought they'd have more time to get Sam away. Maybe that's why he has mud all over his jeans. Maybe he really *is* that scheming, that devious.

'You knew who she was,' I say accusingly.

Drew looks hurt. 'We *both* did.'

'Not until the police came and spoke to me,' I say. 'I didn't know until then. You knew before that. Why didn't you tell me?'

Drew breathes in deeply, an exasperated sound, then throws both hands up in the air. 'I tried,' he says, his voice an agonised croak. 'I tried to talk to you.'

'When?' I frown.

'So many times, Hope. So many bloody times.'

I feel a stirring of self-doubt. 'When? When did you try and talk to me?'

'All the time!' Drew bursts out. 'All the bloody time, right from very beginning.' He pauses and shuts his eyes. 'When Sam was having his operation . . .' He breathes in and out deeply, then opens his eyes again. 'And then numerous times after that. A couple of months ago, even. After a while, I wondered if you even remembered what happened, and that's when I stopped trying. I thought you'd blocked it out, and God knows, you'd have had good enough reason to do that, Hope. But please don't tell me I didn't try to talk to you, because I did.'

We both sit in silence for a moment as I turn this thought around for a bit, then tuck it away for later. I say, 'Her number's on my phone. Can you get it, please? You call it. You speak to her. But put it on speaker so I can listen.'

Drew nods, and goes down the stairs to get my bag from where it's fallen. He takes out my phone and brings it back up to me. I find the number, then hand it back. He calls it, holding the phone out so that it's between the two of us. It rings out.

'It's not switched off, at least,' Drew says. 'So we'll just keep trying until she answers.'

I nod and Drew sits down on the stairs beside me again.

It has started to rain hard and the landing window is rattling noisily. The overhead light is way too bright and is hurting my eyes. There's a ringing sound in my ears and my head hurts.

I swallow hard and cover my eyes with my hands, thinking about what Drew just said about me lying to the police, and how he'd tried to talk to me, and that maybe none of this would have happened if I'd just listened to him.

I try to think back to what I said to those police officers and whether it was actually true or not, but I can't remember. Maybe it wasn't? Maybe I lied – to myself, and to them?

PART FOUR

Seven Months Earlier

20

Drew

I sit in the family room at the hospital and stare down at my trembling knees, trying to think, but my mind has frozen. Maybe it has raced so fast for so long that it has stopped working. Like a faulty phone battery. Or a faulty heart. I close my eyes and force myself to breathe. My baby is – at this very moment – in Great Ormond Street Hospital having emergency life-saving surgery to close the hole in his own tiny heart. A space came up on the surgeon's list and then he was gone. The obstetrician called it a 'scoop and run' and the phrase made me wince. It was freakishly apt.

After the ambulance left, Hope went back to the maternity ward. I thought we might talk, but she turned her back on me and said she needed to sleep. So, I found my way to the family room, where I ejected a Styrofoam cup of coffee from a machine in the corner and sat down to wait. And here I am. I've been here for two and a half hours and had three Styrofoam coffees and a bag of ready-salted crisps that sat on my tongue like scraps of cardboard, as did the croissant I ate for breakfast. But I have to stay strong, for Hope. I have to be here for her. How can I leave her now?

The silence in the room is deafening. I look up at the TV, which is on with the sound down. The news has finished and *The One Show* has started, the screen in front of me incongruously – almost mockingly – filled with happy faces and silent laughter. I look around for a remote, but I can't see one. I get up, but I can't turn off the TV manually, so I sit down again and instead look at my phone, which is on the empty plastic chair beside me. As I reach out to pick it up, it bleeps and flashes and my heart leaps so violently that I think I might pass out.

I grip the edge of my seat for a second and then I reach out again and check the notification on the screen. It's my dad. I've had several missed calls and messages, but I can't bring myself to talk to anyone. I should tell him he's a grandad. I wonder if Hope's called her parents. She's no closer to them than I am to my father, besides which, Hope's parents are weirdly self-centred and childish; it's almost as though she's the adult and they are the kids. I wonder how that conversation will go.

I try to think of someone else to call, someone who will tell my dad for me. There's my sister, Milly, in Australia, but she's always so busy with her job and her children, and anyway, it's the middle of the night there. There's my brother, Max, who I'm closest to out of all my family, at least since I lost my mum, but he struggles badly with depression and I don't want to burden him with what's happened to us. I have friends who know my dad, but I don't want to talk to them either. I can't, not without telling them everything, and how can I do that? They'll just tell me to go to the police and they won't be able to do anything to help, and it won't make me feel any better.

I need to talk to Hope. She'll have had some sleep by now. She'll know what to do. The thought brings with it a rush of relief and I stand up quickly, gathering up all my empty cups and crisp packets, fumbling and dropping them, then picking them up again before stuffing them into the bin by the door. I realise I can't wait to leave this room, which has begun to feel like a prison cell.

As I walk back onto the ward, a nurse looks up and smiles at me. I flash her a faint smile back, but inside I'm thinking, *If you only knew*. It then crosses my mind that maybe she does; maybe she's smiling because she knows that someone from hospital management is about to come for me – a man in a suit and tie, accompanied by a police officer. I imagine them arriving in the corridor up ahead and walking onto the ward. I force myself to breathe as my legs give way underneath me for a moment, so that I have to stand still and put my hand against the wall to steady myself.

'Are you OK?' the nurse asks me.

I nod. 'Yes. Just a bit dizzy.'

'I'll bet you haven't eaten much. I'll get you a biscuit,' she says cheerily. 'And how about a cup of tea?'

I nod, unable to speak. I look around, disorientated. I can't remember which room Hope is in.

'She's in there,' says the nurse, pointing.

'Right.'

They gave Hope a room on her own, which I'm guessing was so that she didn't have to see the other new mothers holding their babies. She is facing away from me when I go in, as she was when I left. I call her name gently, but she doesn't move. I hover by her bed for a moment, then sink down into an armchair next to her. It feels better to be here with Hope than in that waiting room on my own; even her scorn and anger will be a welcome break from the silent recriminations running on repeat through my head. There's a newspaper on the bedside cabinet. I pick it up and open it out, but it's a tabloid, two days old. It can't be Hope's – she hates the tabloids. I fold it back up and put it down on the beside cabinet again, and as I do so, I notice my hands trembling violently. My knees are shaking too.

Hope stirs and turns over so that she's now facing me. She opens her eyes and I'm overwhelmed with relief, even though she's actually the last person who is likely to be pleased to see me. I watch her face as she realises where she is, what's happening, that I'm there next to her, that I am, indeed, the last person in the world she wants to see.

'Is there news?' she asks quickly, her voice croaky and thick.

'No, not yet.'

She clears her throat.

'Do you want some water?' I ask her.

She gives a brief nod.

I pick up the jug from the stand. Hope leans on her elbows and moves into an upright position. I pour a glass of water and put it on the overbed table in front of her, but my hand is still shaking and I spill some.

'Sorry.' I pull a tissue from a box on the nightstand and drop it onto the spilled water. We both watch as the liquid seeps through. Hope picks up the glass and drinks.

'So, you've not heard anything at all?' she asks, putting the glass back down.

I shake my head. 'No.'

She looks directly at me and we sit in silence for a minute, each waiting for the other to say something.

'Hope—' I begin.

She cuts me off quickly. 'I don't want to hear anything about *her*.'

I nod. 'Yes. Yes. Of course. That's fine. I wasn't going to—'

'Sam's all that matters right now. Until we know for sure that he's . . .' She stops and clears her throat. I fall silent, waiting for her to finish her sentence. 'That he's OK,' she says, swallowing back tears. 'That everything's OK . . .'

I take a chance and reach out and touch her hand very lightly, my fingers grazing hers. I know Hope so well. I know the fact that she's even talking to me like this means she's stopped being angry and has decided to be pragmatic. She's a remarkable person. She has an incredible ability to see through the worst of situations and switch into a practical, grown-up mode when she needs to. It's something to do with having had two hippy parents who never grew up, no doubt; *she* pretty much had to parent *them*, which is why I've always known she will make an amazing mother. That's one of the many, many things I love about her. Right now, there's nothing I want more than to accept her terms, pretend that nothing else has happened and slip into a safe, warm haven with her and shut out the world.

But what if the police come for me? What do I say? We need to agree on this. I'll do whatever Hope says, of course. I get up to close the door, but as I do so, the nurse comes in with a cup of tea and a plate of biscuits. I step back for her to enter and wait as she puts the plate down on the nightstand. She hands me my tea and asks Hope if she'd like a hot drink and Hope says she would.

'We need to talk,' I say, when the nurse has gone and I've shut the door behind her.

Hope shoots me a warning look. 'Is it to do with *her*? Because I mean it, Drew, I don't want to know.'

'It's not about the . . . my affair,' I say clumsily, and Hope flinches. 'It's about . . .' I glance at the closed door behind me and whisper, 'You know.'

Hope shakes her head, her blue eyes gazing straight into mine. 'No,' she says firmly. 'I don't.'

The door opens again, making me jump. The nurse comes back in with Hope's tea.

'Still no news about Sam?' Hope asks.

'Nothing yet,' says the nurse regretfully. 'But I promise I'll come and tell you as soon as I find out.'

The nurse leaves and I get up and shut the door after her for a second time. 'You know what I'm talking about,' I say, turning back to Hope. 'Don't make me say it.'

Hope sips her tea, holding her saucer in one hand, the cup in the other. Her expression is unreadable.

'Hope,' I say, swallowing back my tears and taking a deep breath, 'I feel terrible.'

A flicker of mild satisfaction crosses my wife's face. 'Well, I'm afraid that's your problem, Drew. If you're look-ing for forgiveness, then you've come to the wrong place.'

'Sure. I get that. But . . .' I lower my voice again. 'Should I call the police?'

'The police?' Hope frowns. 'For what?'

I stare back at her. 'To admit what I've done.'

Hope gazes at me in baffling silence for a moment. 'You want to tell the police you had an affair?'

I swallow, glancing towards the door again. 'Hope, I'm not talking about that.'

'Good,' she says defiantly.

'But, Hope . . .'

She puts down her cup. Her chest rises and falls and her lips part as though she's about to say something, but a second later there's a knock on the door and we both look up to see the obstetrician standing there.

There's a clatter behind me as Hope drops her cup and saucer onto the overbed table and my heart jumps for what seems like the hundredth time. I lean over to help her, but then I turn back to see that the obstetrician is smiling, and I honestly start to wonder which way is up and which way is down and what's real and what isn't as he tells us that our baby is back from London, and that the operation has been a success.

21

It's a cold, bleak morning. The sky is dull and grey. Tiny buds have appeared on the rose bushes bordering the front garden, but the trees are still bare. Three weeks have passed since our little boy was born, and as I close the front door and walk across the gravel drive towards the garage, I feel the familiar resurgence of guilt that's with me just about every waking moment of every single day. But I've been over and over what happened. I've turned it round in my head and looked at it from every possible angle, and I just don't know what to think any more.

After Sam came back from his operation and Hope and I could begin to breathe again, I went home for a shower and a change of clothes. In the bedroom, I gazed at the Moses basket, all ready for our baby – our miracle baby – on Hope's side of the bed. I imagined having to wrap it in bin liners and put it in the loft, along with all the soft toys and baby clothes in the nursery. The pram in the garage. I'd have to return that to the shop or give it away. We couldn't keep it, have it sitting there, a reminder every time we went out there. Hope is nearly forty and this is almost certainly her last chance to be a mother. It would have killed her to lose this baby; it would have destroyed her. I turn it all over and over in my mind and then I conclude – as I do each and every time the memory begins to haunt me – that I did what I had to do.

'Morning,' says a voice from behind me. I swing round to see my neighbour, Nick, who is standing on his drive behind the waist-high fence bordering our two properties, car keys in hand. He takes a closer look at me. 'You OK, mate?'

'Sorry,' I murmur. 'I was miles away.'

'Course,' he says, his face falling in sympathy. 'How's it going? How's the baby?'

'He's still on the ventilator,' I say. 'But he's doing well. Hope's at the hospital with him now.'

'And how's *she* doing?'

I hesitate, meeting his gaze, then clear my throat. I haven't seen Nick to talk to properly since before Sam was born, and he's not someone I'd usually confide in.

'I'm not really sure, to be honest.' My voice is thick with silent tears and there's a moment of awkwardness. I fake a smile, feeling ashamed. Nick is on his way to work. He's stepped out of his house and walked to the car and he's just asked after Hope out of politeness.

'I'm sorry, mate,' he says. 'I didn't mean to pry, but . . . well, you know, Jess has been asking after her, and we're both so sorry you two have been through such a tough time and . . . and, well, Jess wanted me to ask you if there is any-thing we can do.'

'It's fine,' I murmur, wiping a tear from my eye and wish-ing I could spare him my grief and ineptitude. Nick and I are good friends, but our relationship has largely been built on fun and games, on adolescent, alcohol-fuelled teasing and morning-after hangovers and recriminations. We have never talked like this before. I clear my throat again. 'We'll be fine. Don't let me keep you,' I say. 'Work going OK?'

Nick eyes me, his expression softening further. 'Come on, mate,' he says gently. 'You can talk to me.'

This is new, but he looks genuine. Hope is always telling me that if I opened up more, I'd have better friendships, and right now, a friend is what I need. I pause, trying to sort out my feelings into the ones I can talk about and the ones I abso-lutely can't.

'I had an affair,' I confess. My skin prickles as I say it. But Hope must have told Jess; she's bound to have done.

Nick stuffs his car keys into his pocket and moves closer to the fence. 'Mate,' he says gently, and I can tell he did already know this. 'But it's over, right?'

I briefly wonder if Jess has put him up to this. But his expression is sympathetic, not judgy – and besides, we may not have talked about our feelings, but I've known Nick for a while now, and he's not the type to gossip, even to his wife.

'Yes,' I say, truthfully, because it *is* over. 'But . . . it's cast a bit of a shadow,' I add. 'Over everything.'

He nods. 'I can imagine.' And then he asks, 'Are you worried she's going to leave you and take the baby?'

I swallow. 'I don't know. I don't know what's going to happen. I really don't know what's going on, if I'm honest.'

He frowns. 'What do you mean?'

I take a breath. 'She's acting kind of . . . weird.' I pause. 'Kind of . . . detached.'

Nick nods. 'It's understandable that she's going to be cold towards you. It's going to take a while.'

'She's not even being cold,' I say. 'It's . . . it's as if nothing has happened. All she talks about is the baby and how he's doing and the practical side of things. I mentioned the affair once, soon after Sam was born, and she said she didn't want to talk about it, and that was that. But now . . . she's . . .'

Nick waits for me to continue. I realise that he's actually really good to talk to.

'I don't think she's well,' I say finally.

'You mean . . . mentally?'

I nod. 'Please . . . don't ever quote me on that. Hope wouldn't like it. She's a psychotherapist. It's her job to help other people with their problems. But I can tell she's not herself. I mean, she's always been one to put a positive spin on things. Rose-coloured glasses and all that. It's one of the things I've always loved about her, to be honest. But it's like she's . . .' I hesitate, checking myself, checking I don't say too much. 'It's like she's in denial.'

'Maybe it's just her way of coping?' Nick suggests. 'And, mate, I'm sorry to tell you this, but therapists are real people with their own problems.' He gives a faint smile. 'Jess says that's why they go into it. She says no one with normal parents and a normal childhood becomes a therapist.'

I give him a faint smile back.

'No offence, mate,' he says, making a sorry face.

'None taken,' I say, meaning it, thinking about Hope's parents. It's actually surprising Hope is as normal as she is, having grown up with those two. But I don't say this; it would feel disloyal. It's nothing Hope wouldn't say herself, but I know the rule: we're allowed to complain about our families, but we'll fight anyone else who takes a pop.

'Look, I'd better get to work,' Nick says finally. 'But I'm around this evening if you fancy a drink?'

'I'll be at the hospital,' I say. 'But thanks for the chat. It's really helped.'

Nick looks pleased. As he opens his car door, he nods towards Hope's Honda Civic and calls out, 'Haven't seen the old Porsche in a while. Is that what you're driving now?'

'Only until I find something bigger.'

'So, what's happened to the Porsche? Have you got rid?'

'Thinking about it. Only because of . . . well, Hope,' I say. 'You know. She wants a family car.'

'Of course she does, mate,' Nick says. 'You're a dad now. Time to put the toys away.'

I look back at him uncertainly. He and Jess don't have children and he could afford to buy my Porsche; they've got plenty of money. But I can't have it sitting on the driveway next door, taunting me. If he asks, I'll have to invent a problem with it. Put him off.

'I'm going to take it up to the West Wyebridge show-room,' I say. 'I've seen an SUV up there. A Range Rover Sport. A seventy plate.'

'Nice,' Nick says. 'You're going to trade in the Porsche?'

'I'll see what they offer,' I say, although I know I won't sell it there. I'll sell it in one of the specialist trade mags, and I'll make sure the buyer lives miles away. 'The SUV's not a bad price for a showroom,' I tell Nick. 'I'll give it a test drive when I get a chance.'

We agree to grab a pint together soon and Nick says goodbye, gets into his car and heads off to work.

I open the garage door and step inside, feeling a range of emotions as I gaze at the Porsche, at the glossy bonnet, the low, tinted windscreen, the spoiler on the back. She's so unique; you don't come across many convertibles with aero kits. The thought of saying goodbye to her fills me with sadness. But I can't keep her. I know that.

I open the door and lower myself down into the driver's seat, start her up and rev the engine a little. I'll leave it running for a bit. Keep her ticking over that way. But no driving her out and about any more. Anyway, she won't be mine for much longer. She's going, and that's that, and it will make Hope happy. I should have sold her a long time ago. My eyes flicker guiltily towards the passenger seat. No wonder Hope hates the Porsche. It must have all kinds of bad associations for her, what with me having had another woman in

it, sitting right there next to me. I was pretty much conduct-
ing my affair in this car.

But it's over. This time, it is *definitely* over, and as soon
as Sam is off the ventilator and out of the woods, I will focus
on putting the Porsche up for sale. But before I buy another
car, before I make that investment, I need to know where I
stand with Hope, and we're not in a place to discuss that yet.
I sigh, thinking of Hope and Sam in the hospital. Hope's
right. Our baby comes first, I know this. He's all that matters.

22

Lauren

When I pull up outside my house, the first thing I notice is that Charlie's car is gone. It hits me like a rock: there was only ever room for one car on the drive, and as Charlie's was the family car, we agreed it should be his and that I'd park mine on the road. But now, the clear stretch of gravel seems wider than it's ever been. It's more than just an expanse of stones – each pebble is a reproach, an accusation. *You. You did this. You're to blame.*

Fumbling in my bag for my keys, I walk up the path and unlock the front door. As I step inside, I feel the urge to call out, 'Hello, hello!' – our usual family greeting. As I turn and catch sight of myself in the hallway mirror, I realise I've lost weight, and even though I've looked at myself in the hospital bathroom, the hollowness of my cheekbones and the shadows under my eyes still take me by surprise. My hair is longer too – straight, dark and straw-like. I've always worn it short, but since the accident everything has changed. Maybe this gaunt new version of myself is here to stay.

I step into the living room and look around, trying to remember what it was like the last time I was here. It's been two months, but I've lost all sense of time. Most days, my mind has wandered so far from the present that I barely remember what I did. Is that why I can't remember what happened? I've done so many car journeys in the past where my mind has been so preoccupied that I don't even remember getting from A to B. I can sometimes remember what I was thinking about, but nothing about the route I took.

At first, after the accident, I was too unwell to speak when the police came. Later, they came again, but I couldn't tell them anything. It's all a complete blank and that just compounds the guilt I'm already feeling. I know it was my fault, but that's all I know.

I look around the room, at the louvred blinds in the box bay window, at the sofas in a beige-and-pale-blue-checked wool, arranged at right angles pointing towards the chimney breast, at the log burner, at the painted white bookcases on either side. I thought I might start to remember if I came home from hospital by myself, if I came into the house to find it exactly how it was the last time I saw it, but although I remember everything else in the room, I don't remember these sofas. I don't understand what they are doing here.

I turn and walk down the hallway into the dining room,

which, like the living room, is neat and tidy, empty of all the usual clutter. I feel a stab to the heart as I realise: Sam's baby gym and all of his other toys are gone. I carry on through to the kitchen and glance over towards the breakfast table. His bouncer is gone, too. In fact, as I look around, there's no sign that a baby ever lived here. The worktops are spotless, the sink gleaming. Even the tiles above the cooker have been wiped down and the crumbs under the toaster swept away. I sigh. Mum. She's been here.

As if on cue, the doorbell rings. I walk back through the dining room and out into the hallway, but the front door is already open and she's inside.

'You didn't wait for me,' she complains, pulling her key out of the lock and lowering a bulging Asda bag for life full of groceries onto the floor. She turns to face me, looking confused. 'I was coming to collect you, remember?'

'I'm sorry. I called a taxi. I just wanted . . . needed a moment. I needed to do this by myself.'

She looks wounded. 'Do you want me to go?'

'No. No, of course not, Mum. I'm sorry. Come on in.'

She turns and closes the front door, picks up the Asda bag and also my hospital case, which I'd left in the hallway. I try to take it from her, but she shrugs me away. 'I've got it. You shouldn't have been carrying it anyway.'

'Mum, I'm fine. Just leave it there. I'll take it upstairs later.'

'*I'll* take it upstairs later. Remember what the consultant told you. You need to take it easy, Lauren.' She drops the case at the foot of the stairs, then follows me through to the kitchen with the groceries and begins to unpack them. 'Now,' she says, 'sit yourself down while I get the kettle on.'

I pull out a seat at the breakfast table. It's the chair I always sit in, next to Sam's missing bouncer. I'm upset that all his things are gone, but I don't want to talk to my mum about it. It hurts too much. Everything hurts. Even pulling out a chair to sit down hurts my neck. My mum sees me wince and turns to face me, hands on hips. She walks over and sits down opposite me, her expression plaintive. 'Why don't you come and stay with me, love?'

'Mum,' I say. 'We've been over this. I'm not moving back to London. My job's here, for a start.'

'You can't go back to work, not until you're fully recovered. And when you're ready, you can get a new job.'

I don't care about my job. It was just something to say. I handed in my notice before the accident, and although my boss has been incredibly kind and has offered me the job back and has even carried on paying my wages, I don't want to go back. I should be in Spain – *we* should be in Spain.

She reaches out and strokes my cheek. 'Stay with me until you sell the house and then you'll have plenty of time to find something nice for yourself. You need a new start, love.'

'I had a new start, remember?'

My mum makes a sad face and heaves a sigh. She gets

up, fetches two mugs from the cupboard and makes the tea. I discover that sitting down makes my back ache, so I get up and stretch a little, then move over to stand next to her. I force a smile and tell her I'll be OK. I tell her that my consultant is here, my GP is here, the hospital outpatients is here, my job's here, my friends are here – although the last part isn't true. All my Oxford friends are work friends, and all my Stow friends are antenatal-class and mother-and-baby-class friends, the friends I made when my life was new and fresh and exciting and I still had something to live for. The thought of being around them and their babies is too much to bear.

'What about Anna?'

'What about her?'

'Well, she lives in London.'

I sigh. 'She lives in Shoreditch, Mum. It's the other side of London. And all my other London friends have moved away. My life's here now. Everything's here.'

It isn't, though. There's nothing here for me now. There's just the hospital, and this house. And the memories.

When we've drunk our tea, I tell her I'm tired and that I'm going to lie down. I climb the stairs to the bedroom, hesitating on the landing. I push open the door to the nursery, my heart beating rapidly.

It's a beautiful room, dual aspect, with adjacent windows overlooking the park opposite. I loved it the first time I set eyes on it. It was just perfect for a child. My eyes land on the blue-and-white bunny curtains, which I chose to match the duvet. A giant panda flops against the bookcase. I sink back against the wall next to the cot, the cot that he didn't even get to sleep in. I pull my phone out of my pocket and I find Charlie's number in my call log. I take a deep breath and tap the call button. It rings out and goes to voicemail. I catch my breath as I hear the familiar greeting: *Hi. It's Charlie. I can't get to the phone right now. Leave a message and I'll call you back.*

I hang up and call again. And again. Every time I hear his voice, I get more and more angry, until the anger begins to overwhelm me and I begin sobbing, furiously. But I am only angry with myself.

The sound of a car door slamming outside breaks into my thoughts, along with hushed voices on the path below the window and a rat-a-tat-tat at the front door. The door-bell rings. I hear my mum walk down the hallway and then her footsteps are on the landing. I can hear her out-side my bedroom door, calling softly, 'Lauren. The police are here.'

I push myself up into a standing position and open the door to the nursery.

My mum looks briefly worried when she sees me in there. 'I'll make some tea,' she says, squeezing my shoulder as she passes. I go into the bathroom and run the tap, scooping cold water over my face, then follow her downstairs.

The police officers are in my living room. They're the same two that I've met twice before at the hospital – uniformed traffic investigators, one male, one female, a PC Jenkins and a PC Walsh. They've taken a sofa each, and PC Jenkins, the male officer, gets to his feet to make room for me.

I wave him back down. 'I'm fine standing,' I say. 'It hurts to sit.'

He nods, gazing at me pensively. He's thinking that I'm lucky to be alive, but I'm not feeling lucky. I'm feeling like shit.

I stand on the hearth in front of the log burner, my back to the mantlepiece. My mum comes in with a tray and places it on the coffee table. The female officer shifts over and my mum sits down next to her.

'So, we've come about your car . . .' PC Jenkins begins.

I sip at my tea. It's still too hot. I turn to put the cup down and a searing pain shoots up my neck. I grip the mantlepiece.

'Are you OK?' someone is asking.

'She gets these muscle spasms.' My mum is answering for me. 'She'll be OK in a minute.'

I wait for the pain to subside, then take a deep breath and slowly turn to face them. 'What about the car?'

'The collision experts have finished their examination,' says PC Jenkins.

'And?'

'And,' he says, 'the results are . . . inconclusive.'

'What does that mean?'

'It means we're going to release it. We need you to sign a disclaimer. I'm afraid it's a write-off, and so . . .'

'It's fine. I'll sign it,' I say stiffly.

No one speaks. The officers give each other knowing glances.

'Is there something else?' I ask.

'We also have some property to give back to you, Lauren. Things that were inside the car.' PC Jenkins picks up and places a package on the sofa next to him. 'I'll leave it here. Is that OK?'

I nod again. I mustn't cry. I won't cry.

'Is there anything else you can remember about that day, Lauren?' PC Walsh asks. 'Anything at all?'

'No. I remember waking up in the car, the firemen talking to me and . . .' I bite my lip. 'And then waking up again in hospital. But that's it.'

I've told them this over and over. I wish I could remember, but I can't.

'That's OK, Lauren,' he says. 'Your mum's account has been very helpful, and we have the conclusions of the collision experts.'

I nod. 'That it was all my fault.'

'No, Lauren,' my mum says forcefully. 'It was an accident.'

PC Walsh looks at me sympathetically.

'The collision experts say . . .' PC Jenkins begins.

'Go on,' I prompt him.

He hesitates, choosing his words. 'That because of the position of the sun and the type of road you were on, it's likely you swerved to avoid a wild animal – a deer or pheasant, perhaps. That your perception response time wasn't affected by drugs or alcohol, but that—'

'She hadn't been drinking,' my mum jumps in. 'Of course she hadn't. She would never.'

'But I was driving,' I say. 'It was still my fault.'

There's a pause as everyone hears the sharpness in my voice and waits for someone else to step in and blunt it. 'The average perception response time is one second in normal conditions,' says PC Jenkins, 'but at that time of day, heading west towards a setting sun on a country lane, it would be closer to two.'

'It's my fault, not yours, Lauren,' my mum says. 'It was lovely of you to come and visit me and I should have encouraged you to set off sooner. I should never have insisted that you stay for tea.'

I say, 'It's nothing to do with that, Mum. It was five o'clock. It wasn't dark.'

'It could have happened to anyone,' my mum says, looking from one officer to the other. 'Right?'

The officers don't argue, but they don't say she's right either. I know they blame me. They might not have enough evidence to prosecute, but they aren't going to commit themselves to absolving me.

The room falls silent again and then PC Jenkins says, 'Is there anything you want to ask me?'

'No.'

The officers look at my mum, but she shakes her head.

PC Jenkins puts the disclaimer form on the coffee table

and hands me a pen. I stoop down and sign it. I don't want the car back. I never want to see the car again.

'Feel free to get in touch if you remember anything,' PC Jenkins says. 'Anything at all.'

As my mum shows the officers out, I tentatively pick up the property bag from the sofa, my fingers trembling. My mum comes back into the living room and stops in the doorway. 'It wasn't your fault, Lori,' she says firmly. 'You just heard them say it.'

'They didn't say that, Mum.'

'Lauren,' she protests. 'They did. The crash experts said it was an accident. They said—'

'That it was inconclusive. Which means they aren't going to prosecute me.'

'They were never going to do that,' she insists. 'Nobody blames you for this. You need to stop doing this to yourself. It isn't doing you any good. Please listen to me, love.'

Her eyes glisten and my gut wrenches. I want her to stop talking, but I don't know how to tell her without hurting her even more. 'I'm going to have a bath,' I say instead.

She swallows and nods.

I look at her red-rimmed eyes and feel the weight of everything. I'm a horrible daughter. I'm a horrible person.

I take the property bag upstairs and put it in my wardrobe, then lie down on the bed and close my eyes.

23

Hope

I wake from a dream about Drew and Sam. It's the usual dream I have from time to time, where Drew hasn't cheated on me and everything is perfect. Sam's home, asleep in his Moses basket next to me, and Drew's here in bed with me, his head next to mine on the pillow. His face is turned towards me and he's smiling into my eyes. We aren't touching, but I can feel the intensity between us. It feels so good to be this close again, to know I am the most important person in his life.

I swim up out of the dream, briefly disorientated, and remember that Sam is still in the NICU and the reason Drew isn't here next to me is because he now sleeps on the sofa bed in the dining room. As I open my eyes, I can tell by the slant of the light through the curtains that it's late. *We're* late. Drew should have woken me by now. We've fallen into a routine. Each day, we get up early and he drops me off at the hospital before going into the office for a few hours.

He then joins me at Sam's bedside sometime in the afternoon and we stay all evening. In the beginning, I'd stay the night too, but lately the nurses have been encouraging me to go home and sleep in my own bed. I struggled with that at first. Leaving Sam behind was hard. But the nurses said a good night's rest was going to be better for my breast milk, and so I listened.

I reach across to the nightstand for my phone. I can hear movement in the kitchen downstairs. Drew's up, making tea. My instinct is to be angry with him for not waking us both sooner and I know he'd take it on the chin, just as he's been taking everything on the chin for the past two months since Sam was born, swallowing every grievance I have about the most minor transgressions – crumbs on the kitchen worktop, muddy boots on the mat. He even accepts my complaints about things that are not really his fault. But this morning, I feel differently. Blameless, faultless Dream Drew is still lingering in my thoughts, and I realise that I want to keep him there for a little longer, along with the image of Sam sleeping beside me. That part, at least, could soon be true.

A warm glow of optimism spreads through me as I think about this. Yesterday was the best day ever for Sam. The staff at the NICU took him off the ventilator for a short while and they let me hold him and feed him myself for the very first time. He latched on well. He snuffled and stopped for breath, but his suck was firm, and Jenny, our nurse, said he shouldn't need the ventilator for too much longer. She said they are going to withdraw it slowly this week and next and then move on to a CPAP machine. But she said he is getting so much bigger and stronger that he shouldn't need that for long either and they are already planning his next move onto the 'feed and grow' ward. She said I should now begin to feed him myself for a little while, several times per day.

I get up and go along the landing to the bathroom. When I come back out into the bedroom, Drew is coming upstairs in his bathrobe with a mug of tea for me. I wait on the landing at the top of the stairs and take the mug from him.

'Thanks,' I say.

'Sorry,' he says, at the same time. 'Overslept.'

'Me too.'

He looks up into my eyes, recognising the softening inside me. 'How are you feeling?' he asks.

I shrug. 'Excited about Sam.'

He smiles. 'Me too.' He hesitates, then asks, 'Is it OK if I come in with you this morning?'

'Don't you have to work?' I ask, surprised.

'There's nothing that can't wait. I'd really like to see you feeding him.'

The thought that Drew would want to skip work to witness me breastfeeding our baby is a real tug at the heartstrings. I seek out his eyes and he flushes, but I realise he means it. He genuinely wants to see our baby having his first proper breakfast.

Tears spring to his eyes. 'I just never allowed myself to imagine us getting to this stage, you know?'

'I know. Me neither.'

He smiles through his tears. 'He'll be home before we know it.'

I smile back, the thought warming me for the second time. 'Yeah. I really think he will.'

Drew gives me a look that makes me think he's about to ask the question that has sat, unspoken, between us: *And what then?* But he simply says, 'Can I grab some clothes?' and nods towards the bedroom.

'Of course.'

I move aside to let him pass, then go down into the kitchen with my tea. I put a slice of bread into the toaster and then have second thoughts and add another. I'm eating for two, after all. The thought is like a warm meadow on a summer's day. I fetch the butter and jam – the brand is Bonne Maman! – and take a plate out of the cupboard, then sit down at the table to express some milk. As I stare out of the window at the blue sky and the wild daffodils and primroses now blooming in the front garden, I think about how everything goes full cycle. There's darkness and cold and rain, but spring flowers and sunshine always follow, as sure as night follows day. I allow myself the luxury of skipping forward to the day Sam arrives home with us for the first time. I try to imagine the three of us together but not together, the way Drew and I are at the moment – and I can't. I just can't imagine it. I can't imagine it, I realise, because it's not what I want. What I want is blameless, faultless Dream Drew. I want us to be a proper family. But Dream Drew doesn't exist. There's only

Drew – this Drew – and I need to decide how I'm going to live with this.

I know, in my heart of hearts, that I'm not going to be a single parent. I don't want that; I never wanted it. And what good is kicking Drew out going to do? What is it going to achieve? We'd have to sell the cottage – our beautiful dream home. How else will Drew be able to afford to buy himself a flat? I don't want him renting. What's the point in that? That will just be money down the drain, money that could go into Sam's university fund – and for what? So that Sam can grow up being bounced back and forth between two separate homes and two lonely parents? Or – more likely – two parents and two step-parents. And that's if I ever meet anyone I like enough to trust with my baby. I might just end up sitting in some kitchen that's not half as nice as this one, lonely and bitter, while Drew and his new wife play happy families with my son.

My stomach twists as I picture this. The thought of Drew and another woman is bad enough, but the thought of Drew smiling at another woman while she holds my baby in her arms is like a stab to the heart. There's no way Drew would just walk away and leave me with Sam. He might agree to it initially, but he would want shared custody of his son, and he would fight me for it. I know what this will be like. I've done enough mediations, counselled enough clients in this situation to know that it will bring me nothing but pain. Drew doesn't deserve forgiveness, I know, but what's the alternative? That I punish him for ever?

Lurking just inside me is the knowledge that everything that's happened could be behind us if I wanted it to
be. Drew has sworn to me that his feelings for this other
woman weren't real, that it was her vulnerability that drew
him back in. He felt guilty that her marriage had ended, that
she was on her own, that she needed him – he could see she
needed him in a way I didn't, emotionally, at least. He said
I have always been so strong and self-reliant and he liked
the feeling of being indispensable, and then when she said
she was leaving town, he felt compelled to fight for what he
couldn't have.

But as soon as I went into labour, he realised that whatever he had with her was no more than a crush – a childish
game, he said. When I discovered the texts between them,
it was the wake-up call he needed, the one that would bring
him to his senses and catapult him right back into the real
world. He said that everything that has happened since has
shown him that he is ready to say goodbye to her, and to his
mum, too, whose death he has never really dealt with. He
said he's ready to be a grown-up and that, if I let him, he will
spend the rest of his life making it up to me and Sam.

They're just words, I know, but they are good words.
They are the words I want, the words I need. I am a long,
long way from forgiving Drew for what he's done, but our
baby has a father and a mother, and this is what I want for
him. The only thing I know for sure is that I don't want to
bring him up alone.

I think once again about all the things Drew and I have

together, all the things we share. We have our cottage. We have our nice things. And now we have our son. We have everything we ever wanted. There's no denying that it's been a bumpy road, and even without that, without all the loss we have suffered, it's hard enough for most couples to keep the romance alive when you know everything about each other, when nothing is new or surprising. But the other side of the coin – and there is always another side of the coin – is the shared history that has fused us together. We have been through so much together. We know each other inside out and we can take that and build on it if we want to. If *I* want to.

I am always telling my clients that the path to true freedom and happiness is the ability to move on from the prison of our past and to be able to choose our response to what's happening in the present. No matter what Drew has done, I can choose for us to begin again, *if I want to*. Today is a new day. That was then and this is now. My *scripted* position would be to kick Drew out, to push him away into the arms of this woman, or some other woman, and to watch from a lonely distance as he played happy families with her. But I'd no longer be the most important person in Drew's life. I'd end up watching his happiness with someone else from the sidelines, just as I spent my childhood watching my parents together, never being able to break into the bond they shared.

But I don't have to follow my script.

I turn the breast pump off, seal the bottles I've filled and put them in the freezer. As I hear Drew coming out of the bathroom and moving around in the bedroom upstairs, I decide to play a game with myself. I'll let Sam decide. If Sam is off the ventilator by Friday, it's his way of telling me that I should definitely forgive Drew.

24

Lauren

It's morning, a week later, and I'm in the car with Anna, heading to the hospital. The road we're on is the same one I crashed on. It takes us through the Chiltern Hills. Anna asked if I wanted to go a different way, along the motorway or along the Chinnor Road, through Ashcombe Ridge, but I said it would be a good thing, that it might jog my memory. And I think it is, because I remember the trees, the miles upon miles of trees lining the road. It's spring now, but it was winter then, and I can picture the skeletal trunks and branches silhouetted against the light of the sun. *There's a lorry in the distance—*

'Lauren?'

I turn slowly.

'What is it?' Anna asks. 'You look as though you've seen a ghost.'

'There was a lorry,' I murmur.

Anna frowns. 'You mean, the one we just passed?'

I twist round to look at the road behind us, but my neck goes into spasm. I clutch my head in my hands and let out a long, soft moan.

'Are you OK?'

'Yes. Give me a minute,' I say breathlessly. I close my eyes and breathe deeply in and out. I count to ten and the pain eases. I moisten my lips and sit back in my seat, col-lapsing against the headrest. 'There was a lorry,' I say again, after a moment. 'On the day of the accident.'

'I thought you didn't remember anything?'

'I didn't, but . . . I think there was a lorry on the road at the same time as me.'

Anna frowns. 'On your side? On the other side?'

'I'm not sure . . . I don't know.' I lift my hands to take the weight of my skull in between my fingers and gently stretch my neck, massaging the top of my spine.

Anna gives me a sideways look. 'Is that meant to be hap-pening still?'

'The consultant said it could take a while.'

She glances at me again, then says softly, 'I'm so sorry, Lauren.'

I feel a surge of irritation and look away, out of the window. 'Please don't pity me, Anna,' I say. After a moment, I add more gently, 'It's just that . . . it doesn't help.'

Anna fixes her eyes on the road ahead, falling silent. It's hard to see her at the moment, to be reminded of her life. She has a husband who worships the ground she walks on and two daughters she gets to talk to every day. They're twenty-three now – all grown up, but still attached to her. Everyone is attached to Anna. She's so bright, so capable, so annoyingly *right* about everything. She's a lawyer, after all. I feel weak and helpless in her presence, even though I know she doesn't encourage this, even though I know she's willing me to get stronger. I love her and I don't want to lose her, but I can't stop myself from pushing her away.

There's a bit of a wait at the hospital. Anna has gone out to feed the parking meter when the consultant calls me in. It's a woman I recognise from after my operation. She checks my blood pressure and my pulse and hits my knee with a small hammer to check my reflexes. She asks about tingling in my arms, hands and fingers and then looks through the X-rays of my neck and spine.

'You've been extremely lucky, Lauren,' she says, bringing up the images of my bones on her computer screen. 'Your fractures have healed nicely and there doesn't appear to be any permanent damage to your spinal cord or to the vertebrae in your neck. The structure seems fine. There *is* damage to the ligaments and to the cartilage around the cervical flexors and it will take time to heal. The physiotherapist will give you some exercises to help with that.'

She shines a bright light into my eyes then, and asks me a series of questions that she already knows I know the answer to – about the date and time and who the prime minister of the day is. And then she talks about the accident. I tell her what I've told everyone else: that I can't remember anything about that day except waking up and being cut out of the car by firemen. I tell her about the lorry and she says that it may or may not have been there. She explains how the brain works – and more importantly, she says, how it doesn't work – and she says that memory is unreliable, and that the lorry may simply be a present-day image which I've superimposed onto the moment of trauma. She says my recollection of what happened might never return.

I tell her that I feel irritable and angry a lot of the time, but at the same time incredibly guilty.

'It's normal to feel all these things,' she says. 'I'd like to refer you for counselling. Talking therapies are proven to have a significantly better success rate than drug therapy in cases like these, and I'd like to start to get you off these medications. The longer you're on them, the more risk there is of forming a dependency. Better to let your mind and body learn how to deal with the trauma the way nature intended, if you can.' She softens her face, then asks, 'Do you have much support?'

I nod. 'My mum and my best friend seem to be taking it in turns to stay with me.'

'Well, that's good. They may notice a personality change. Again, it's normal and there's some helpful information I can give them.'

She tells me to see her secretary outside who will give me the literature, some phone numbers, a prescription for another month's worth of painkillers and an appointment for four weeks' time. Afterwards, I head to the pharmacy, where

I have to wait for a bit. When I get out to the lobby near the hospital doors, I look around for Anna. I check my phone and see that she's sent a message to tell me she's moved the car and is now parked in a street outside the hospital. I tell her I'll find her. She gives me directions: turn left, past A & E, past the Women's Centre, through the long-stay car park and through the exit at the back.

I walk out of the double doors at the hospital entrance and follow Anna's directions, turning left past the short-stay car park and past a separate building, stopping briefly to check the sign outside. It's the Women's Centre; I'm going the right way. And then, as I cross the road to the long-stay car park, I hear the growling of an engine and a flash of colour catches the corner of my eye. I turn to watch as a bright, shiny sports car rounds the corner and pulls into the car park next to the Women's Centre. A sudden wave of emotion courses through me. I watch, trembling, as a man gets out of the driver's side, locks the door and walks over to the pay-and-display machine. He's tall and fair, smartly dressed in a navy suit – nice-looking, I notice. He plunges his hands into his pockets to search for change or his wallet or something, and I watch as he feeds the meter and walks across the road towards me. There's something vaguely familiar about him.

I feel a flush of heat prick my forehead and my heart starts thumping as I cross the road and approach the car. As I get close, I can see that it's a Porsche 911 Carrera, a 2002 two-door convertible. It's a spotless burnt yellow, the colour of the setting sun. I stare and stare at it. I'm almost certain that I've seen this car before. I pull out my phone and take several photos of it, moving round from the front to the side and the rear. I then walk back over to the Women's Centre. I don't really know what I'm doing. Looking to see if the man who owns the car is inside, I suppose.

I reach the double doors at the entrance.

'Nice, isn't it?' says a gruff voice. I turn to see a man in his sixties or early seventies, a hospital staff member, I'm guessing from his uniform, who has come outside for a smoke. 'Lucky bastard,' he adds, smiling.

I stop, my heart still fluttering. 'Do you know him?'

He takes a long pull on his cigarette. He has a heavily lined face and curly grey hair tied back into a ponytail. 'I just work here, love,' he says, his accent distinctly cockney.

'You've seen him before, though?'

He crushes his cigarette underfoot. 'Well, you don't forget a car like that.'

No, I think. *You don't.* 'Does he come here often? Does he work here? Or is he visiting someone?'

'Sorry, love,' he says, giving me a kind smile. 'I can't really answer that. Confidentiality.' He stretches the word out like a poem, and the long vowels remind me of home.

I nod and go through the entrance to the Women's Centre. The foyer is large, clean and empty. I scan the chairs and tables, look across to the lifts. I then sit down and think hard for a moment. What is it that I think I know? Have I really seen the Porsche before? Or is this just my brain playing tricks on me like the consultant said it would? Are the car and the man and the lorry all really no more than present-day images I've superimposed onto the past? I open the gallery app on my phone and look again at the photos I've taken of the car, at the low, tinted windscreen, at the Porsche logo and headlights – a button nose in the middle of the bonnet between two round, wide, startled eyes.

My phone bleeps in my hand and makes me jump. Anna! Christ. I'd forgotten all about her. Maybe there really *is* something wrong with my memory. But I don't want to go home just yet. Something about the car is tugging at me. My life in the past two months has felt like one long dream sequence. This is the closest I've felt to reality in a very long time. And then it hits me: there's a way I could find out if this is all an illusion. Suddenly I feel empowered, back in control. In charge of my life.

But I also know Anna will try and talk me out of it, so I find her number and ring her. 'Anna, I'm so sorry,' I lie when she picks up. 'They want to do some blood tests. I'm so stupid. I picked up my meds and I was supposed to go to phlebotomy. I completely forgot.'

'Don't worry,' she says cheerfully. 'I'll have to find somewhere else to park, though. I'm in a one-hour space and a traffic warden just walked past and gave me the evil eye. How long do you think you're going to be?'

'No, don't wait,' I say hurriedly, knowing she'll argue.

'It's no problem,' she begins. 'I'll—'

'Please. It could be ages. You know what it's like. I don't want you to have to hang around.'

'I don't mind.'

'I know you don't. But I'm actually feeling really good about being on my own, about managing on my own. I'll get a taxi home. I'd like to just . . . spend some time by myself. Is that OK?'

She pauses. 'A taxi will cost an arm and a leg.'

'It's not that much. I got one the day I left hospital,' I remind her. 'And Mike's still paying my wages. I'm not broke yet.'

The line goes quiet for a minute, then, 'Are you sure you'll be OK?'

'I *need* to be OK, Anna?' I say. 'You and Mum can't be here for ever. I need to start . . .' I hesitate, feeling the weight of the lie, although I know it will please her, '. . . moving on . . . getting back to normal.'

She hesitates, then says, reluctantly, 'Well, OK.'

'So, do me a favour,' I continue, trying to sound upbeat. 'Go back to mine, put your feet up in front of the TV. And why don't you stop off first at the Co-op in Stow and get us a bottle of wine?'

'OK. I could get some food. Cook us something nice?' Anna suggests. 'Have it ready for when you get back.'

'Perfect,' I say, buttering her up.

'So, what do you fancy?'

'Anna,' I say, 'you're the best cook south of Watford. Anything you make is going to be delicious.'

'Well . . .' she says. 'I'll take that. I am pretty good.'

I end the call. Next, one eye on the lift and the double

doors to the stairs, I call the taxi firm that I stored in my contacts the day I left hospital and order a cab. I tell the call handler that I'm going to Stow from the Woodley Ridge Hospital in Wyebridge, but I'm going to have to get the driver to take a detour and I don't know how long I'm going to be. I'm told it's fine, they'll have someone there in ten minutes. I give instructions for the driver to pull into the short-stay car park opposite the entrance to the Women's Centre and then I get up, go outside and cross the road to where the Porsche is parked and check the parking ticket in the window. It has over an hour left to run.

I hover in the car park, in the sunshine. When the cab arrives, I ask the driver to park up a couple of rows back from the Porsche. I explain that I'm waiting for someone to come out of the hospital and I can't say exactly when we'll be leaving, but I understand the clock will be running.

'You're the one paying,' says the driver, shrugging, his back to me. 'No skin off my nose.'

I get out of the car and walk over to the parking meter. I don't have any change, but there's a phone number you can call, so I punch it into my phone, making a mental note of the location code. I follow the instructions to park for an hour and look around to take a note of the taxi's number plate, then walk back to the taxi, where I hover for a moment with the door open. I discover that I have a reasonable view of the hospital entrance from inside the taxi, so I get into the back seat.

The taxi driver doesn't attempt to engage me in idle

chit-chat, for which I'm grateful. I lean back against the seat, my eyes on the hospital doors, intermittently looking at my phone and checking the time. It's now forty minutes until blue-suit man's ticket's up.

Then thirty. Then twenty.

Fifteen.

And then I see him.

'OK,' I say to the taxi driver. 'It's time.'

25

Drew

Hope was in really good spirits when I arrived at the hospital this afternoon. Sam was asleep in her arms and when I leaned down to kiss him, she lifted her hand and touched my cheek and then she leaned forward and kissed *me*, right on the lips. It really took me by surprise. This past week, since Sam came off the ventilator, she's behaved differently towards me. It's subtle: a hand against my back as she passes me in the kitchen, a grin of acknowledgement as I make a tentative joke. When she smiles at me, the smile reaches her eyes and is totally different from the weird, fake smile that's been plastered on her face for the past two months.

This afternoon, after work, I drove to the hospital in the Porsche. I told Hope I had an appointment and that it was going to be a surprise and I'd come back for her later. I think she knew what I was doing, because she shot me a look that told me she was glad, and as I drove into Wyebridge, I really started to think about the future. There is the real possibility

214

that we might now be able to talk things through properly. For weeks, I've been immobilised by fear of what might happen to Hope and Sam if I'm not around to take care of them. The cottage, for example. It's my wage that pays the mortgage. Hope can't work, not with a baby. She might be able to see a client or two, but she'd never manage financially on her own, and her parents don't have any money. Every time I start to think about it, there's a blockage in my mind. I just can't get any further without talking to Hope. Every time I start going down that dark road, I have to stop and force myself back.

It feels strange and a little uncomfortable to be driving the Porsche again, but although I'd prefer to sell it privately, I should at least see what they'll give me for it on a part exchange. It's been in the garage for two months now and I don't want to buy the SUV on finance, so trading it in might be the easiest way. I'll get a valuation at the showroom and test-drive the SUV and have another last quick look around, but hopefully I'll get a good deal on both. Then I can decide.

It's four o'clock and the traffic slows as I head through the suburbs and into the town centre. The schools have finished for the day and the pelican crossings are teeming with young children in school uniform and parents pushing buggies. Clusters of teenagers block the pavements outside the newsagents and fried-chicken shops. Wyebridge is an old market town, once known for its sawmills and still known for its university, but it was redeveloped and expanded in the 1960s and is now mostly known for its huge shopping centres and concrete car parks. I know it for the Crowthorpe development, a new build of affordable housing between Stoke End and Woodley Ridge that I've been working on for the past year and a half, a development that's now come to a standstill due to issues with the contractors. *It's where I met her for the first time.* The thought enters my mind unbidden and I push it away.

As I move on through the town centre towards the Sandford Industrial Estate, I check my rear-view mirror and notice a taxi behind me, which I am sure was also behind me as I left the hospital. This seems a bit of a coincidence as I'm travelling west now, on the road out of Wyebridge, almost back out into the countryside again, and there's nothing but the car showroom up ahead. I don't think much of it as I pause and wait for a gap in the traffic, scanning the forecourt for the SUV I saw last time, the one I have my eye on. It's still there, and it's still stunning: a Range Rover Sport in Carpathian Grey with black tinted windows.

I turn right into the showroom and drive through a gap in the cars to a car park at the back. As I get out of my car, I notice the taxi taking the next right into a housing estate. It's someone who lives there, then. That makes sense. I park the Porsche, then walk back out of the car park towards the showroom entrance. There are a couple more SUVs on the forecourt, including another Range Rover. They are all slightly older and a little less expensive than the one I have my eye on and I walk around, taking a look at each of them, but I still prefer the 70 plate. The sales guy comes out and

I tell him I want a valuation for the Porsche and to test-drive the Range Rover, then I follow him inside and wait while he arranges both. I think about Hope's face when she sees the new car. If all goes well, I could pick her up in it later. She'd be so happy. It could even be a cause for celebration. Maybe.

The sales guy hands me the keys to the Range Rover and I get into the driver's seat and start it up. He gets in beside me and directs me east, back into Wyebridge and then south towards the motorway, circling back through the industrial estate. En route, he points out all of its great features – low mileage, full service history, heated seats, sunroof – giving me the hard sell. But I've already made up my mind. The car is a beauty. Smooth, roomy, easy to drive. Back at the showroom, I put down a deposit. The valuation for the Porsche is lower than I expected and I reluctantly agree to come back for the Range Rover in the morning. I need time to think about the part exchange. I may have to buy the Range Rover on finance after all, but one way or another, Hope is going to have it by tomorrow lunchtime, and as for the Porsche, we'll see.

I almost turn back for the hospital, but then I remember: Hope won't want me turning up to collect her in the Porsche. That won't go down well. I'll need to go back home first for her Civic. It shouldn't take long. My mind is full of this as I get back in and start up the engine. I exit the car park, indicate right and swing out onto the road, heading west towards home. The traffic tails off considerably as

217

trees, farms and garden centres replace the housing estates and builders' merchants. Soon, the road splits off in two directions and most of the cars behind me turn north. As they do so, I notice that there it is again behind me – the taxi. It's the same taxi that was behind me all the way from the hospital. It's keeping its distance, and I understand now that this is far from a coincidence. I'm being followed. A burst of adrenaline pulses though me and I lower my foot over the accelerator, getting ready to slam it down.

The Sandford Road turns into the Old Chiltern Road and I head out into the countryside, one eye on my mirror. We're still in a thirty zone, but the street lights soon give way to trees on both sides of the road. I can see the black-and-white circle up ahead that indicates the thirty is about to turn into a seventy, and as soon as it does, I take off. This is what the Porsche is good at. It can go from nought to sixty in five point two seconds, as I've just demonstrated. The taxi driver steps on the gas to try to catch me up, but he can't. He won't.

The evening sun is dazzling, almost blinding, but there are no other cars on the road and I push my foot down harder until the bank and undergrowth beside me and the slope of the fields beyond are all a blur. I'm conscious that I've succeeded in losing the taxi long before I get to the turning for Chorley Common, but it's not until I've driven through the winding roads and into the village and pulled up onto the drive and locked the Porsche back in the garage that the banging in my chest stops.

26

Lauren

I wake slowly, the sun orange on my eyelids. I'm on the swing on our patio and I know without opening my eyes that Anna has brought me a cup of tea, which is welcome because my mouth is dry. The painkillers do that. They make me sleepy, too, especially the codeine. It also gives me nightmares, sometimes. But most of my dreams are sweet, filled with Charlie and Sam. I once read somewhere that when your real life feels like a nightmare, you have nice dreams. Otherwise you'd go mad.

'Thanks,' I say, levering myself up onto one arm and reaching for my tea. I take a sip, then drink some more, propping myself up on a cushion. 'Where's Mum?' I ask.

'She's in the kitchen doing the washing-up.'

'We have a dishwasher,' I remind her, shielding my eyes from the sun. 'She doesn't need to do that.'

'I know. But she's going home later. She wants to help.'

Anna and my mum both work, but either one or the other,

or both, is here most days, particularly at weekends. Last Sunday was Easter Day and they both came and did their best to help me through it without Easter eggs or cake or anything to remind me that it was a special day, a family day. I'm not sure how we'd have celebrated, but Sam would have been three months old and he'd have been able to look at an Easter egg and touch it and marvel at the pretty foil wrapping. Every time I think of something like this, of what might have been, it feels as though I've been punched in the stomach, where there's a ball of pain, tightly wound and heavy. Sometimes I want to punch back, but I don't know who to punch because there's only me. Sometimes I just want to close my eyes again, to sleep for ever. In my dream life, I am blameless and I have everything I ever wanted.

'It's cooled off a little,' says Anna, looking up at the sky. 'Glorious weather, though.'

The sky is a deep blue and cloudless. Sometimes I imagine that it's a vast ocean I could dive into and just . . . disappear.

'I don't suppose you could get me another one?' I ask when I've finished my tea. I hold out my cup.

'Of course.' Anna jumps up.

When she's gone, I pull my phone out of my pocket and find Charlie's number in my call log and tap the green phone icon under his name. The call rings out and goes to voicemail. I catch my breath, as I aways do when I hear the greeting: *Hi. It's Charlie. I can't get to the phone right now. Leave a message and I'll call you back.*

I end the call and stare into the ocean-sky for a while.

'Is it illegal to follow someone?' I ask Anna as she comes back into the garden with a fresh cup of tea for each of us. She places the mugs on the table and sits back down in the rattan garden chair next to me. The chair is part of a set that Charlie and I bought soon after I found out I was pregnant. We spent a lot of time sitting out here last summer. Charlie always sat in the chair Anna's sitting in; I always lay on the swing. Sometimes I think Anna is Charlie when she sits down next to me. She often does so without speaking. She's tall and slim – a similar height to him.

'Follow them . . . how?' she asks.

'Like . . . tailing them in a car.' I think about this. 'Or trying to find out where they live.'

She looks concerned. 'Well, it depends how often you do it, and whether it's troubling them. And the reason you're doing it.'

'To find out about them,' I say. 'To find out what they're hiding.'

Anna sips at her tea. 'Who are we talking about here, Lauren?'

I can feel my heart beating just a little too fast. 'So, is it illegal? If you're not bothering them?'

'If it's once . . . then probably not.'

'What if it's twice, but you're not bothering them?'

Anna frowns. 'Well . . . whether you're bothering them is subjective. It depends on how they perceive it.' She hesitates. 'And it all depends on whether you knew or ought to have known it would bother them. And that's an objective test. You ought to have known it would bother them if a reasonable person in possession of the same information would think it would bother them.' She hesitates. 'Why are you asking me this?'

I think about this for a moment. 'If I tell you, will you drive me?'

She eyes me for a moment. I know she can't do anything illegal, which is why I'm asking. But I know she feels sorry for me, too.

'Where do you want me to drive you?' she asks.

I pull out my phone and open Google Maps. I open the page I've bookmarked and pass the phone to her. 'There's a minor road that turns north off the Old Chiltern Road between Ardeley and Stoke End. I followed a car the other day, the day we went to the hospital.'

Anna looks dumbstruck. 'You did what?'

I clear my throat. 'I followed a yellow Porsche. I know I've seen it before.'

'Where?'

'I can't remember. That's why I'm trying to find it. If I can put it into some kind of context, it might trigger a memory.'

Anna takes the phone, giving me a sideways look. 'You drove? I thought you weren't ready to do that?'

'I was in a taxi.'

Anna frowns, remembering our trip to the hospital, how she'd left me there. 'You said you remembered a lorry,' she reminds me.

'I remember a lorry *and* a Porsche. I'll never find the

lorry, but the Porsche was distinctive. It was yellow. A cab-riolet, a soft-top. I did some research and it's a rare car, in a rare colour. So, to see one around here twice would be unusual. I don't think it would be that hard to find it.'

Anna looks at my phone, examining the route I've saved. 'So, you want to drive through the villages north of there?'

'Yes,' I say. 'And that's all I want to do. Just to see if I can spot it. Where it turned off must have been the road to Chorley Common and Water Oak. They're both tiny vil-lages and they don't lead anywhere except up to Ashcombe Ridge. But, look. Here.' I point to the map on my phone. 'If you wanted to go to Ashcombe Ridge from Wyebridge, you'd just go along the Chinnor Road.'

'So you wouldn't take that route unless you were going to either Chorley Common or Water Oak, is that what you're saying?'

'Yes. Exactly that. So, we check those two villages, and then maybe Horsley and maybe the Hampdens.'

Anna sighs and hands me back my phone.

'Anna,' I plead. 'I need your help. Just this once, I prom-ise. I was in the taxi last time, so even if they saw me, that's what they'd be looking out for. They're not going to recog-nise your car.'

'*They?*' Anna looks bewildered. 'Who are *they*?'

'It was a man driving.'

Anna frowns. 'So you remember the car but not the driver.'

'His face was . . . kind of familiar. But . . .'

'What? Where do you think you know him from?'

'I honestly don't know,' I say, feeling a little flustered. She's doing her lawyer thing, cross-examining me. 'But he definitely has something to hide.'

Anna frowns. 'How do you know that?'

'Because he gave me the slip.'

'What? You mean he knew you were following him?'

'Yes. Which means—'

'Where? Where did you follow him? And for how long?'

'From the hospital through Wyebridge and then out towards West Wyebridge and then he stopped at a car showroom.' Anna gazes at me in silence. 'He went in and test-drove a car and then he got back into the Porsche and carried on, heading in this direction, and then . . . and then he must have seen us, because he suddenly put his foot down. He took off really fast.'

'Because he noticed you following him,' Anna says, still looking worried.

'Well, yes.' I realise with a jolt that she's not on my side about this, that she's not going to help me. 'Probably,' I murmur.

Anna sighs. 'You can't just go tailing people, Lauren. Apart from the issue of whether it's legal, you don't know who you're dealing with. There are some crazy people out there.'

'Crazier than me?' I challenge her.

She looks sorry. 'Lauren, you're not crazy,' she says gently. 'But you have been through something traumatic, something no one should have to go through alone. No one thinks you're crazy. We just think you need someone to help you through it.'

I sigh. 'You're talking about therapy,' I say, sounding disparaging, although I actually have mixed feelings about this. I've been dismissive every time Anna has suggested it, but I have started to wonder whether it might be a good idea. If nothing else, I'd get a second opinion about the snatches of memory that have been resurfacing. My mum and Anna are trying to protect me from any more pain, I know that, but it's not helping. The idea of having some-one to talk to other than my mum and Anna – someone independent, someone who isn't hurting too, someone who might actually listen and be interested in what I have to say – suddenly doesn't seem such a bad idea after all.

Anna comes again the following weekend and is really pleased when I say that maybe I will give the counselling a try. It actually feels like the only thing left that I have any control over, and so I hunt out the paperwork my consult-ant's secretary gave me at my last appointment and we run through the list of therapists together. There are ten of them, and Anna advises me to call every single one and interview them. See which one is the best fit for me.

'Go with your instincts,' she says. 'The one you feel most comfortable talking to.'

A third of them are men and I dismiss them straight away; I know I'd feel more comfortable with a woman. The one

I like best lives in Amersham, but I'd hoped for someone nearer, and none of the others feel quite right, so I abandon the hospital's recommendations and do an online search instead, filtering it for distance and credentials. There are over eighty bereavement counsellors in a ten-mile radius, so I narrow my search further and pull up a new list. I filter out all the ones in Stow – it feels too close to home; I don't want to bump into my therapist in the fruit and veg aisle in Waitrose – and on the second page, there is one I like the look of. She looks friendly and has a welcoming smile. She focuses on trauma and bereavement and has impressive qualifications. And then I see where she lives and I get really interested. She lives in Chorley Common, one of the two villages I'd seen the Porsche turning towards last Friday.

Anna has gone out to the supermarket and is pleased when she comes back and I tell her I've found someone.

'So, what's she like?' she asks.

'I don't know yet,' I admit. 'I haven't spoken to her. But you know what? I think she's the one.'

Anna frowns and leans over my shoulder, peering at the laptop. I've hidden the filter that shows the therapist's address. All it's showing is the first half of a postcode, which will mean nothing to Anna. 'She looks nice,' she says. 'And she looks experienced. But why her?'

'Just a hunch,' I say.

I don't tell Anna what my hunch is. I don't say anything else except that I am going to get in touch with the therapist after the bank holiday on Monday. I'm not sure if Anna believes I am really going to go through with the whole therapy idea, but she makes pasta and salad for dinner and we watch TV and drink some wine and I hug the truth about my 'hunch' to myself for the rest of the weekend.

The truth is that Chorley Common is a small village where, no doubt, everyone knows everyone else and their business, and possibly even who lives in the neighbouring villages. And what car they drive.

PART FIVE

Five Months Earlier

27

Lauren

I'm eight months pregnant, and when most women are nesting – cleaning and painting and getting a nursery ready for the baby – I'm planning to leave my home for good.

In the living room, I lean against the door frame and gaze around the room at the box bay window, at the log burner, at the painted white bookcases. I look up at the corniced ceilings and down at the original wooden floorboards. This house meant so much when we moved in. It was the perfect family home and we'd planned on living here, raising a family together. It's hard to believe that's not going to happen now.

A strip of sunlight has filtered through the blinds and is casting a slatted shadow across the wall, reminding me of the villa in Mantilla de Mar where Charlie and I stayed on our first holiday together. We'd struggled with the heat and had slept the afternoons away in the bedroom behind the venetian blinds, a sheet we'd soaked in the bathtub draped across us, an ancient fan that came with the villa blowing warm air. We'd wake around five and make love, then swim in the pool before heading down the steps to our favourite restaurant, where we'd eat paella and drink crisp white wine and look out across the shingle at the sea shimmering in the distance.

There were one hundred and fifty-eight steps from the town to the villa. Charlie and I would curse them as we climbed back up languidly every evening, sweating and gasping in the heat. We would be carrying heavy bags full of water and our favourite wine – a fruity Verdejo Rueda – along with waxy packages of cheese, tubs of fat olives and soft, juicy nectarines from a small supermarket we'd found in the old town, and we'd stop to catch our breath and shake our heads at our slow, plodding pace. But the climb would be worth it: the view from the balcony outside the villa was to die for. This was our favourite part of the day: we would cool off in the shower, pour the wine and arrange the food on a tray, then we'd sit on the balcony, looking down across the red-brick rooftops, past the eleventh-century church and out to sea. At nine thirty, the church clock would chime and then the lights would come on across the town and around the bay. We'd delight in this: '*Here come the lights,*' one or other of us would say, as if this had been our daily ritual for ever, as if this was our life now – and then we'd clink glasses and sip the crisp, cold wine and put our feet up against the wall so that our toes were touching, and we'd talk and talk, whiling away the hours between dusk and dawn.

We'd only been together for four and half months by then and we were still in the honeymoon phase (though it wasn't our actual honeymoon – not yet). We had met on-site at a project I was overseeing in Oxford, an ambitious redevelopment to upgrade a historic building in keeping with my firm's most recent mission statement pledging a fifty per cent increase in carbon-neutral construction over the next three years. The building was in the centre of Oxford, near St Giles, and belonged to the university's science faculties. It had initially been scheduled for demolition, but the plan now was to restore it to create a state-of-the-art science museum to rival the Ashmolean, with a restaurant on the top floor and a glass-walled viewing terrace looking south over the dreaming spires.

It was an exciting project and I was enthused to be part of the team that had been put together to save the building; environmental engineering and regeneration had been my specialism at university, and reducing a building's carbon footprint through innovative design and construction was my passion. Charlie was working for the electrical contractor and we'd got chatting as we queued for lunch in a café across the street. We'd hit it off immediately and found ourselves sharing a table in the same café at lunchtimes, until one day Charlie had asked me to stay behind after work and let him take me out for dinner. The following evening, instead of taking the train back to London, I'd booked myself a single room at a small, inexpensive B & B in Iffley village. We'd eaten lobster linguine at a restaurant on the high street and he'd walked me back through Christ Church Meadow and along the river and we'd held hands and kissed at Iffley Lock. Romance had turned to passion and Charlie had ended up sharing my small bed. We hadn't got much sleep that night.

It had been his idea to book a two-week holiday in Spain. Charlie lived with a housemate on Botley Road. And following a break-up with a long-term boyfriend two years earlier, I'd gone back home to live with my mum in West London and hadn't yet found anywhere of my own. The holiday was our chance to be alone together, far away from the prying eyes, winks and smiles and calls of 'Here come the two lovebirds' from our colleagues – although, while I faked embarrassment, I secretly enjoyed the teasing because I was totally besotted with Charlie and proud to be seen with him.

The truth was, he was gorgeous. He had longish but well-cut dark brown hair, a broad chest, strong-looking arms and a confident way of carrying himself. My stomach did cartwheels every time I saw him up a ladder with a drill in his hand. He had navy eyes that crinkled in the corners when he laughed and a smile that could light up all three floors of the museum. The first time I saw him, he'd flashed that smile as I passed and I'd cringed and thought, *Here we go. He's going to whistle in a minute.* But as it turned out, he wasn't just another annoying, yet-to-evolve contractor looking for a bit of sport by eyeing up and humiliating the females on-site. There was so much more to him than that.

We met properly in the café over the road two days later. I'd glanced back over my shoulder and there he'd been, right behind me in the queue.

'It's Lauren, isn't it?' he'd asked. That smile again.

'Sorry. Do we . . . do I know you?'

'Charlie Hopwood.' He'd held out a hand, then lowered it when I didn't take it. I hadn't meant to be rude; I was just wondering how he'd found out my name. The contractors and engineers didn't really have anything to do with each other on-site.

'OK. Full disco. I googled you,' he admitted.

'You *googled* me?'

'Well . . . you work for JMB, so—'

'And . . . did you just say "*disco*"?'

He grinned. 'Ah. Yeah. Got it off the telly. Some Australian thing. Thought I'd try it out. But you don't like it. I'll stop. I promise, I will never *ever* say "disco" again. Not unless I'm actually going to a disco, of course. Not that I make a habit of going to discos, but . . . you know. If I did.' He hesitated. 'Do you like discos?'

I looked at him cautiously, thinking that this guy was too attractive to be genuinely interested in me. I'm not confident about my appearance. My friend Anna has told me that I'm the sort of person that people notice when I walk into a room, but I've never really understood what that means.

'Um . . . yeah. Rock . . . disco. I like a dance,' I said, feeling a little sorry for him. Just because he was good-looking and friendly didn't automatically make him a dick.

He looked relieved. 'You've got to like Chic, right?'

'You've got to like Chic,' I agreed.

It was my turn to be served, but I didn't know what I wanted, so I told him he should go in front of me. He ordered a flat white and a lasagne and I immediately wanted a lasagne too. I suffer from food envy. I love food. Trying a new dish and finding it's delicious is the best thing ever for me – but I fear making the wrong choice, so I asked for a lasagne too. But there was none left; Charlie had got the last portion. I said it didn't matter, that I'd have something else, but Charlie hovered behind me, insisting that I take his. I protested. He said the lasagne should have been mine by right and that we should at least share it. So we found a table by the window and I gave him half my salad, and when the lasagne arrived we cut it in two. (It was OK, seven out of ten.) We talked shop for a while. He said that he'd fallen into electrical work by accident after leaving school and abandoning his A levels, that he didn't like working for other people and wanted to work on his own renovations. We both loved old buildings, we discovered, and I was impressed to find out he was a member of the National Trust. Soon we were eating dinner together and sleeping together and visiting Hughenden Manor together and walking around the Ashmolean together, and then . . .

And then Spain. We read and talked and swam and walked and explored the architecture in the old town. Charlie was as much of a food lover as I was, keen to explore the local cuisine and taking as much pleasure as I did in finding a delicious new dish or bottle of wine. But I was cautious. I was thirty-three. Most of my friends were getting married or settling down into long-term relationships round about the same time I'd become newly single, which had been tough on me. I wanted to meet someone new – I needed to meet someone new – but my previous break-up had been a difficult one to recover from and experience had taught me to expect the worst. Since Charlie and I had started seeing each other, part of me had been waiting for the inevitable argument, the unmasking of the irreconcilable difference that would drive us apart – because this was too good to be true, wasn't it? We were having such a good time.

But the argument never came. Every time I woke to find the bed beside me empty, I'd wonder if this was it: the moment he'd gone off to think about whether he'd flung all of his eggs into the wrong basket, whether he felt more *himself* without me than with me, whether we were moving too fast. But no . . . a moment later, there he'd be, grinning in a wet towel or bringing me breakfast in bed, having been for a shower or a dip in the pool, or out for bread and milk (down, down, down and up, up, up all those steps to and from the town). And so the lazy, sun-drenched days and magical, moonlit nights went on.

And then, *the* conversation; the one I'd always remember.

'Let's buy a house together,' he'd said, as we sat on the balcony on the last night of our holiday.

'Charlie!' I protested, laughing. 'We've only known each other a few months.'

'So?'

I grinned at him. 'You just don't like renting.'

'Well, yeah.' He nodded. 'I hate renting. It's a waste of money. And Jonno's a geek.'

It was true; his housemate *was* a geek. He was thirty-two, but he was still working at the same video store he'd worked at when he was seventeen. He watched *Beavis and Butt-Head* – and he and his friends sniggered together like Beavis and Butt-Head. He slept all day, ate cereal for breakfast, lunch and dinner, and stayed up playing on his Xbox all night.

'So . . .' he said, looking at me excitedly. 'What do you think? We could look for a project. A place we can do up together. With our pooled knowledge, we'd be perfect for it.'

I studied his face, my heart beating faster. 'But . . . that's a big commitment. How do we know if we're . . . you know. Right for each other?'

He turned to look at me with the utmost sincerity. 'But we *are* right for each other, Lauren. Aren't we? Don't tell me I'm the only one who's having a great time?'

My heart jumped at his words. I'd thought my last boy-friend was the love of my life. I'd been scared that he was going to be an impossible act to follow, but now here it was: my second act; my second chance at happiness. But . . . experience had taught me that this first flush of happiness wasn't an indicator of the future, that people changed. Something was holding me back.

'You don't know me yet,' I said. 'Not completely. I could be a psychopath for all you know.'

Charlie laughed. 'You're not a psychopath.'

I laughed too and kicked off my flip-flops. 'But you don't know that for sure.'

He shrugged, frowning, serious now. 'I know all I need to know. I know you're the nicest person I've ever met.'

I looked up at him, touched. Was it really that simple? 'But . . . what if you felt differently once you got to know me. What if I'm not the person you think I am?'

He speared an olive with a fork and shrugged, nonchalantly, confidently. 'I love you, Lauren. There's nothing you could do that would stop me from loving you.'

My stomach flipped, and I said, 'I love you too.'

We went back to Spain the following year, and again the year after, and then in April we went again and it was there I found out I was pregnant.

That was the moment our lives began to change for ever. I didn't know what I was doing. But Charlie knew, and that was good enough for me.

28

Hope

I'm having a boy! I'm over the moon. Never mind eating for two; I seem to be eating for a whole football team. But I don't care and neither does Drew. I'm radiant, he says. In fact, so says everyone who knows me. 'Pregnancy suits you,' said my mum last week, looking at me sideways, surprised, as though my bump was a hat I'd tried on that she had tried to talk me out of buying. But here it is. It fits!

So . . . (drum roll!) I had the twenty-week scan and all was fine. The sonographer told us that he (he!) is developing just as expected. In another three weeks we will reach a major milestone: at twenty-four weeks our baby can survive without me, even if things go wrong, which they won't because I'm being so careful, taking it so easy and making sure that there is absolutely zero stress in my life.

When the sonographer told us the sex, it was a thrilling, magical moment. We walked out into the waiting room and Drew grabbed hold of me, kissed me and then shouted,

'Yes!' out loud and punched the air. And then we were both crying and laughing at the same time. Drew said that he'd secretly been hoping for a boy and now I feel as though I've done something amazing, because I catch him looking at me in the most special of ways, as though I really have done something incredible. He looks at me as if I've made all his dreams come true.

He's been so sweet and kind. He brings me breakfast in bed every morning before he goes to work and brings home flowers on a Friday. He cooks and clears up after dinner. He runs me baths and cuts my toenails and rubs my feet and back. He calls me from work to ask if I'm resting and encourages me to take naps. If I seem ridiculously smug and joyous, it's because I thought this day would never come and because it hasn't always been like this. I've already lost three babies and this pregnancy has been tainted not just by the fear of losing another, but by the thought that's been teetering on the edge of my consciousness: *Drew's with me out of guilt. It's her he loves.*

Normally, I'd dismiss the thought quickly; I'd squash it down and put a lid on it. I'd focus instead on something positive – after all, I'm very good at that. But the baby is strong, it seems, and I, too, now feel mentally strong enough to invite the memory in, to unwrap it, open it up and examine it so that I can put it in context, deal with it once and for all and then, hopefully, put it away, back in its box.

We were supposed to be making a baby that evening, the evening I found out. I was ovulating. I had it all planned.

Drew was on board. We'd discussed it before he left the house that morning and he'd smiled and kissed me and promised to be home by six. It was a warm day, but I'd put a shepherd's pie in the oven because it was Drew's favourite meal and because I could set a timer and let it sit there until we were ready. I'd opened a bottle of red wine and poured us each a smooth, velvety glass. When Drew got home, we would need to get straight down to it. I'd need to lie with my feet up for at least half an hour afterwards (not proven to be more effective, but why argue with gravity?). We'd eat dinner in bed in front of the TV and then Drew would go downstairs and crack open a beer and watch *Peaky Blinders* or *Luther* or something else on the big TV in the lounge. But I wanted to be asleep by nine, because research *has* shown that a good night's sleep aids fertility.

It had only been two months since we lost our third baby, but my online searches had brought up studies that had shown it was fine to start again early, and as far as I was concerned, the sooner the better. So, this was the evening. At five past seven, when Drew still hadn't come home, I picked up my phone from the bedside table and found his number. The call went straight to voicemail, but I forced myself not to be angry because I didn't want anything to spoil the mood.

It was around eight when I heard Drew's car outside, the engine revving, the gravel crunching. I listened from the living room as the car door slammed and the front door opened, and then I got up and went into the hallway.

'Hi,' I said.

'Hello.' His greeting was clipped and strangely formal. I didn't know what to make of this, so I watched in silence as he closed the front door and hung his jacket over the banister at the foot of the stairs, loosening his tie with his other hand. He turned to face me, his blue-grey eyes seeking out mine. They were filmed over with tears. He pushed his fair hair away from his face – something he does when he's nervous – and his Adam's apple bobbed in his throat. 'I'm sorry,' he said, his voice breaking.

'Hey. It's OK.' I stood on tiptoes to kiss him, winding my arms around his neck. I didn't need to know why he was late. I brushed his ear with my mouth and said, 'We still have time.'

Drew took my arms and removed them from his neck, holding me away from him as if I had a virus. I drew back my dressing gown, smiling temptingly and giving him a glimpse of what I was wearing underneath, which wasn't much.

'Stop, Hope,' Drew sighed, sounding tired. 'Just stop.'

Shame made me flush. I could feel the heat in my cheeks and neck.

'I need to talk to you,' he said.

'What . . . now?' I asked. 'Can't it wait?'

He shook his head. 'No. No, it can't.'

My heart sank. I didn't understand what could be more important than making a baby. This wasn't how things were supposed to go.

I stepped into the living room and sank down onto the sofa. Mild panic rose inside me. Has he lost his job? I wondered. My work as a therapist was not enough to pay the mortgage. And besides, I'd been hoping I could scale things back.

Drew followed me and sat on the sofa opposite, gazing at me wistfully. 'I'm sorry,' he said again.

'What for?' I asked. 'What's happened?'

'You're not going to like this, Hope.'

'Just tell me.'

He cleared his throat. 'I've been seeing someone.'

I felt my heart flutter. 'You mean . . . an affair?'

He nodded and moistened his lips.

'Who? Who is she?'

He looked at me, his face ashen. 'Someone I work with. You don't know her. It was a mistake. It's over now.'

I waited for him to continue.

There were so many questions, so many emotions, I didn't know where to begin. It was with shame that I acknowledged the thoughts lingering foremost in my mind: *He hasn't lost his job. We can still pay the mortgage. He says it's over. Can this be resolved somehow, or put aside, so that we can have sex tonight?*

Although why was he telling me this now, tonight of all nights?

I felt a chill run through me. 'Is she pregnant?' I asked, my voice cracking. The fluttering of my heart turned into pounding.

'No.' He shook his head vehemently. 'No, Hope. No. We were careful . . .'

He paused as I flinched at the mental image of Drew unrolling a condom. Her putting it on.

'How long has it been going on?'

'A few months.'

'How many?'

'Not many.'

I waited.

'Since Christmas. Before Christmas.'

I thought about Christmas, about what we were doing. We were having a baby – that's what we were doing. And then we were losing a baby. Bile rose in my throat.

Drew leaned forward. 'It's over, Hope. I'm so, so sorry I've hurt you. But it's over. It's *you* I love.'

'So why tell me?' My voice was shriller than I'd meant it to be. 'Why tell me now? Why spoil tonight?'

Drew swallowed. 'Her husband has found out.'

'And he's threatening to tell me?'

'He's threatening to tell everyone.'

I sat up straight. 'Everyone?'

'Everyone I work with. Everyone she works with.'

I thought about this. I thought about why he had been late this evening. I pictured them together in the second-floor conference room at his office, or in a cosy pub on the corner, or in his car, as she tearfully told him that their juicy secret was no longer a secret. I thought about his boss, Graham, and Jim Key and Marissa, Graham's secretary, and everyone in the whole goddamned planning department – maybe everyone in every single department of Wallingford District Council – knowing that Drew had been fucking someone else, someone that wasn't me. It might even be in the local paper. It would be all round the village.

It was more than I could bear

At the time, I thought there was no way I could forgive Drew. I was so, so angry. But I wanted to be a mother and I wanted this more than anything. Drew swore that it was over, that it was me he wanted – me and our future baby. It took me a couple of months to move on and, yes, forgive him, but the thought of losing everything we'd built up together was too hard for me. I was nearly forty. What were the chances of finding someone else before it was too late, someone I loved enough – someone who loved *me* enough – for us to want to have a baby together? They were just about zero. If I wanted a baby, this was it: I had no choice.

Now, Drew's reaction to the scan has convinced me I made the right decision. I smooth my hand over my belly and smile to myself. The baby is due in April next year, so there's a long road ahead yet, but this is the furthest I've ever got, and as for Drew's affair, it's in the past. I have to believe that. If experience has taught me anything, it's that I'm resilient. I can do this. They say we see the world not as it is but as who we are. I can choose how to look at things, and I've chosen to believe my husband when he says this fling of his meant nothing and that I'm still the most important person in his life.

And what was the alternative? To throw away everything, including my last chance to be a mother? No. No way.

In the end, no one at work found out and Drew's reputation remains intact. So no harm done. Well, who knows what it was like for her and her husband? But for us, all is well.

29

Drew

I saw her today. I walked past her after I'd parked the Porsche and our eyes met, just for a second. She looked sad – so very sad – and I found all sorts of feelings surfacing, but I didn't stop. I felt ashamed, the way I just kept walking as if she was nothing to me, no more than a stranger in a car park. I could feel her watching me as I went into the office, and I couldn't think straight for the rest of the day.

I don't want to be that person, that cliché: the man who cheats on his wife, then makes it up with her and goes on to ghost the other woman as if she never existed, as if she's the one to blame for what we *both* did. It's not in my nature to treat another human being that way. But I told Hope it was over, and I have to stick to that. I owe it to my wife to be completely, one hundred per cent loyal and that means no contact with her – none whatsoever. I can't change what I did, but I can change what I do now.

I don't know why I did it – the affair. I've never done

anything like it before and I swore I never would, not after I got my own heart broken. I was nineteen and I'd met an amazing woman. She was older than me and she seemed so worldly-wise, so mature, although she was actually only in her early twenties and, looking back, I can now see that she was barely an adult herself. But she had her own flat and her own car and when she asked me to move in with her I felt so grown-up, living with a woman like that, at my age. I was wildly, deeply in love with her and we were deliriously happy for a while. But then I came home early from college one day and found her in bed with my best friend. The pain was indescribable. I made a rule after that: always finish one relationship before you start another. I didn't ever want to put anyone else through what I'd been through.

And now I have. Hope says it had something to do with it being the anniversary of my mum's death the winter before and because of us losing the first two babies. But I think that's probably just an excuse. I've hurt two people – three if you count her husband – and I'm not proud of myself. Hope is the kind of person who bounces back from everything. But I know she's still hurt, deep inside, even though she's so happy about the baby, even though we've talked and talked about it and even though she says she's forgiven me. My mum's death from cancer *was* a hard loss to bear, and then soon after that we lost the second baby, so maybe something about that third pregnancy – the expectation of more loss – triggered something in me. Maybe I was frightened of the inevitable – or at least it had come to feel inevitable.

And Hope says that many people have a midlife crisis after they lose a parent. It can make you think about how you are living your life, or it can make you want to be alive, or . . . something.

I'm grateful she sees it that way, but if I were to be completely honest with myself, I think I just wanted sex with someone new. I'm ashamed to admit it, and of course I'd never say that to Hope. Deep down, I suppose I didn't want to hold my breath about the baby, to think of it as real, because after what we'd already been through, a part of me couldn't believe that it was really going to happen. But was that why I cheated on my wife? I don't know if it's really that complicated. I think I just liked being near her, liked the fact that she was new and fresh and different from Hope. Maybe I have low self-esteem and was flattered that she liked me. Maybe it's because we worked so closely together on the planning appeal. I've noticed over the years that when I work closely with a woman, I can sometimes start to develop romantic feelings for her. You spend all week in the office together, after all – more time than you spend with your family. That's changed for a lot of people since lockdown, of course, and hybrid working is now the norm for most people, but if I'm not out on-site, I'm in meetings with developers and contractors most mornings and afternoons, and so it's never become the norm for me.

Anyway, there she would be, on-site on the Crowthorpe development when I arrived in the morning, and I soon started to look forward to it. Something drew me to her pale skin and green eyes, the way they would look up at me from behind her protective glasses, tendrils of soft, dark hair escaping from her hard hat. We'd watch the concrete going into the footings together, look over the plans together and argue with the contractors together. She's clever, like Hope, and we were a team, in the way that Hope and I are a team. I suppose she became my *work wife*, except, of course, that work spouses are supposed to remain platonic.

I did try. I tried to push away my feelings – and our relationship *was* platonic for a while. Then, there she was at the office Christmas party, standing on her own under the mistletoe and streamers. Gone were the site boots and the hi-vis coat. She had tinsel in her hair and was wearing a green velvet dress that matched her eyes.

The thought of her still thrills me. She's slim-hipped and dark, while Hope is curvy and fair. If anything, I love Hope's curves more, but it was never really about her body. Something just compelled me to kiss her that night. It was a chaste peck, of course, all above board in front of our colleagues, but the spark was there and we talked all evening. Later, we agreed to share a cab home together, except that we didn't – go home that is, at least not straight away. We went to a hotel in Watlington instead.

By the time things ended between us, the planning appeal had concluded and the Crowthorpe development had been put on hold due to issues with the contractors, so she asked to be moved to another site. I don't know the ins and outs because we never spoke again, but my sense was that this was the deal she'd cut with her husband. Although I heard on the grapevine that things weren't going well between them. Maybe he's left her, and if so, I do feel bad about that, especially now things have turned out so well for Hope and me.

So, seeing her today was a little unsettling. I suppose it was inevitable that our paths would cross again at some point, given the business we're both in, but it's a bit strange that it was today, what with it being the anniversary, almost, of when we first got together. (Anniversary! Christ! Don't let me ever say that word with reference to her again, and especially never in front of Hope.) What I mean is that it's almost exactly a year since we first got together at the office Christmas party. The weather is the same, too: there's a chill in the air, damp leaves on the ground, my breath is coming out in small, foggy clouds. So, it's weird that I saw her again today for the first time since it ended. I guess that's why it's dragged things up. But I won't be going to the work Christmas party this year. Hope and I have fixed things and now I'm going to be a father – for real, this time. It's finally happening. I finally see my future. I've been such a fool, but it's over and my wife still loves me and I'm going to have a *son*. A son! I can't believe my luck.

30

Hope

I am twenty-four weeks pregnant today, and it's the best Christmas present ever. Twenty-four weeks means the baby can survive without me. It would be touch and go if he came this early, obviously, so we are praying that doesn't happen, but I now have something to cling on to, because he would have a sixty per cent chance of survival. (I know that leaves a forty per cent chance of something else, but I'm not thinking about that. The odds are in our favour this time.) There would be nothing *inevitable* about him coming this early, not like the other times. He would be considered premature – a 'preemie', a baby worth fighting for.

Drew took a few days off before Christmas and we drove into Wyebridge and bought a crib, a beautiful wicker Moses basket for our little Moses, with a sweet cream hood and a lace trim. He's not really going to be called Moses, but that's what we're calling him for now until we can decide on a name. I like Adam or Harley. Drew likes Drew Junior, which

I absolutely refuse to name our baby. When he says this, he says it tongue-in-cheek, smiling, and I know he knows that's not going to be *the* name. We both know I'll be the one to make the final decision. Like I said, he owes me, and I'll be making him pay for a good while yet.

The only battle I'm not yet winning is over the car. When we were out shopping for the crib, I also saw a pram I liked and I wanted to buy it, but it wouldn't fit in the back of Drew's Porsche. I have been nagging him again about getting rid of it, about exchanging it for a family car. Drew says there's no need – he says that it's a good car, solid and steady – and that we can fit a rear-facing child's car seat in the back, and a buggy too, if we find a smallish one and are creative about it. He says the Porsche will be the perfect father-and-son-mobile (he says it like he's Batman and it's the Batmobile). But I keep telling him no, it's not practical. It's old, for a start, a 2002 plate. He's absolutely not going to be taking my son out in a car that's almost twenty years old. Besides, he got it because it's fast – as Drew has been fond of telling people, it can go from nought to sixty in five point two seconds – and the thought of him driving that fast with our son in it is just . . . well, it's not going to happen. I only allowed pregnant *me* in it the day we went shopping because he promised to drive slowly, and because we've had a cold spell and my Civic wouldn't start.

He bought the Porsche with the money his mum left him and I'm more than aware that it's all wrapped up with her death, a compensatory behaviour, no doubt, to deflect him from accepting that she was gone and that he needed to grieve for her – an attempt to replace her with something that would make him feel alive. I didn't try to stop him. I knew he had this deep need inside him all of a sudden to live life to the full, to put the top down and zoom off into the sunset with the wind in his hair. I assumed it would be a passing phase, that one day he'd wake up crying and we'd cuddle and talk and he'd acknowledge the pain and sadness and wouldn't need the car any more.

Well, I hope I'm right about this, and that he didn't buy it to attract women. I couldn't help thinking, when I was sitting in it, heading to Wyebridge, about the fact that it was the car he had when he was seeing *her*, that she sat in this seat next to him, the way I do, as if *she* were his wife instead of me. I can't help thinking that they must have had all their cosy chats in there and maybe they even had sex in there too – if that's possible. If they did, I hope it was bloody uncomfortable and that someone got a cold, hard handbrake in their vagina and a gearstick up their arse.

OK, I'm blaming the other woman, which is deeply anti-feminist, I know, but then what she did to me wasn't very sisterly, was it? She was fucking my husband when I was carrying his baby. She knew I was pregnant; he says he told her. What kind of a woman does that? He says she felt bad about it, and they kept trying to stop, but they can't have tried very hard because they didn't stop for four and a half months, even after I lost the baby. I know it's not cool to treat the other woman as the scarlet temptress who lured away your husband. I know he could have and should have resisted her, but I suppose, if I'm honest, I just expect more from women than I do from men.

And anyway, I'm not letting him off the hook; it's just that he has something I want. I want to be a mother and I want to be the mother of a baby that has *both* its parents. Besides, I love Drew and I know he's a good person. I don't know her and I can't be responsible for whatever was going on in *her* life at the time. It's easier to be angrier with someone you don't know.

I suggested to Drew that his reluctance to get rid of the car was because of her, because of the association with her, but I didn't really believe it, even as I said it. The reason he doesn't want to get rid of it is because it's unique. You don't come across many convertible Porsche 911 Carrera 996s with spoilers, apparently. He says it's going up in value. Drew has always been a bit of a collector and so this makes sense. But I now see it as his last-fling car, the car he had when he made the kind of reckless, stupid decisions a man makes before he settles down and becomes a father. I don't hate the sight of it, but I don't associate our new life with it. He bought it on a whim and he had a fling with her on a whim – the same whim. That whim is over. We're going to be a family now.

So, I'd like him to get a more sensible car before the baby comes. In the meantime, we have my car. It's a Honda Civic five-door saloon – perfectly practical and big enough for a family, but we could do better. We could get something far more comfortable. We could afford a newish SUV if he sold the Porsche.

I thought that was going to be my Christmas present, to be honest. On Christmas Eve, in the morning, Drew said he had to go into Wyebridge, alone. He gave me a look that said, 'Don't ask,' and, of course, I knew what that meant, but at the same time I was a little disappointed. I'd thought we were going to spend the day together, wrapping presents, baking canapés and drinking coffee (decaf for me) in the morning, watching old Christmas movies in the afternoon and . . . well, getting festive and excited about Christmas. I had a goat's cheese tartine recipe I wanted to try for the first time in preparation for our drinks and nibbles with Nick and Jess on Boxing Day. I'd been hoping we could do this together (Drew is a *very* good cook). And afterwards, I had imagined us curled up together on the saggy (but incredibly comfortable) old peacock-blue sofa beside the fire.

'So, how long are you going to be?' I asked as he tugged his coat on in the hallway.

'I'm not sure. I'm not sure how long it will take.' He wrapped his scarf around his throat.

I frowned, but it was a nice frown, a puzzled frown. A frown that said, *What on earth can it be?*

'It's a secret,' he smiled. 'Trust me, you'll like it,' but then his smile faded. *Trust me.* It was a throwaway comment, entirely Christmas-present-related, but we both felt awkward at the implication that he might be going out to do something secretive that *wasn't* to do with Christmas, and that I had a very good reason *not* to trust him.

But I did. I honestly did. And so I baked in the kitchen, drinking coffee and eating mince pies with Jess, who'd come through the back gate to help me, and then we each put on a peppermint face mask and swapped notes on the presents we'd bought our husbands – a tan Maxwell-Scott Italian leather briefcase for Drew, a new iPhone for Nick.

'So, what do you think it is?' Jess asked. 'Your mystery present?'

I shook my head. 'I have no idea!'

Jess grinned. 'I think I know.'

And so it was Jess who put the idea into my head. After she left around two, I thought I was going to hear the gravel crunching and that Drew was going to pull up in a sparkling new four-by-four, all ready for Christmas. So I was disappointed when I heard that familiar howl on the road outside. I was sitting on the sofa, feet up. Drew came in, blowing his fringe off his face and stamping his sleet-dampened feet on the mat, and he jumped when he saw me through the living-room door. He was carrying a huge rectangle wrapped in brown paper, which was obviously a painting. I pretended not to notice what he was holding, but I knew what it was – he'd got me a very pretty oil on canvas of some sunflowers, which we'd seen in an auction room and I had admired.

I love the painting, and it was a really thoughtful present, but I'd have much preferred a new family-friendly car.

31

Drew

I wish I'd never met up with her again, but I did and now I can't get her out of my head. It's just like that Kylie Minogue song; my brain is doing the same desperate, dirge-like *La-la-la. La-la-la-la-la* thing, on repeat. (It's a clever song, in that way, a real earworm.) But I need her out of my head because it's Christmas and my wife is having our baby and *that's* all I dare think about.

I never intended to meet up with her. I *really, one hundred per cent* never planned it. I only ever intended to go to the auction in Stoke End, or, if I didn't win the painting, to the big John Lewis in Wyebridge – my backup plan. But on Friday as I left work she messaged me and said she needed to talk. She said it was important. I couldn't just ignore her for a second time. It felt so cruel, so disrespectful, and a small part of me was worried about what might happen if I didn't reply. I've never thought of her as unstable or erratic. She's a strong, strong person, as strong as Hope, I'm pretty certain of that. But I care about her. How could I not? I'm not a monster. So I messaged her back. She asked if we could meet for coffee the following day.

The following day was Christmas Eve and I'd already got a good reason to go out on my own, so it wasn't as if I had to lie to Hope. The painting was listed as lot number 102 and I estimated it would come up at about eleven thirty. The guide price was £500 to £800. It was an original by a semi-famous local artist, a landscape of the fields north of Ashcombe Ridge, and I knew there was a good chance it would go for over the guide price. It's not that there's a limit on how much I'd spend on Hope – she deserves a bloody medal, not a painting – but I also knew that she'd look at the auction website and see what it went for, and that she wouldn't want me to pay over the odds. And so John Lewis was my backup plan in case the bids went too high and it went for ridiculous money. They would have something nice at John Lewis.

I was distracted the whole time I was at the auction, knowing what I was going to do afterwards, and I had to focus hard to keep my mind on which lot we were up to. The auction room was busy; I'd say there were a lot of men looking to get last-minute Christmas presents for their wives. The despicable irony of the situation wasn't lost on me: I was there to buy a painting for my wife and then I was going to meet my mistress. I'm a cliché, a pathetic excuse for a human being, I know this. Anyway, I got the painting for £850.

We met in the car park at the Crowthorpe development, not for sentimental reasons, but because we knew that no one would be there. The dispute with the contractors was ongoing and the build was still on hold. The entire site was fenced off and gated and I knew none of the engineers would be there on Christmas Eve.

She was waiting when I arrived, her lone Nissan parked in the middle of the empty car park. I pulled up next to her and jumped out quickly, tapping on her passenger door. She opened it and I got into her car with her. Hope had been on at me about the Porsche lately, asking me to get rid of it on the basis that it was the car I'd sat in with my mistress. (Hope actually called her that, and when I asked her not to, she asked what else I should call her and gave me a challenging, Hope-like look, and I couldn't answer that.) Thinking about it now, it's all just completely messed up. As if us sitting in my mistress's car instead of my own would make what I was doing all right.

When I saw her, my heart melted. She was wearing a green woollen bobble hat, and the colour matched her eyes, just as the dress had done, the one she wore to the Christmas party. Her clear, Celtic skin was pale and her black hair hung in long waves around her shoulders. She looked so young and so cute that it was all I could do not to kiss her.

'Sorcha—' I began.

'I'm going back to Ireland,' she said, interrupting me. 'My sister's had a stroke.'

'Your . . . younger sister?' I asked, shocked.

She nodded, a tear escaping. 'It was out of the blue. One minute she was fine and then she just collapsed. She was at my mum's when it happened, thank God, or they might not have found her for hours . . . or days, even.'

'Can she talk?'

'Just about. But she has no mobility. I'm going back home to help my mum look after her.' She looked into her lap, her eyes glistening. 'And then I'm going to find work in Dublin.'

'You're not coming back?'

'No.' She pulled off a glove and wiped her cheek. 'I wanted to say goodbye.'

'Is Paul going too?'

She shook her head. 'He's staying here. It's over between us.'

She started crying then, so I took her in my arms and held her.

And that was it. That was all. There was a kiss. It was on the lips, and it was perhaps not the kind of kiss you'd give your brother or sister, but it was *fairly* chaste – and that's all that happened. The woman I loved a little, but not as much as my wife, was leaving for another country and I don't think this was even an ultimatum, my chance to stop her, to tell her not to go. She'd already made up her mind. Her sister needed her, and my wife was six months pregnant with my first child. I had nothing to offer her, and we both knew that.

And so we said goodbye and I opened the car door to

leave, and then I shut it again and told her – completely unfairly and *completely* irresponsibly – that I wished she wouldn't go.

She said I had no right to say that.

I agreed, apologised and then left.

I drove home with the painting and I looked at my lovely, pregnant wife and I convinced myself that I had done the right thing. I'd said goodbye and I'd come home, hadn't I?

But Sorcha played on my mind all of Christmas Day and all of Boxing Day. That evening, we had drinks with our neighbours, Nick and Jess, and I laughed and joked and played the part of the perfect husband and the perfect host, but now it's three days since I last saw her and I just can't get her out of my head.

32

Lauren

Charlie pushes the pram gently back and forth in the hallway.

'Is he asleep?' I ask from the sofa in the lounge.

'Nearly.' Charlie puts a finger to his lips. 'He's desperately trying to stay awake,' he whispers. 'He doesn't want to miss anything.'

I smile at the image of Sam's eyelids fluttering drowsily, pausing, half-open, then finally closing. I can almost smell the sweet, milky scent of him as he lies swaddled in the mint-green blanket we chose from . . . where did we get that blanket? I can't remember. Oh my goodness. We only bought it a few months ago. Baby brain!

I yawn and stretch my legs out, closing my eyes and tucking a cushion beneath my head. I need to sleep, too. 'When the baby sleeps, you sleep,' my mum had said insistently, soon after Sam was born. 'Turn off your phone. Forget the housework.' I tug at the duvet Charlie has laid across me and imagine I'm lying on a sunbed in Mantilla de Mar. I can feel the heat. I can hear the gentle drone of insects and the distant hum of the tourists eating at restaurants down in the bay. *Bliss*, I think to myself. *It will be sheer bliss*. This *is* sheer bliss. The sleepless nights are torture, of course, the on-demand relentlessness of Sam's waking hours a complete shock to the system. And then throw in all the mood swings as my hormones adjust from nine months of pregnancy. I am either crying or laughing most of the time. But it's bliss, all the same.

When the visa comes through, Charlie will be able to work in Spain. He'll need to get certification and his work will have to be signed off by a Spanish electrician, but we'll have the rent from this house until we sell it and then we'll be able to buy something we can renovate and make our own. When Sam is a little older, I'll cross-qualify too. In the meantime, the cost of living in Mantilla is way lower than it is here in Oxfordshire. We'll both be able to work less and spend more time with Sam and with each other. My mum's sad about it, as is Anna, but as I've told them, there's nothing to stop them from coming out to join us. My mum says she's thinking about it. Anyway, it's only a two-hour flight to Barcelona. She can come and see her grandson whenever she likes.

Near my waist, I feel the sofa sink a little as Charlie leans in and strokes my hair, planting a kiss on my cheek.

I open one eye.

'Sorry. Were you asleep?' he asks softly.

'No. Not yet.'

'I'm sorry,' he says again. 'I'll leave you to have a nap.'

'Don't go yet,' I say drowsily, taking his hand and kissing it.

He grins, his navy eyes crinkling at the corners. 'You don't know where that's been.'

'I think I do. Same place mine has been.'

'I don't care,' he shrugs. 'I still want to have sex with you.'

'No. No way. Not until Sam's at least ten and I'm through the menopause. I'm not risking this happening again.'

Charlie laughs. 'You just need some sleep. And then I'd say it's game on. You know you want to.'

He's joking. He knows it's out of the question. I had ten stitches in my perineum three weeks ago and it's still sore as hell.

'Yeah, I want to,' I smile. 'Just not for another ten years.'

He smiles down at me and then his eyes move to the sofa I'm lying on. 'We need to get some new sofas,' he says. 'Before we go.'

'Really?' I frown. 'Is there any point?'

'We'll sell this place quicker. Everything else is new or in good condition. The sofas let this room down. First impressions, right? They say that people make up their mind if they are going to buy a house within the first two minutes. And this is the first room they'll walk into after they come through the front door.'

I nod. 'Yeah, I guess you're right.'

'So, a trip to Ikea, then?'

'Sure. Why not.'

'When?'

I yawn. 'Not this week.'

'You have to factor in the delivery time. The visa could come through any day and then there's nothing to stop us putting this place on the market and booking our flights. The estate agent says it will go quickly.'

'With new sofas.'

'With new sofas.' Charlie looks down at me for a moment. 'OK, you're tired. I guess it can wait a couple of weeks. In fact, we could go on my next day off.'

I smile. 'The one you booked off for Valentine's Day?'

Charlie looks sheepish. 'Yeah. But . . . that's OK, isn't it? It would be good to go on a weekday. The traffic on the North Circular is horrendous at the weekend, even on a Sunday.'

'We could go to Milton Keynes?'

He thinks about this. 'But if we go to Wembley, we can call in and see your mum on the way back.'

The thought warms me. 'Sure.'

'I know it's not ideal, but . . .'

'It's fine,' I smile. 'That's a nice idea. She'll like that.'

'And then,' he said, winding an arm around me, drawing me close and planting a kiss on my lips, 'we'll have all the time in the world to celebrate Valentine's Day – and all the other days, and the rest of our lives – when we've settled in our new home in Spain.'

As I drift off to sleep, I think again about leaving Stow. When Charlie first came up with the idea of emigrating, it seemed so spontaneous and a little crazy, but that's Charlie.

He says I inspired him, I'm not sure how or why, but he has definitely pushed me to do things I'd never have dreamed of. We hadn't even planned to have a baby or get married. Things just turned out that way.

We had been together for two and a half years by the time I fell pregnant. By then, we'd bought the house in Stow and moved in together. I was working for a small civil engineering firm in Oxford. But I was nearly thirty-six and when would there be a better time to have a baby? We were both beyond happy at the prospect of becoming parents and Charlie proposed to me the same day I told him. We had already started talking about moving out to Spain and we didn't have any money left by then, so we got married at the town hall in the city centre on a cool September day. We'd invited just our parents, our siblings and Anna to the ceremony, which took place in a wood-panelled room with stained-glass windows. Charlie and I spent the whole service grinning at each other, relishing the secret we were saving to announce at the reception. I still wasn't showing very much at five months, and Sam (or soon-to-be Sam) was concealed behind a bunch of white roses under my empire-waist wedding dress. Afterwards, outside on the steps, my veil blew off and my brother caught it; I simultaneously dropped my roses and my mum leaned in to pick them up. As she did so, she glanced at my belly and at that moment – she later told us – the realisation dawned on her. The photographer captured all of this in a single magnificent photograph that Charlie and I chose as the one we'd have enlarged and printed in black and white and framed in cream to hang on the living-room wall. It encapsulated everything about the day for us.

I open my eyes and look across the room at the photo now, the one I love so much. I'm looking skywards, my eyebrows raised, my mouth a wide 'O' as my veil takes off across the pavement. I've already flung my roses, which are suspended in mid-air. My brother is also suspended in mid-air behind me, his arms outstretched – a well-dressed goalie. My mum is leaning in, her eyes on my belly. Charlie's holding my hand – the one that wasn't holding the roses – and gazing at me adoringly, oblivious to all the chaos. Even though I've seen the picture a hundred times, my heart lurches at the thought of where we were back then. Not *where* we were (on the steps of the town hall in Oxford city centre), but where we were in our lives. *The first picture of us as a family*, Charlie had said softly, after we hung it. He's senti-mental like that.

And now he wants to go sofa shopping on Valentine's Day, which is most unlike him because he's usually so romantic, but I know that's just a measure of how keen he is for us to get the house sold and leave for Spain. Besides, I like that he was thinking of my mum, about letting her see Sam so that she gets to spend some time with him before we leave for Mantilla. It was thoughtful. My mum is going to miss her grandson so much.

I snooze lightly for a while, probably only twenty minutes, but it's all I needed. When I wake up, Charlie is standing in the doorway.

'Hey,' he says. 'I've taken a photo of Sam. For the passport. Want to see it?'

I nod, smiling.

He pulls his phone out of his pocket and opens his photo gallery, then holds it up. It's Sam in his pram, fast asleep.

'He's got his eyes closed,' I point out, laughing.

'It doesn't matter.' Charlie shakes his head. 'It's allowed for babies.'

'He's three weeks old!' I smile. 'He'll look completely different by the time we fly.'

'Doesn't matter.' Charlie shrugs. 'It will be valid for five years. Those are the rules. So shall I apply for it?'

'Sure.' I smile. And then I add, 'I love you, Charlie Hopwood.'

Charlie leans forward and whispers in my ear, 'I love you, too, Lauren Hopwood. And thank you.'

'What for?'

'For him.' He nods at Sam's pram, where our son is still sleeping. 'Isn't this just going to be the best thing ever? The three of us starting a new life together in Mantilla de Mar?'

I nod dreamily, my eyes closing again. 'It really is.'

33

Hope

I'm in my usual counselling room in the extension of our house. But it's a cold day and the floor-to-ceiling glass windows and bifold doors can cause it to get a little chilly in here in winter, so I've closed the screen door and got a small heater on.

My ex-train-driver client sighs and rubs his eyes.

'She wanted to die, Clive,' I remind him. 'She threw herself in front of a train. You don't do that unless you're serious about ending your life.'

'I know. I know what you're saying,' he murmurs. 'But she was only eighteen. How could she have been sure that's what she really wanted?' His voice breaks a little as he looks up at me with a pleading expression that's now very familiar.

I decide not to encourage this with a response. We've talked a lot about the girl who died, the pain she must have gone through. I want him to talk about *his* pain, what *he's* going through.

'My wife says the same as you,' he says, after a moment. 'But I was the only one in the cabin. Nobody knows exactly what happened except me. If I'd stopped in time, she'd have survived, she'd still be here and then they could have got her the help she needed. *She* could be the one sitting here in counselling with you. *She* could be the one dealing with whatever it was that was causing her so much emotional pain. I can't stop thinking that if only I'd been paying that little bit more attention . . .'

'The inquest exonerated you,' I remind him. 'They said you weren't to blame.'

'But they weren't there, were they? I was the only one – and I know I wasn't paying attention, not *full* attention.'

'You'd had the breaks required by law. You weren't using your phone. You were driving within the legal speed limit.'

'I know, but the speed limit's just a guide. That's what it says on the organisation website. You don't have to drive as fast as you're allowed to legally.'

'But you had to get the train to Cardiff on time. You had a duty to your passengers, to your employers.' I add gently, 'The inquest found you weren't at fault, Clive.'

'I know, but I can't help but think that if I'd been going just five miles slower, then . . .'

'Then she'd have waited until you were a little closer before she jumped in front of you.'

Clive looks up. He can't find a counterargument to this. We always end the session with him accepting what I say and agreeing to do some deeper work on the underlying cause of his inability to let himself off the hook. But then he goes back home and his old behaviours start up again: poring through the transcript from the inquest and picking out anything that doesn't positively support his actions in the crucial final moments, or searching online for arguments that will prove he made a mistake. We've discussed survivor's guilt and the fact that it's one of the classic symptoms of PTSD, which manifests most commonly as flashbacks and self-blame. But, in my experience, the root of the problem often goes deeper. Clive is hiding in his head, dealing with it intellectually – which is appropriate once you've allowed yourself to feel your feelings. My challenge with Clive has been to get him to go back to the *original* trauma, the one that confirms his deeply held belief that he is to blame for most things that have gone wrong in his life. He has felt this way before, after all. It's his script.

After he has left, I put the kettle on and sit at the kitchen table with my laptop and type up my notes, then I make a cup of tea and get the steak out of the freezer for the special Valentine's Day meal Drew is cooking us tonight. The thought of the cosy meal warms me as I return to my wing-back chair in the extension and look out through the patio windows onto the back garden, at the beds of hellebores and cyclamen that have survived the winter frost. At the end of the garden bordering the fields, I can see two beautiful long-tailed pheasants sitting on the picket fence. I hope the foxes don't catch them; they're nesting nearby. I heard them mating last month – I could hear the screams from the bracken behind the woodshed. They scream to attract a mate and then they hunker down until spring and the vixen lets the dog run around after her. I chuckle to myself. I've been the same, only in my case it's, 'Drew! Drew! Can you bring me a cup of tea!' But I'm getting so big now, it's easier for him to run up and down the stairs.

I stroke my bump and smile to myself. The fox cubs will be born in the spring, the same time as our baby, only the vixen will have been pregnant for just fifty-three days. Fifty-three days! I wish! But I'm thirty-two weeks now. I can't quite believe it. Just another two months and our little Adam or Harley will be here.

As I pick up my phone, switching the sound back on, I see I've missed a call from Drew. There's a voicemail message from a number I recognise as his office landline. I swipe the keypad and play it back.

'Hope, is my phone there?' He sounds fraught. 'I can't find it. I'm sure I picked it up this morning, but it's not here – and it's not in the car either. Can you check and call me back at the office?'

I call his number, but it goes to voicemail. I heave myself out of my chair and walk into the kitchen, have a quick scan for it, then go upstairs to the bedroom. It's there. I can see it, still charging on the bedside table. I walk round to Drew's side of the bed, pick it up and pull out the charger cable.

Immediately, I spot the notification on the screen.
Call me.

It's a simple message, but that's what makes my heart leap – the brevity, the familiarity. *Call me.* It's from someone who's saved to Drew's contacts as 'Barry, Crowthorpe'. I've never heard Drew mention anyone called Barry in connection with the Crowthorpe development – in fact, I've never heard the name before, and anyway, I can't think of anyone Drew works with who would send a message saying *Call me*, not without adding the word *'please'*. His boss is called Graham, and as head of planning, almost everyone else defers to Drew. The developers, the architects and the contractors are beholden to him to stay part of the framework agreement. I can't think of anyone who'd be that curt, or that familiar. My gut instinct is that Drew is keeping something – or someone – from me.

Time stops for a moment. I can feel my heart racing, which is not good for the baby, but I can't stop it; I can't calm down. I try to take deep breaths as I sink onto the bed, but – call it women's intuition or whatever – I know. I just know. 'Barry, Crowthorpe' is not a colleague from the Crowthorpe development. He's still seeing her – that woman. It's still going on.

It only takes me two tries before I crack the PIN. Drew is not that imaginative and he's also forgetful – it would have to be something he'd remember easily. It's his mum's birthday, of course, which I also remember because, unlike Drew, I remember all of the family birthdays. I'm the one who always bought his mum her presents and birthday cards.

I try to take deep breaths, but I can feel my blood pressure rising as I scroll back through the messages. They aren't sexy or salacious or even particularly intimate, they're worse: they are loving and caring – at least the ones from Drew to *her* are loving and caring. The ones from her are sad and despairing and hopeful and conflicted. They are a couple trying to find time for each other, trying not to hurt me, but needing each other's company. They are tormented, and therefore romantic – after all, nothing is more romantic than forbidden love.

There are hundreds of messages, stretching back to Christmas – to Christmas Eve, in fact. My stomach swoops as the realisation hits me. Christmas Eve! The day Drew went out in the Porsche to pick up my Christmas present – the day when I'd sat in the kitchen laughing and joking with Jess and secretly hoping he'd gone out to get rid of that bloody car. I'd believed him and trusted him and thought that what he was doing was about *me*, about *us*, when all the time he was looking for an excuse to sneak out to see *her*.

She'd messaged him first, it seems, the evening before.

I need to see you.

Drew had agreed. They'd arranged to meet, and then there was nothing for a few days after that, but judging from the messages that followed, he must have been thinking about her the whole time. He must have been thinking about her all of that evening and on Christmas morning when he was stroking and talking to my bump as we lay in bed; he must have been thinking about her when we were opening our presents and eating our Christmas dinner, and all of the time we were snuggled up together on the sofa in front of the fire, watching *It's a Wonderful Life.*

Angry tears spring to my eyes, but I wipe them away and shuffle back onto the bed, propping myself up with a pillow and leaning back against the headboard as I begin to read the messages that follow. It's Drew first, on New Year's Eve.

I can't stop thinking about you. Can we meet again? Can we talk?

I'm in Ireland. I told you, she replies.

You're coming back for your things, though?

Yes.

When? For how long?

On the 3rd. For a week.

Can I see you then?

Drew, you have a wife. A pregnant wife.

I know. I'm sorry.

What do you want from me?

I know this is wrong of me, but I don't want to lose you, Sorch. When I saw you, I knew. I can't let you go.

I let out a short, loud gasp of agony. The tears well up in my eyes again and begin streaming down my cheeks, but – even though I know this will cause me nothing but more pain – I carry on reading. I read on and on, and on.

At some point, as the low afternoon sun shimmers through the trees and slants in through the bedroom window, I become aware of a dull ache across my lower back. I shift into a better position on the bed and carry on reading, but twenty minutes later it's still there and it's more than a dull ache now – it's a familiar ache, an ache I now recognise, an ache that fills me with an ice-cold dread as I think about what to do next. Call the midwife. Call Drew's office. But I hate Drew. I hate bloody Drew. I don't want him here; I don't want his help.

Midwife. Midwife first. Where's my phone, though? I must have brought it upstairs when I was calling Drew's number, but I can't see it. I pick Drew's phone up from my lap and enter his PIN again, then call my own number. I can hear it ringing; it's somewhere in the bedroom. I drop Drew's phone onto the duvet and slide off the bed. But as I push myself to my feet, I suddenly, urgently need the bathroom, and that's when the cramping starts.

34

Drew

I fire off a quick email to Graham, my boss, then grab my coat and leave the office. It's not yet four, but I'm worried about Hope; it's been a good couple of hours since I phoned and left a message and she hasn't returned my call.

Luckily, the roads are quiet and I'm home in less than half an hour.

'Hope,' I call out as I put my key in the latch and swing the door wide open. There's no answer, so I slam it shut and glance left into the kitchen, then right into the living room. I take off my coat and hang it over the banister, and that's when I hear the wailing sound. It's coming from upstairs.

'Hope?' I yell at the top of my voice. My chest tightens and my breath catches in my throat as I grab at the banister and launch myself up the narrow stairs. I take them two at a time, hitting my head on the beam on the landing in my haste to get to the top. I can see my wife through the bath-room door, which is slightly ajar. She's on her hands and knees, crying, leaning with her forearms resting on the edge of the bath.

I stride across the landing towards her, push the door wide open and fall to my knees beside her. 'Hope. Sweetheart. What happened? What's going on?'

She turns her head to face me. Her eyes are wide and glassy, her hair is damp on her forehead and all the colour has drained from her face. She glances down, her eyes directing me to the bathmat underneath her, and I can see that it's soaking wet. There are also splashes of bright red blood.

'Oh my God, Hope. The baby's coming?' I say, shocked.

Her jaw sets in a hard line as she says through clenched teeth, 'Call the midwife. Call an ambulance.'

I think about this, my heart racing. 'It will take too long. Let's go. Now. In the car.'

Hope looks unsure for a moment, but then she's clutching her belly and groaning again. 'OK,' she agrees.

I put my arms around her and help her to her feet, then glance around and grab a couple of clean towels from the airing cupboard. I hand them to her.

She grimaces. 'You're worried about your precious car seats?'

I peer at her, confused. I know she's in pain, but her tone is distinctly unfriendly. Is she angry with me for not yet having got rid of the Porsche?

'You'd better get your phone,' she says, clinging to the bathroom door handle.

'You found it?'

'It's on the bed,' she hisses.

'OK,' I say soothingly. 'Wait there.' I stride quickly into the bedroom. I can see my iPhone. It's next to a pillow that's propped up against the headboard. There's a miniscule, split second of relief that it's not lost before I realise that it wasn't me sitting up against that pillow this morning. That's not where I left my phone.

No. No. *No no no no no*. Hope knows. She knows about Sorcha. She's guessed my PIN and she's read our messages, all our hundreds of messages, and she's gone into labour and she's only thirty-two weeks pregnant, and it's too soon and it's all my fault. This sudden onslaught of clarity knocks ten tons of crap out of me. Everything is now crystal clear: I've been such an ignorant fool, chasing a ridiculous fantasy like some lovesick teenager. My wife is frightened and in distress and our baby could die and *I've* done this. This is *my* doing. I am one hundred per cent to blame.

I snatch up the phone from the duvet, push it into my pocket and step quickly around the bed. Hope's phone is on the floor. I pick it up and go back out onto the landing. Hope has made it along the hallway and is clutching her belly and leaning heavily against the newel post at the top of the stairs.

'Hope. I'm sorry. I'm so, so sorry,' I say, wracked with shame.

'Just get me to the hospital,' she retorts through clenched teeth, her eyes blazing back at me with fear and anger. 'Just get me to the fucking hospital, Drew.'

'Yes. Yes, of course.' I spring into action and leap down

the staircase. I turn round to face her and hold out my arms. 'Lean against me,' I say. 'Just lean on me.'

Hope lets out a satirical snort at the suggestion that I am actually someone she could depend on, but she does as I tell her and lets her body weight fall against mine. I put my arm around her waist and together we move down the stairs and out to the car. I let go of her for a moment as I reach back to slam the front door shut behind us and then blink the Porsche lights on and open the passenger door.

I look back at Hope, who's still standing near the house.

'The Civic, Drew,' she pants. 'We need to take the Civic. I can't get in there, can I?'

'Yes, you can. It's faster,' I plead. 'Please, Hope, this is going to be quicker, I promise you.'

Hope reels in pain again, groaning and gasping, and allows me to guide her towards the Porsche. Luckily, she fits in OK and I'm able to swing her legs in and get her seatbelt on. I race around to the driver's side. Within ten seconds we're out of the drive, and in less than a minute we're out of the village and onto the open road to Wyebridge. It's late afternoon and the sun is low in the sky, but it's still light and the road is quiet. I put my foot down and the Porsche takes off. I vaguely think to myself that at least Hope will see the car has its uses now.

We pelt along the winding road, Hope slumped in her seat, intermittently silently accusing or gasping and moaning in pain. I want to tell her how sorry I am, how desperately fucking sorry I am. I want to reassure her, tell her everything's going to be OK. But I've lost that right. I've probably lost everything, and there's nothing I can say or do except get us to the hospital as fast as I can. That's my one job now: to get us to the fucking hospital before this baby comes. I can't allow myself to think about what happens next for us as a family, whether I'll ever be forgiven, whether my wife will leave me. I just need to keep praying that our baby isn't going to be delivered by the roadside, that he isn't going to die.

The road curves through the Chiltern Hills, banks of peat and moss rising steeply on either side of us, the jutting trees lining the road like sentinels. Rays of dappled light filter through the branches, but we're driving east, away from the setting sun, and my vision ahead is pretty clear. Soon the banks are replaced by hedgerows and open sky. I know this road well. We're not far from Stoke End, which means the turning to Woodley Ridge is just a few more miles away.

'We're halfway there now,' I say to Hope, trying to sound reassuring. I take a bend at a clear seventy and Hope lets out a whimper, but she doesn't ask me to slow down. If she's afraid of the speed we're going, her cries of fear are indistinguishable from her labour pains.

As we round the bend and out onto the straight again, I can see a lorry up ahead.

'Oh, God. Seriously?' Hope says, panicked.

'And there's a car behind it.'

'Fuck!' Hope closes her eyes.

The lorry looms larger and larger until we've almost

caught it up and I'm forced to put my foot on the brake. We slow right down to a frustrating thirty and fall into line behind the car in front of us, which I can now see is also a sports car, an M4. I can tell by the way it's tailgating the lorry that the driver is also eager to get past.

'Can you overtake?' Hope asks.

I glance at the solid double white lines on the road ahead. 'Not yet. But don't worry. I'm sure I can. As soon as it's safe.'

We both fall silent, watching the road. A minute later, the single white line on our side becomes a broken one. With no indication, the M4 suddenly swings out sharply and begins to overtake the lorry. I watch, my adrenaline rising. I have no idea what the length of the truck is – we're on a straight road and all I can see is the gigantic back of its trailer, almost blocking out the sky. But if it's safe for the M4 to get past, then it's safe for us, surely? This could be our only opportunity. We might otherwise be stuck behind this lorry all the way to Wyebridge. There's no time to hesitate. If I'm going to go, I need to go now.

I edge out a little, trying to get a glimpse around the trailer at the road ahead. The M4 is travelling steadily forward about twenty feet in front. I can't see anything beyond it. I hover in the opposite carriageway for a split second, then move back, still trying to decide whether to stay or go. But then Hope lets out a long, low guttural groan and my mind is made up. In one swift movement, I throw my gearstick forward into third, revving the engine and swinging the

Porsche around the tail of the lorry and into the carriageway opposite.

'Drew?' Hope murmurs anxiously, her voice a question mark.

'It's OK,' I say.

The M4 is still up ahead, around forty feet in front of us now, nearing the cabin of the lorry. I put my foot down to catch it up, but it suddenly picks up speed and swerves back into the left-hand lane, cutting up the lorry before speeding off into the distance ahead, leaving us for dust.

To my horror, there's a car heading straight towards us. I'm in the wrong lane, but the lorry's still moving forward, closing the gap. I realise with a searing jolt to the stomach that I'm not going to make it: I can't get through.

'Drew!' screams Hope. 'What the fuck!'

It all happens in slow motion: the brakes slamming on hard, the car veering off the road and hurtling through the hedgerow. I can see it moving at speed in my peripheral vision as I swing round in front of the lorry and back onto the left-hand side of the road.

'Shit. Oh my God. Fuck. What the fuck have I done?' I stutter as I regain control of the Porsche. 'Hope. What do I do? I need to stop.'

But I can't stop. I can't slow down. If I brake, the lorry will go straight into the back of me. I have to keep going until I've put enough distance between us and the lorry. I keep on going, but I'm shaking so hard it's all I can do to drive in a straight line.

Hope is silent in the seat next to me. I glance across at her. She's white as a sheet.

'I'm going to have to stop, Hope,' I say again, my heart still thumping wildly. 'There's a lay-by ahead – or I think there's a petrol station in Stoke End. I could pull in there.'

Hope still doesn't answer and I glance at her again, then check in my rear-view mirror. There's no sign of the lorry. Has it stopped?

'What shall I do?' I ask. 'Shall I just pull over at the next lay-by?'

'No,' Hope says firmly.

'What? What do you mean, no?' I ask, confused.

'I mean . . . no,' Hope says through gritted teeth. 'Don't stop. You can't stop. You need to carry on.'

'Hope?' I whimper. 'I can't. I . . . we need to call some-one. We'll call an ambulance for you and we'll call the police. Put your Bluetooth on.'

Hope closes her eyes and begins to groan like a wounded animal. For a moment, she doesn't speak. But then she catches her breath and she turns and screams at me, 'The baby's coming, Drew! I need to get to the fucking hospital! Just drive. Just fucking drive!'

PART SIX

Now

THAMES VALLEY POLICE – MAJOR CRIME UNIT

Pre-interview legal briefing

OFFICER(S) NAMES:

DC Suzy Hibbert

DC James Foley

BRIEFING LOCATION:

Polar Park Police Station, Heathrow

TIME: 14.55   DATE: Monday, 8th July 2024

LEGAL REPRESENTATIVE DETAILS: Sarah Kellerman

DETAINED PERSON(S) DETAILS: Andrew John Faris

OFFENCE(S):

Murder x 2, contrary to Common Law

Attempted Murder contrary to S.1 of the Criminal Attempts Act 1981

The CIRCUMSTANCES are: -

At around 17.00 on Monday, 14th February 2022, LAUREN HOPWOOD was driving her husband's Audi A6 estate on the Old Chiltern Road in Buckinghamshire. Her six-week-old baby SAMUEL HOPWOOD was in a rear-facing car seat on the front passenger seat next to her. Her husband CHARLIE HOPWOOD was in the back of the car. The family had been for a day out in London, first to Ikea in Wembley and then to JENNIFER CAMPION'S house in Northolt. JENNIFER CAMPION is the mother of LAUREN HOPWOOD and grandmother of SAMUEL HOPWOOD. The family had spent the afternoon at Lime Tree Park in Northolt and had then gone back to MRS CAMPION'S house where they had tea before leaving at around 16.30. They had taken the M40 as far as Handy Cross, then had turned north and continued west along the Old Chiltern Road between Wyebridge and Stow.

At approximately two miles past Stoke End, the Audi is known to have left the left-hand carriageway of the Old Chiltern Road, where it crashed through a hedgerow, then through fields and into a forest and collided with a tree. CHARLIE HOPWOOD died at the scene. LAUREN and SAMUEL HOPWOOD were rescued by fire services and taken to Woodley Ridge Hospital. LAUREN HOPWOOD went on to make a full recovery; however SAMUEL HOP-WOOD died later from his injuries.

At the time of the incident LAUREN HOPWOOD had no recollection of what had happened and no witnesses came forward. Collision experts could not find any road markings or other evidence to explain why the car had left the road. Traffic investigators concluded that this was a single vehicle accident, likely caused by MS HOPWOOD swerving to avoid a wild animal.

On 10th June 2022, LAUREN HOPWOOD called police to say she now remembered that a yellow Porsche Carrera had been on the road on the day of her accident and believed it to have been responsible. She also said she thought a lorry may have been involved. She gave police the VRN of the Porsche, along with several photographs she had taken. The VRN was CW02 XEG.

At the time of the accident, your client was the owner of a yellow Porsche Carrera VRN CW02 XEG. However, on Monday, 24th April 2022, he traded in this vehicle by way of a part exchange for an SUV, with the proceeds of the sale of the Porsche being received by him in cash. Meanwhile, a finance agreement was entered into for the SUV.

On 25th July 2022, traffic investigators attended your client's home address and spoke to his wife HOPE DUNSMORE, who confirmed he had been the registered owner of the vehicle in question on 14th February 2022 and that she and your client were travelling in it towards Woodley Ridge

Hospital on that date at the relevant time, as she was heavily pregnant and had gone into labour. She stated that your client was driving. She stated that while your client had overtaken a lorry and had temporarily travelled into the opposite lane, he had done so safely, and that neither she nor your client had encountered any other vehicle on the road, other than a BMW M4 which your client had also overtaken prior to overtaking the lorry. She said that the Porsche had left both the M4 and the lorry behind on the road and had safely reached the hospital at around 17.15 that evening, where she had then given birth to her son SAMUEL DUNSMORE-FARIS. She stated that neither she nor your client were aware of any accident or any car leaving the road.

As MS HOPWOOD had not been able to recall any specific details of how the Porsche was alleged to have been involved in the crash that killed her family, and because a regional news campaign had been run at the time which had not resulted in a lorry or any other drivers coming forward, and because there was no CCTV on the road or any other independent evidence, the traffic investigators concluded that there was insufficient evidence to pursue this line of inquiry and that their original conclusions about the accident had been correct.

At 13.15 today (Monday, 8th July 2024), your client attended the Station Duty Office at Heathrow Polar Park Police Station. He stated to the officer on duty that he was responsible for the deaths of two people and that he wanted to confess. It is believed that your client was referring to the road traffic incident in which LAUREN HOPWOOD was seriously injured and in which CHARLIE and SAMUEL HOPWOOD lost their lives.

On his arrival in the SDO your client further stated that he believed his girlfriend was presently being held in police custody in relation to an allegation of child abduction. He wanted police to know she had done nothing wrong. He named his girlfriend as LAUREN HOPWOOD. He asked to speak to the officers dealing with her case. He said he would give these officers a full and frank account of how he had caused the deaths of his two victims, but only on the condition that they released MS HOPWOOD from custody and discontinued any charges against her.

The SDO checked with the custody sergeant on duty who confirmed that LAUREN HOPWOOD was in custody at Polar Park at that time. She had been arrested by uniformed police officers in the presence of myself (DC Hibbert) and DC Foley at Heathrow Terminal Five on an inbound flight from Girona via Paris Orly which landed at 12.10 today. She was booked in at 12.55, just twenty minutes before your client arrived at the SDO.

DC Foley and I therefore attended the SDO and spoke to your client, who told us that MS HOPWOOD had

gone to live in Spain in September 2022, taking his son
SAMUEL DUNSMORE-FARIS (then aged 7 months)
with her. Mr Faris further stated that while his wife
HOPE DUNSMORE had previously reported this as an
abduction, this was not the case. Your client stated that his
wife had not known that he and MS HOPWOOD were
in a relationship or that he had asked MS HOPWOOD
to leave the country and take his son with her. His intention had been to leave his wife and join MS HOPWOOD
and SAMUEL DUNSMORE-FARIS in Spain as soon as
he could.

MCU officers at Thames Valley Police had already
been investigating the disappearance of SAMUEL
DUNSMORE-FARIS, who was last seen in September
2022, seven months after the accident which killed MS
HOPWOOD'S husband and son. It was believed that the
two incidents were linked. Your client was therefore arrested
at 13.55 today.

Because of your client's statement that he had been in a
relationship with LAUREN HOPWOOD prior to the
deaths of her husband and son, it is now believed that
the car crash was deliberate and that all three victims were
intended to die.

We would like to question your client about his involvement in the deaths of CHARLIE and SAMUEL

HOPWOOD and the serious injuries caused to LAUREN HOPWOOD.

Your client has no criminal convictions. We are not prepared to disclose anything further at this time.

35

Drew

I stop reading, close my eyes and lower my head into my hands. My tongue seems to be stuck to the roof of my mouth, and I make a gluey sound when I try to speak.

'Here. Have mine. I haven't touched it.'

I look up as Sarah, my lawyer, pushes her plastic cup of water towards me. My hand is shaking as I pick it up and take a gulp, then another, and then I finish it all.

'I'll get us some more,' she says, sliding out from the bench opposite me and opening the door of the tiny, cell-like room we are in. She disappears into the corridor outside, returning a moment later with two more plastic cups of water, which she puts down on the table in front of me. 'They're for you. Have them both.'

'Thanks.' I take another swig. It doesn't seem to matter how much water I drink, though. I glance up at the cameras in the corner of the room. 'Are you sure we're not being bugged?'

'If we were, it would be a serious breach of the Police and Criminal Evidence Act,' Sarah says, sliding back down onto the bench opposite me. 'Of course, you can never guarantee what kind of tactics the police will resort to, but I'm fairly confident it doesn't happen very often. They wouldn't be able to use anything we say in here in evidence, and it could damage their case against you if they did anything illegal to gain intelligence. The CPS or a judge would not be pleased, put it that way.'

I relax just a little at this and wait for her as she pulls her laptop back round to face her, swipes the trackpad and quickly types something. She's in her early forties, I'd say, possibly slightly younger. Hope's age, maybe. She's casually dressed in a T-shirt, jeans and trainers and her wavy fair hair is pulled back into a ponytail. Despite her informal appearance, she's really good at her job, this Sarah Kellerman, I can tell. She's smart, bright and efficient. I'm in safe hands. Lauren was right.

But it doesn't stop the flame of fear flickering wildly inside me as I think about what I'm being accused of. Murder. Trying to kill Lauren. I was expecting a charge of death by dangerous driving, but this? This wasn't part of the plan. I take a long, deep breath as I think about the chain of events that set all of this in motion, about everything that has happened in the past few hours since Hope ran out onto the driveway, tapped on my car window and handed me her phone.

Sarah finishes typing, then looks up. 'So, was it Lauren who told you to ask for me?'

I hesitate, then nod. 'She called Hope this morning, just as I was leaving for work. She was on her way back from Spain, waiting for a connecting flight. She called to say she was going to be arrested and she gave me your name.'

I watch Sarah for her reaction. 'Well, I'm sure you must realise that I'm stepping into dangerous territory here. Each of you is a victim in the case against the other. There's got to be a huge conflict of interest. I can't act for you both.'

'Yes,' I say quickly. 'You can. There's no conflict of interest.'

Sarah looks at me sharply.

I take a deep breath and say, 'We both want the same thing.'

'Which is?'

I take another long, deep breath as the flicker of fear lights up inside me again. 'Can I really talk to you in complete confidence? Without you telling anyone?'

She nods. 'Absolutely. I can't repeat anything you tell me. I'm bound by my professional rules. Be aware, though, that I can't let you put forward anything in interview that I know not to be true.'

I think about this again for a minute, but I know I have no choice but to be open with her, as must Lauren. We have to tell Sarah the truth and let her advise us both. She'll know what the right thing is for each of us to do.

'I'm going to admit everything,' I tell her. 'I'm going to go to prison, and Lauren is going to give Sam back to Hope. That's what we want. It's what we agreed.'

She gazes at me. 'You're going to admit that you caused the crash intentionally?'

'No. Not intentionally,' I say, my voice cracking a little at the thought of this. 'It was an accident. I know I told the police I knew Lauren, but I didn't, not then. I didn't know her and I didn't know her family. I had no reason to hurt any of them.'

'So . . . you weren't in a relationship?'

'No.'

'Ever?'

'Ever.' I feel myself flush at my admission of yet another lie. 'But I'm Sam's legal parent and so if I gave him to Lauren, they can't prove she abducted him, right?'

Sarah looks thoughtful, but she doesn't answer my question. 'And she asked you to say this?'

'No,' I say quickly. 'It was my idea entirely. That wasn't why she called.'

'So, why did she call?'

'She wanted to make sure Sam has a mother if . . . if there's a court case and we both go to prison. We wanted to leave Hope out of it. But then I thought of a way to leave Lauren out of it too, to get them to withdraw the charges against her. I told them both – Lauren and Hope – that everything that happened was my fault and that I was going to take responsibility for it. All of it. And because we all want the best for Sam, they agreed.'

Sarah takes this in. 'So when did you really meet Lauren for the first time?'

'The day she turned up at the house saying she'd lost an AirPod and asked me questions about the Range Rover.'

'That really *was* the first time?'

'Yes. I mean, I'd started to suspect who she was before that, or at least, I had guessed it was something to do with the accident. I guessed pretty much as soon as I noticed I was being followed in the taxi that day. I thought it was going to be someone who'd seen what happened and had come to blackmail me. The lorry driver, maybe. But when she started having therapy with Hope and turning up at our house and talking to Hope's friends, it didn't take me long to put two and two together.'

'But she told Hope her name was Anna?'

'Her real name was reported in the local newspapers. You know, at the time of the crash. There were photos of her, her husband and their little boy. I looked them up.' I pause as a wave of self-hatred rises up inside me for the millionth time. 'Look,' I sigh. 'I did the wrong thing then, but I can do the right thing now. I want to get her out of trouble and put the blame back where it belongs. On me. I'm the one who started all this. Lauren has promised to let Hope have our son back, and so now I just want to keep my end of the bargain.'

Sarah looks me hard in the eye. 'The police might not be able to prove you caused the accident unless you tell them.'

I shrug helplessly. 'I promised Lauren I'd put my hands up to it, and I'm not going back on that. But it was an accident. I swear, everything I told you is the truth. Hope had gone into labour and we were on the way to the hospital, and the hospital records will show this. How could I have planned for my wife to go into labour at the exact same moment Lauren was coming the other way? How could I have planned any of it?'

Sarah nods.

'And just so you know, I wasn't in any financial difficulty,' I continue. 'That's not why I sold the Porsche, or why I sold it for cash. I admit that I didn't want to be seen driving it any more, for obvious reasons.' I feel myself flushing for the hundredth time. 'But, like I said, I was already going to get rid of it before the accident happened. Hope wanted a family car.'

Sarah types a little before pausing again.

'And I took the SUV out on finance because I knew Hope would have to give it back if I went to prison.'

'So, you already knew there was a good chance you would go to prison?'

'Of course,' I say, swallowing. 'Look, I was going to hand myself in, but I was scared for Hope and our baby, and . . .' I squeeze my eyes shut, fighting back tears of shame. 'And so that's why I carried on driving. That's why I did what she asked. I'd cheated on her and I'd caused her to go into labour and she was screaming in pain, so I kept on going, and I'm so ashamed of myself for doing that, for not calling an ambulance immediately. But I promise you, it wasn't because I wanted anyone to die.'

There is a long silence. 'Look,' Sarah says at last, her

forehead creasing. 'I think they're bluffing, Drew. I don't think they think you killed anyone intentionally. I think they know it was an accident. I think they're just trying to get you to talk to them.'

Mild relief runs through me. 'What makes you say that?'

'Let's just say they misled me. Let's just say that the last time I spoke to anyone from the Major Crime Unit, they led me to believe all three of you – Lauren, you and Hope – were involved in some kind of illegal adoption-slash-human-trafficking scam.'

'What?' I ask, incredulous.

She shrugs. 'I think that was just a ploy to get Lauren back to England. In other words, they were using the same tactics as they are using with you now. They haven't mentioned it since, and while they often hold something back in disclosure, I don't think that's the case this time. My guess is that they've told us everything they know and they're not sure if they're going to make any charges stick, so they've made the case against each of you appear more serious so that you'll both talk to them, blame each other and give them the evidence they need.'

'Can they prove anything against Lauren?'

Sarah shrugs. 'I'm not sure yet, if I'm honest.'

'What about Hope?'

'Well, if you admit causing the accident, then I'd say, yes, they can. They have a statement from her which gets you off the hook. She could be charged with lying to protect you. Assisting an offender. It's a serious offence.'

My heart plummets. We missed something. We bloody missed something. 'I know how it looks,' I say, pleading with her. 'But Hope has always been as honest as the day is long. She would never lie to protect me. But she was in this weird, detached kind of state after Sam was born. I can't explain it. She's always been an optimistic kind of person, but this was more than that. At first I thought she was in denial, but then I started to think that maybe she didn't see what had happened, or had blocked it out, what with the trauma of three miscarriages, then going into labour at only thirty-two weeks and thinking she was going to lose a baby again. She must have been so frightened, in so much pain, and all of this was straight after finding out that I hadn't ended my relationship with Sorcha after I promised her I had. The stress would have been intense.' I close my eyes, feeling sick at the thought of what I put my wife through, about her reading all those messages between me and Sorcha and then going into labour. 'I really do think she had detached from what was happening due to the stress of the moment. It was bad enough for her finding out I'd been cheating on her again.'

'Well, if she was suffering from some form of dissociative disorder or PTSD, she may have a medical defence,' Sarah says slowly.

I lean back against the wall behind me, the flicker of fear blowing up inside me again. The thought of Hope going through a trial is horrific. It could take months. Years. She could be remanded, go to prison. And even if she got bail, would they give Sam back to her? And what if she lost?

'If she was convicted, how long would she get?'

Sarah's eyes are kind, but she has no choice except to be straight with me. 'It would be something close to what you would get, I'm afraid. Sentencing for assisting an offender is linked to the gravity of the index offence. Her sentence would be commensurate with yours.'

I nod, trying to remain calm. 'So, how long could we get? Both of us?'

'For double murder and attempted murder? You'd get life. Thirty years minimum. But only if they can prove you intended to kill or seriously injure the Hopwoods.'

'And if they can't?'

'We're probably looking at either manslaughter or death by dangerous driving.'

'How long for that?'

'Maybe eight to nine years.' Sarah's eyes soften. 'I think you can at least expect that. But it very much depends on the circumstances.'

Another flicker of fear makes me lose myself for a moment.

'I'm talking about what happened after you drove away,' Sarah prompts me.

I swallow. I can't meet her eye as I say, 'The circumstances were not good.'

36

I did exactly as Hope said. I drove. I drove like the wind. I don't remember anything else about the rest of the route we took. I remember arriving at A & E, where I abandoned the Porsche in a loading bay and helped Hope inside. By now, she was having contractions every couple of minutes and was barely able to walk. She stood at the reception desk, groaning in pain, and gave her name and address and a couple more details, and then it all happened quickly: a nurse appeared and helped her into a room just off the main lobby and soon afterwards they got her onto a trolley and wheeled her down to the delivery suite.

I knew pretty soon that something was wrong. People kept arriving: midwives, doctors, nurses pushing a trolley with a heated bed and a light over the top. The midwife told Hope to push, and Hope was crying and saying she couldn't do it, but she did and at eight minutes past seven, our son was born. He came out flat and pale and so, so tiny. He wasn't breathing.

The midwife tried to resuscitate him and then the obstetrician and the nurses with the heated bed and light took over.

Hope was still crying and saying, 'My baby. My baby,' over and over again. I wanted to put my arms around her and tell her that everything would be OK, but I couldn't, because my promises meant nothing and because I'd betrayed her and I didn't dare touch her and have her push me away. I couldn't take that on top of everything else. So, I stood beside her and watched, numb with fear, as they intubated our little boy and put him on the ventilator and then took him in an incubator to the neonatal unit, where he was quickly surrounded by more doctors and more nurses and plugged into machines, monitors and drips. They measured his oxygen and his carbon dioxide levels and then the radiographer came in to do a chest X-ray and then they did a head scan and a heart scan and took his blood for tests.

It all happened in a long series of jolts. Hope was in the delivery suite being stitched up, and so I went on my own to the neonatal unit. I remember hearing the words 'cardiac' and 'acidotic' and being told that the baby's sats were too low. I stared and stared at him, not knowing how to feel. Did I dare love him? Of course I loved him, I loved him more than anything in the world, but all my senses had been blunted by guilt and dread. The nurse showed me how to hold out my finger and let him hold it and I did that for a long time, even when my arm ached. As I looked down at his tiny fist, at his fluttering fingers, I couldn't believe any human being could be that small.

I slept in a chair next to him. At some point during the night, I woke and Hope was in the chair opposite. In the morning, a cardiologist came in and told us that the baby needed to go to a specialist children's cardiac centre for an operation on his heart. A surgical space had become available at Great Ormond Street and he needed to go quickly. We weren't allowed to go in the ambulance with him; they said it was going to be what they called a 'scoop and run'. They said there was no point in me travelling to London, that he'd go straight into surgery, they'd do the operation and bring him straight back.

Hope was in pieces at this, I knew, but she'd stopped crying and was being practical, in the way that Hope always is in an emergency. She wanted to name him before he left for London and I agreed, telling her it could be any name she wanted. (I had no right to be arguing about whether he was going to be Adam or Harley, and of course I wouldn't have dared suggest Drew.)

But then the obstetrician walked into the room and Hope surprised me by asking him his name.

'Sam,' he replied.

'I like that,' said Hope. 'Sam. Yes. He will be Sam. He *is* Sam.'

Hope looked at me and I nodded. I liked the name – very much, in fact – and I said so. The nurse arrived at that point and overheard and she smiled and said, 'It's a lovely name. Solid. Traditional.' She took out a pen and changed the name tag from 'Baby Dunsmore-Faris' to 'Samuel

Dunsmore-Faris' and I was just grateful that my name was in there somewhere, because Hope could have just as easily decided that our baby was going to be a Dunsmore. I took this as a good sign for our relationship, although I knew I was clutching at straws. But Hope had let me stay through the birth and now it was mid-afternoon the following day and she still hadn't asked me to leave. These were all things to cling on to and I needed something. I was a drowning man.

After the ambulance left with Sam inside, Hope went back to the maternity ward. I thought we might talk, but she turned her back on me and said she needed to sleep. So, I found my way to the family room, where I ejected a Styrofoam cup of coffee from a machine in the corner and sat down to wait.

All I could think was that I had to stay strong for Hope and Sam. But my nerves were in shreds, not just because my baby was in the middle of a life-saving heart operation and my wife had read all my stupid, *stupid* love-struck messages to Sorcha, but because there was now something else occupying my thoughts, something I should have thought about sooner: I'd left the scene of an accident. I'd left the scene of an accident *I caused*. I hadn't called the emergency services.

I *still* hadn't called them.

The shame and fear I was already feeling intensified to an unbearable new level. I remember being glad that the family room was empty so that no one could see me cry. There was a TV on the wall opposite and *Pointless* was on with the volume down. I usually enjoyed the show, but now it seemed impossible that the contestants were standing there, smiling and joking and laughing while I was staring at the screen through a swell of tears, waiting to find out exactly how much my wife hated me, whether the police would come and arrest me any minute, and whether my baby would die.

The tension was too much for me. I stopped crying and picked up my phone, my right thumb hovering over the number 9 on the keypad. I had to call the police and tell them what had happened – of course I did. But what would I say? It had been almost twenty-four hours since we came to A & E. How could I explain the delay? I gripped the phone as I rehearsed the conversation with the police: '*I planned to call you as soon as I got to the hospital, but my mind was elsewhere for the whole time we were in the delivery suite and then our baby was born and he wasn't breathing and he was taken to the neonatal unit, and then it slipped my mind.*'

But it hadn't slipped my mind. I remembered. I did. I remembered when we were in the delivery suite and again later that night. I just didn't know what to do. I didn't want to get arrested, not then. I know how pathetic and selfish it sounds, but I was thinking of Hope, of our relationship, of our baby. I didn't know what Hope would want me to do. I *couldn't* get arrested, not until I knew Sam was going to live and that Hope would get by without me. But . . . but then, what about the occupant – or occupants – of the other car?

I forced myself to think about what must have happened after Hope and I drove away. The lorry driver would have seen the car veer off the road; how could he not have done?

He'd have stopped and called the emergency services. They'd have been on the scene quickly and the people in the car would have been treated by paramedics and . . . and so what was done was done, wasn't it? What difference would it make if I handed myself in now or later this evening . . . or even tomorrow? I wiped away my tears. When Sam's surgery was over and once I knew he was OK, *then* I'd make the call. And I'd just be honest. I'd tell the truth. I'd tell the police why I waited. In the meantime, I needed to focus on Sam and Hope and try to shut everything else out of my mind.

I fixed my eyes on the TV. By now, *Pointless* had finished and the *Six O'Clock News* headlines were flashing up. Suddenly it hit me: it would be on the news, wouldn't it? Not the national news, but the local news – or at least it would be if it was anything serious. And if it wasn't and there were no reports, then I'd know it had all turned out OK. My adrenaline rising, I opened up my web browser and, with trembling fingers, typed in 'car crash near Wyebridge'. The Wi-Fi signal wasn't great and I had to wait for several seconds, but when the results loaded, there was nothing. I tried out a few different search options, but still I found nothing.

A combination of mild relief and exhaustion overcame me, and I slumped back in my hard chair and dozed for a while. When I opened my eyes, there was a reporter talking into a microphone on the TV in front of me. She was standing on a road in front of a blue-and-white police cordon, a single tow truck in the background behind her, along with several police vehicles with flashing blue lights. A surge of terror ran through my body as the camera zoomed in at a huge, gaping hole in the hedgerow bordering the road, beneath which two or three bunches of flowers had been laid. I realised with a cold, sudden dread that this must be the regional news I was now watching. I knew where this was. I knew what must be happening – and why.

I drew myself upright in my chair, my shoulders rigid as I watched the scene playing out in front of me. The camera was now back on the reporter, who continued to mouth silently while the wind lifted her hair. *Overnight, concerns were raised about a missing family of three*, the subtitles on the screen read. *They hadn't been seen since yesterday at around four thirty. Relatives have been laying flowers as tributes to their loved ones while they try to make sense of what's happened here.* The family were named: they were a man and woman in their late thirties and a six-week-old baby. The woman was now in a critical condition in hospital. The man and baby were both dead.

The woman would be here in this hospital, I realised with a heart-stopping lurch. It was the nearest hospital. Her baby had been alive when they found him, but had later died – here in this very hospital. *The bodies of the man and baby would be here in this hospital.* I watched in stunned stillness. I now had the answers I'd been searching for. But this was worse than anything I had allowed myself to imagine. I now knew the severity of what I'd done.

For a few days, I went to pieces. I didn't sleep. I couldn't eat. I managed to hide my inner turmoil from Hope, who seemed to have absolutely no recollection of any of it when I tried to talk to her. We were both worried about Sam, and no doubt she assumed that's why I was so spaced out and tired, but, in truth, the accident was pretty much all I could think about. I waited, my stomach in knots, fully expecting the police to come for me at any moment.

But they didn't. *They didn't come.*

So I waited some more, watching all the local news reports and scouring the papers. The police were appealing for witnesses, but there didn't seem to be any, and there was no mention of a lorry or any other car on the road. And then I started to think that if no one else knew what had happened, how could *I* be sure? I *thought* I saw something, but I was in the middle of a hugely stressful situation, what with Hope having just found all my messages to Sorcha and going into labour eight weeks early. Hope was screaming in pain beside me when I saw what I *thought* I saw, and most of that was in my rear-view mirror when I was driving away from the scene. What if the car *I* saw had simply swerved to avoid me and then continued on its journey? After all, Hope was there too, and she didn't appear to have noticed a car leaving the road.

I'd need to be sure; I'd need to be *one hundred per cent certain.* If I was responsible for this tragedy, I would lose everything: my job, my reputation, my career, my home. Hope would lose her home. She wouldn't be able to afford the mortgage without me. We'd both be vilified in the press and by the online trolls. I'd seen TV programmes about it. Anything to do with the death of a child and people would bay for blood. I'd seen reports of people from the other side of the world – gangs of people – turning up at someone's house, making threats and smashing in their windows. We had a baby now, a baby who was in intensive care in hospital. I had a wife who needed me. (She might hate me, but she still needed me – if only to keep paying the mortgage.) How could I leave her alone with all this? How could I leave my baby? How could I turn myself in to the police without being one hundred per cent sure about what I'd done?

But I was lying to myself, I knew that, and by the time Sam came off the ventilator, I'd made up my mind. I had to go to the police. Hope seemed a lot better, much more herself, and although I was convinced she'd been through some kind of postnatal dissociative condition, I believed she was well enough now to cope with what was about to happen. I would just wait a little longer until Sam had settled into a routine with her at home. Then Lauren followed me home in the taxi and started turning up on our doorstep. I knew pretty quickly who she must be and why she was there. It was almost as if I'd been expecting her. But I didn't want her to spring everything on Hope during a therapy session, and so I asked Hope to stop seeing her. At the same time, I tried again to broach the subject of the accident, but I could tell by then that Hope had either been in too much pain to see what had happened or had blocked it out.

I needed to tell Hope myself, in my own way at the right time, that I was planning to go to the police, that I'd go to prison, that Sam would lose his father and they would both lose their home. In the meantime, I was going to confront Lauren and tell her this, too. But then she stopped coming to our house or to the village and we heard nothing from her in weeks. So I put it off. I decided I would wait until Sam was discharged from hospital outpatients, which was due to happen at the end of August. By early September, Hope was well and happy and had made new friends in the village, and I knew it was time. I was just trying to find my moment, but I swear on Sam's life, I was going to do it. I was going to speak to Hope, make sure she understood the consequences for her and Sam, and then hand myself in.

But then she came back. Lauren. She came and took Sam and said she knew what I'd done. I told her I'd go to the police, and I would have done had she not then told me that Hope had already spoken to them. The minute she said this, I knew instinctively that Hope had lied to them and that this was the reason Lauren had come back again.

I knew Hope was now in as much trouble as I was and that I was in a stalemate, because I couldn't let Hope go to prison. How could I? I had to try to stop Lauren, to plead with her, to make her see sense. But as I followed her through the field to her car that night, I felt the lifeblood drain out of me, because it was then that I realised she wasn't just here to try and teach us a lesson. She was taking our little boy to replace the one I'd killed.

37

Lauren

I stare at the screen of my lawyer's laptop. I'm in the police station at Heathrow, and seeing it all for the first time, reading what really happened to me and my family as I drove back from London that day, feels like a tornado has just blown through the roof of my home. A swell of tears gets a chokehold on me and I can't speak for a moment. Sarah waits, her eyes gentle as she slides a box of tissues across the table towards me. I grab one clumsily and bury my head in my hands.

'I'm sorry,' I say, and then the tears come. I don't want to cry like this in front of her, but I can't stop myself. I sob and sob while she says repeatedly, 'It's fine. Take your time.'

When I've finished, she says, 'He's not looking for forgiveness, Lauren. He's not asking anything from you. He just wants to fill the gaps for you, to help you find peace with what happened.'

I nod. 'I get that.' I blow my nose and wipe my eyes with

the wet, scrunched-up piece of tissue in my hand. Sarah reaches for a waste-paper bin, holding it up for me. I drop it in and take another from the box.

'He also wanted you to read it first because it's going to form the basis of the statement he's going to give the police.'

I feel a fluttering in my chest. 'He's going to hand that into the police?'

'Everything except the last paragraph, the one about you coming to take Sam.'

I swallow hard as I think about this. 'If he lets them carry on thinking we were in a relationship, they might go ahead and charge him with murder. After all, what are the chances of his girlfriend coming along in her car with her family at the exact same moment he was coming the other way?'

'Slim, but it's possible,' she says, shrugging. 'People who know each other do just happen to drive past each other. And the hospital records will support that Hope was in labour, so I can't see a jury being able to conclude that it was anything other than a coincidence. Anyway, he's prepared to take that risk.'

I turn this over in my mind. A huge part of me feels overwhelming relief at the thought that there could soon be closure, that – at long last – someone might be locked up for what happened to my family, and to me. But another part of me just feels more pain, and fear, too, for Sam.

'What will happen to Hope?' I ask, thinking fast. 'If the police read Drew's statement, they'll know Hope was in the car, that she witnessed what happened. They won't believe she didn't see anything.'

'Being in the car when the accident happened wouldn't make her guilty of a crime,' Sarah says. 'She was just Drew's passenger and whether she saw or remembered what happened or not, she had no duty to turn Drew over to the police. The problem arose when she told the police there was no accident. She could be charged with offences relating to that.'

'No.' I shake my head. 'Hope can't get arrested. Hope can't face charges.'

Sarah looks at me across the table. 'I'm afraid I can't guarantee that won't happen. I also can't guarantee that there won't be any charges against you.'

I feel winded suddenly. This has all been for nothing. I should have phoned Hope sooner, but I didn't think of it until after I got on the plane this morning and by then there wasn't much time. Sarah had already warned me that there was a risk of both of them being arrested too, and so, as I flew over the Pyrenees towards Paris, I came up with the best plan I could think of. No matter what Hope had done, what *they'd* done, Sam needed his mother, his *real* mother, and it was in my power to make that happen. It broke my heart, but I knew that no matter what happened to me now, there was no way I would be allowed to keep him. Drew and Hope were eager to cooperate with me and said they would do anything to get him back. But they had no family, they said, or at least no one suitable to take care of him. Hope mentioned Jess next door, but Sam wouldn't remember her. She would be a stranger to him, and besides, I remembered Jess telling me she didn't want children. They knew no one who would be both willing and capable of looking after him.

I want to tell Sarah that I'll hide Sam, refuse to tell the police where he is, that I'll die before I let him go into foster care. He's the reason I came back to face up to this. I can't let him live out his childhood in the social care system or with someone who doesn't want him. He deserves to be loved, really loved, the way every child deserves to be loved.

Sarah is typing and so I wait for her to finish. I look down at the table for several moments, trying to figure it all out. There must be an answer. There has to be. And then something makes me realise there's one more question that hasn't yet been answered. 'Why didn't the lorry driver stop?' I ask. 'He must have seen what happened.'

Sarah pauses and looks up. 'I don't know. But I'd hazard a guess that he was doing something illegal. Maybe he was on his phone at the time, or driving without his tachograph card, or with someone else's. The rules are pretty strict about how long they're allowed to drive for, and maybe he was breaking them.'

I close my eyes and squeeze them shut as another spasm of pain grips me. It's hard to hear this, to think about how my baby might have been saved if only everyone had done the right thing. Maybe the lorry driver assumed Drew would do the right thing, or maybe he thought *he* would. Maybe we all believe we will do the right thing.

But would we?

Maybe if I hadn't taken their baby, Drew would have handed himself in to the police like he said he'd planned to, and Hope would have got a medical report about her traumatised postnatal condition and Sam would have grown up with the right mother and I would have got justice for my Sam and Charlie and we would all have been allowed to move on.

I didn't really know what I was doing, of course. Maybe it had been my original intention to show Hope and Drew what they'd taken from me, for them to experience that same devastation and loss. I do remember thinking that, wanting that. But I was lost in grief and by the time I took Sam from them, I was on autopilot, probably much the same as Hope was. I must have been, because I remember very little about that time.

I do remember when it started, though. That same day, the day Mike phoned and I decided I wasn't going back to work, I remember finding the Spanish work visa Charlie and I had applied for in an unopened envelope in the kitchen drawer. It must have arrived while I was in hospital and my mum must have put it there. But then I saw that there was a second unopened envelope underneath it, and I realised it was Sam's passport. I opened both envelopes and there it was in black and white: the evidence of our planned new life together, mine and Charlie's, our new life with our new baby. I remember sinking to my knees and spending the afternoon curled up in a ball on the kitchen floor.

I barely remember the next few weeks, hiding in the field at the back of Hope and Drew's house, packing, booking flights, buying formula milk and nappies and getting Sam's car seat and baby carrier out of the loft.

We drove straight to the airport that night, the night I took him. I can't actually remember the journey, but I do remember the feeling. It was one of calm, of happiness, something I hadn't felt in a very long time. We stayed overnight in the Travelodge next to the airport and got the first flight out to Girona. I didn't know if the passport would be flagged, or if I'd get caught, but they couldn't use biometrics or an eGate for a baby, and when it worked and I got through customs at the other end, I was able to convince myself even more fully that this was *my* Sam, the one I'd lost. He had the same name and he was the same age, more or less. On the plane, a woman asked me if I was on holiday and I found myself telling her that, no, we were emigrating, that Sam's dad was just tying things up at home and would soon be coming out to join us. Of course, it wasn't true, but saying it felt good. It eased the pain inside me and I started to heal. In Spain, as I got better and as the pain lessened over time, I knew Sam wasn't mine, but I couldn't bring myself to give him back.

'I don't want Drew to tell the police about the accident,' I say, finally. 'Please tell him not to. I don't want them to know what he did.'

Sarah looks doubtful. I can tell she's worried this isn't the right thing for me. But my mind is made up. Hope is Sam's mother and Drew is his dad, and all of this needs to stop.

'I'm serious,' I say. 'I don't want him to tell them. So what do I do? Do I tell them I got it wrong about the accident? That I made a mistake?'

'No.' She shakes her head. 'You already told them you couldn't remember any specific details about what happened. They didn't think you'd make a good witness and I can't see how that could have changed.'

'So what do I do?'

'Nothing.' Sarah sits back in her seat, folding her arms. 'As Drew and Hope have already discovered, if you lie to the police, it can give them everything they need to build a case against you. You have the right to remain silent and you need to exercise that right. You need to think instead about what they'll be left with if neither you nor Drew says anything further.'

'Wait,' I say, anxiety creeping up again. 'Drew confessed. He told them he killed two people.'

Sarah shrugs. 'Which two people did he say he killed?'

I think about this. I see what she's getting at.

'You make no comment,' she says. 'Both of you. We put them to proof on all of it.'

'What does that mean?'

'The law says they have to prove the case against you,' she explains. 'It's not for you to prove your innocence. You have the legal right to remain silent. So, we go into interview and see what they've got.'

There's a knock at the door. We both look up. The door opens. It's DC Foley, the male detective who was there when the uniformed police arrested me in the passenger zone at the airport soon after I got off the plane. His eyes are dark, his jaw tight.

'Can I have a word?' he asks.

Sarah turns to me, excuses herself and says she'll be back in a moment. DC Foley steps back and opens the door for her. I can see the female detective standing outside, clutching a notebook. Her expression is sombre too.

38

Drew

The police are not happy. DC Foley is angry. I can hear him from my cell. They are standing in the corridor nearby and he is shouting at Sarah. I can hear everything he is saying and everyone else can too. He certainly means me to hear it. He is telling her she doesn't know what she's doing, asking her how much experience she actually has in a sneering tone of voice. He is telling her she should know that she can't represent both Lauren and me.

'You have a clear conflict of interest,' I hear him say.

I hear Sarah say back, 'That's my decision to make, not yours.'

'Well, I'm not having this. You're interfering with our investigation.'

'I'm doing nothing of the sort. I'm just doing my job.'

'They are on opposite sides of the fence, for Christ's sake.'

'You don't know that,' I hear Sarah reply. 'You don't know my instructions.'

'He's already confessed.'

'No, he hasn't.'

There is a pause and I hold my breath so as not to miss anything. 'This isn't over,' he says, and then it goes quiet in the corridor.

I lie back down on my plastic mattress and listen to my fellow prisoners banging the doors and shouting to each other. Someone calls out, 'That your brief, mate, getting a hammering?' and I say, 'Yes,' and allow them all to laugh at my expense. I don't want to upset anyone by appearing stand-offish. I may as well get used to being a suck-up – either that or toughen up, bulk up and learn how to defend myself, because this is how my new life is going to be. I know the score. One wrong word, one wrong look, and someone could come up behind you and cut your throat with a razor blade melted into their toothbrush. I deserve this. I deserve everything that's coming to me. But not Hope. Please, God. Not Hope. She can't go to prison.

I put my head in my hands and whisper over and over that I'm sorry, that I didn't mean it. I didn't mean any of it. I've hurt so many people, and now my wife and child are going to suffer too. I wonder if I will ever see Hope again. I wonder if I'll ever see Sam again. What will happen to him if Hope goes to prison? And what kind of a life awaits her once it's known that she's there for helping her husband to conceal the death of a child?

It's evening by the time the two detectives come for me.

They stand outside my cell, grim-faced and unfriendly, and pull back the hatch over the window.

'You're up,' says the male one, DC Foley, unlocking my door and handcuffing me again before leading me down the corridor, into the custody area. He shows me back into the same side room, where Sarah is waiting for me, and uncuffs me. When the police have gone out and shut the door, she gets up and opens it again, checking that the detectives are not standing outside, trying to listen in.

'Are you OK?' she asks, closing the door.

I nod, although I'm not OK at all. I've never been worse, in fact.

'Right. This is what you're going to do,' Sarah says, and a ray of hope lights up inside me once more as she tells me that Lauren has answered 'No comment' to every single question in her interview with the police, and that she wants me to do the same.

39

Lauren

After Sarah left for the evening, the police hounded and hounded me to tell them where Sam was, but Sarah said there was nothing they could do if I refused to answer their questions. Later, in spite of the bright lights outside my cell, the rattling of doors, the shouting and the banging on walls, I slept. In the past twenty-four hours since I left Huesca, I had only dozed in brief snatches, nodding off for a few moments in the departure lounge in Girona, and maybe for an hour on the plane. I had been dizzy with exhaustion by the time the police were ready to interview me, and all the way through I could feel my heart beating just a little too fast. But Sarah said I had done well. After the detectives left, I ate the microwaved meal I was offered, then closed my eyes as I lay down on the thin mattress on my narrow bed. It was a light, strange sleep and I dreamed I was already in prison.

In the morning, a custody assistant brought the phone

into my cell. It was Sarah. She said that I was going to be released on bail, pending further inquiries. I could hardly believe my ears. I had been convinced I would be charged. My bail had a number of strict conditions, one of which was to have no contact with either Hope or Drew. Sarah warned me that if we spoke to each other, we could be arrested again, and if charged, I might not get bail next time. I didn't need to be told twice.

When I walked out of the back door of the police station, my mum and Anna were waiting outside. I hadn't seen either of them for almost two years and it was an emotional moment, not least because I had thought this would only happen through a glass window inside a prison. I was also worried that because I had been abroad for all this time, I'd be a flight risk, but Sarah said the police couldn't remand me unless they had enough evidence to charge me and, at this time, they didn't, which only meant they weren't sure yet, but being released was still more than I could have hoped for. I had to sleep at my mum's house every night and report to the police station in Northolt three times a week, which meant I couldn't leave the country, but I was otherwise free.

It was strange to be back at my mum's house, the house I grew up in, sleeping in my old bedroom again. It felt as though a lifetime had passed since I was last here. I wondered if walking through the front door and into the kitchen might trigger any memories of my last day here with my family, but there was nothing. I had a strong sense of déjà vu when we walked across the road to the playground in

Lime Tree Park, but I remembered the hospital consultant saying my brain could play tricks on me, that it could cause me to superimpose random flashbacks onto the things I had been told by my mum and the police. The consultant also said that many people block out the moment of trauma and never get it back, and although I'd like to remember the trip to Ikea and my last hours in this house and in the park with my husband and baby, I don't want the next part back. What happened later that day – that night – is terrifying to think about and I don't want to relive it. I'm content with the speculative, second-hand version given to me.

I haven't dared call Gabe or tried to speak to Sam. Gabe and I agreed before I left Spain that I wouldn't get in touch until it was safe to do so, and following Sarah's advice, I left both my phones behind in Huesca so that the police couldn't take them from me. Anna told me social services might try to get the family court to make an order to bring Sam home, but the court would first have to be satisfied that the child I had with me in Spain was the same child Hope had reported missing, and if they didn't know for sure or have any idea where he was, this was also unlikely.

So there has been nothing to do but wait. I have spent my days sitting and chatting with my mum in the kitchen, or taking her dog Henry for walks around the park. In the evenings, we watch TV together. At first, I would go into the West End with Anna, but then, two weeks ago, the nausea started. I couldn't brush my teeth without gagging, and the smell of my mum's cooking sometimes made me want to vomit, even though it was food I normally loved. When I realised what this was, it threw me completely. I felt bewildered and frightened and incredibly guilty, and as I lay in bed in my old bedroom at night, I would whisper to Charlie and Sam – my lost Sam – that I was sorry and that I hoped they understood.

It's been eight weeks now. It's two o'clock in the afternoon, but it's dark outside. The rain is coming. It's been hot all month, but suddenly summer is over. I always forget that about England in August. One minute it's blue skies and blazing sunshine, the next it's autumn, and it reminds me that although it sometimes feels like it, time never really stands still. Even so, I'm mentally preparing myself for two more days of not knowing what the future holds, because I can't imagine anyone is going to make a decision about me on a Friday afternoon or on a Saturday or Sunday. But then, suddenly, it happens. My phone rings. I lift it from the windowsill where I left it and it's Sarah's name flashing up.

For a split second, my heart freezes.

'Lauren?' she says, and there's a warmth in her voice that tells me this is good news. I brace myself.

And then, just like that, it's over. It's all over. Sarah has spoken to the senior investigating officer, who told her that there is insufficient evidence to charge any of us with a criminal offence.

'We're all free?' I ask her, astounded.

'Yes. You're free. All of you.'

'I can go back to Spain?'

'Yes. No more restrictions. That's it.'

'What about Sam?' I ask, hesitantly. 'Can they try and come for him?'

'No,' Sarah says confidently. 'There's nothing they can do. Let me explain. The birth records from the hospital don't have any genetic information and so there is nothing to prove or disprove the account Drew gave the police last year, which is that Sam is biologically yours. Also, Hope told her next-door neighbour, Jess, that she'd been a surrogate for you and, in spite of her subsequent regrets, had handed the baby over willingly, and the police can't prove otherwise. As you know, I'm sure, surrogacy is legal in this country, and although the government would prefer people to go through one of their recommended organisations, you don't have to. There is no law in this country to prevent an informal surrogacy arrangement between willing parties. And the court has no power to intervene in that arrangement unless asked to by either the surrogate or the intended parent, not without any evidence that the child is at harm. It's usual to ask the court for a parental order so that the intended parent becomes the legal guardian, but that doesn't always happen and there's no law that says it has to. So, in short, they don't have a leg to stand on where Sam is concerned.'

I feel my heart swelling in my chest. 'And Drew?'

'There was insufficient evidence to charge him,' she says. 'When you both exercised your right to silence, all they were left with was Hope's account that they were on the road that day, but not involved in any accident.'

'So that's it?'

'That's it. There will in all likelihood be a social services referral if Sam comes back to the UK, and he may be placed on the Child Protection Register for a while, but Anna says it's highly unlikely that they'd try to remove him from a family member who can provide a safe home, and even less likely that a court would agree.'

For a moment, I am in disbelief. The rain has begun to drum heavily against the bedroom window and as I look out onto the puddles that are pooling on the pavement outside, a surge of energy lifts me out of my chair and down the stairs, where I put on my raincoat and slip into my boots. My mum has gone to the park with the dog and I will go to meet her. I light up inside as I imagine her face when I tell her my good news. We have been close these past few weeks, my mum and I, and as I step outside, I know I am going to insist she comes to visit me in Spain for a while, and I know she will agree when I tell her the secret I've been keeping, as will Anna.

And then I think about the other person I need to tell, the most important person, and my tears of joy mingle with the damp droplets in the air as I stand on the porch waiting for the rain to ease just a little. I am finally able to begin to embrace the idea that there's a new life growing inside me.

Epilogue

Hope

We have arranged to meet in a park just five miles to the west of the city centre in Huesca, near the old town. It's a lovely place, its dusty paths bordered by cypresses and horse chestnuts. There's a fountain and a duck pond in the centre and a sweet little playhouse across the bridge that looks like it's made of gingerbread, straight out of a fairy tale. It's Snow White's house – a tribute to Walt Disney – and apparently Sam loves it, along with the duck pond and the playground and the small zoo. We've been told this park is one of his favourite places to play.

At five to twelve, I catch Drew's eye. He is sitting on the metal bench beside me, looking pale and frightened. He gives me a tight smile, but there's nothing we can say to each other to appease the growing sense of anticipation and excitement we are both feeling as it gets closer to midday, the time we arranged to meet. I go back to watching the birds landing on the water and taking off again, but then, a minute later, Drew nudges me. My heart starts racing as I see them approaching.

There are four adults: Lauren, of course, and a man who must be her boyfriend, Gabe, and then behind them another dark-haired woman who looks exactly like him and must be his sister, and an older, grey-haired woman who must be the aunt. My eyes scan them in less than a second, moving quickly to the blond-haired little boy walking between Lauren and Gabe. He's wearing checked shorts and a blue T-shirt and plimsolls and is holding on to their hands, swinging his legs up, forcing them to lift him up high. We rise to greet the group, and as he sees us, the little boy stops swinging and watches us cautiously, his big blue eyes flickering from the two of us to the Snow White house behind us and back again, as if he can't make up his mind which he is most interested in.

'Hello, Hope.' Lauren speaks first, her eyes landing on mine, then moving between us. She nods. 'Drew.'

'Hi, Lauren. Is this . . .?' I begin, uncertainly.

She nods. 'This is Sam.'

I swallow hard, trying not to cry. I can't stop looking at the little figure on the path in front of me. I instantly recognise his features: the big, enquiring blue eyes. The turned-up nose. The smiling mouth. Everything is bigger but the same. It's unmistakably him.

'He's beautiful,' I breathe softly.

'He has your hair,' Drew whispers to me, and I throw him a grateful smile. It's true. He has my curls.

Lauren ushers him forward. 'Sam. Say hello to Hope,' she urges.

'Hello,' he says shyly, and I hold my breath at the sound of his voice.

'Do you remember what I told you about Hope?' Lauren asks him.

Sam shakes his head.

'Well, she's a very important person for us.'

Sam peers up at Lauren. 'Why?'

'Because she's part of your family. And so is Drew.'

'Is she your mummy?' he asks.

We all smile, but it hurts a little, too.

'She's not my mummy, no,' Lauren says. 'But she *is* a mummy and Drew is a daddy and they have lost their little boy, which has made them a bit sad. So, they would like a little boy to play with. Is it OK if they play here with you for a while, then come to visit you at Lucía and Marta's house?'

Sam shrugs, considering this, looking as if he'd like to help. 'Do they like chickens?' He has a little lisp when he says 'chickens'. It's adorable and I find myself unable to speak.

'We love chickens,' I hear Drew saying next to me, his voice full of enthusiasm, as if Sam has just introduced his favourite subject.

'And cats?' Sam asks doubtfully.

'You have a cat?' Drew is astounded now, as if this is a miracle.

'Yes! Her name is Luna!' Sam announces happily. I can't take my eyes off that smile. I know that smile.

'Well, we'd love to meet her, wouldn't we, Hope?'

'Yes,' I agree enthusiastically, fighting back tears.

'You have to be careful,' Sam warns Drew, wagging a finger. 'You mustn't pull her tail.'

'Promise,' Drew says, then crouches down on his haunches, holds out his hand and extends his little finger. 'Pinky promise.'

And then they're hooking fingers, and Drew is pretending Sam is too strong for him and falls forward onto the pathway while Sam throws his head back and goes into peals of laughter, and I know that laugh. I'd know it anywhere.

'*La casa*,' Sam suddenly shouts in Spanish. '*La casa Blancanieves!*'

'*Sí*,' says Lucía. '*Vamos.*'

'He's talking about the little house,' Lauren explains. 'It's Snow White's house, apparently.'

I nod. 'Can we come to the house with you?' I ask Sam. Sam surveys me for a moment.

'Go,' says Gabe to Sam, nudging him forward. 'Go with Hope and Drew. They want to play with you.'

Sam steps forward, hesitantly, and we walk with him, but we don't try to take his hand. Not yet. Baby steps, I tell myself. One day at a time. Lauren was right. We have to give him time to learn to trust us before we can gently introduce the truth about who we are.

'OK,' Sam shrugs. 'Come with me and I will show you.'

Drew turns and grins at me and his eyes say, *Ready?*

We turn and follow our son as he leads the way across the tiny bridge.

Lauren

We're down at the waterfront at dusk. Gabe has hired a small fishing boat and we're going to sail out, just to the point in the distance where the sea meets the clifftop. It's the point where the last of the lights flickers on in the evenings, just past the last of the bars and restaurants on the north side of the bay. It's not very far. Gabe doesn't want us to go out too deep, not with me being fourteen weeks pregnant, and I understand that, and besides, it's perfect. It's exactly the place where I have often imagined Charlie would want me to leave him and Sam, shimmering on the water together in the morning sun or in the moonlight, where I can see them, always, from the top of the hill above the bay.

The waves break on the beach as we step into the boat, the surf shimmering in the setting sun.

But I can't do it. 'I'm not ready,' I say suddenly.

As usual, Gabe is calm and doesn't ask any questions. He

simply shrugs. 'There's no hurry,' he says. 'No hurry at all. Let's go home.'

I nod gratefully and wait by the water's edge, clutching the bag containing the two urns to my chest, while Gabe takes the boat key back to its owner. Gabe's right. There's no hurry. I am still counting my losses as well as my gains.

But as Hope once told me, there are no rules about this. The important thing is to allow the feelings to ebb and flow like the tide, in the knowledge that nothing lasts for ever. Everything changes. It's the only certainty in this life, after all.

As we walk across the sand and follow the shoreline back into the village, I think for the millionth time about Hope and Drew and their little Sam. 'Will they take Luna?' I ask. 'When they go?'

'Yes,' Gabe says. 'I think they should. Don't you?'

'Yes.' I smile. 'And maybe a couple of chickens.'

Gabe laughs and I laugh too, even though my heart hurts at the thought of Sam leaving the farmhouse and moving into Hope and Drew's new house in the centre of Huesca.

'You want to visit them this weekend?' Gabe asks.

'No. Let's give them some time. Ana and Lucía said they are all doing well, and Hope messaged me this morning to say that Jess is coming from England to visit on Friday. Next weekend, we will go.'

'Sure.'

We fall into a contented silence.

'Thank you,' I say. 'For everything.'

'No.' Gabe shakes his head. 'Thank *you*. I will miss both Sam and Luna, but I have this baby to look forward to now. You couldn't have given me a more perfect gift.'

'I told you I'd bring you back a present,' I say, smiling at him.

'You did. It's the best present.'

I hesitate, then say, with some trepidation, 'I was thinking that maybe, if our baby is a boy, we could call him Daniel?'

Gabe glances at me, his expression unreadable.

'Like Deniel, but . . .' I pause. 'But only if you want to, of course. It's fine if you don't.'

Gabe reaches for my fingers and says, 'Yes. I do. Very much.'

As the sun sets on the horizon, we head on round the bay and up the hill.

Acknowledgements

This was a difficult book to write. I had never before written a story that repeatedly jumps backwards in time until you get to the beginning, and it was hard to begin each new timeline and to know precisely what the characters would now be thinking and feeling about something that hadn't yet happened! It was perhaps a little like it is when you meet an old friend you haven't spoken to for some time and they tell you only very fleetingly about something awful they've been through when you weren't around. Working out exactly where a character's mind would have been then – and where it would be now, as a result – was a challenge for me, so much so that I literally began to write the story backwards, starting at the end and working my way towards the beginning! But I'm now so pleased I did. Thank you so much to Charlotte Osment for the suggestion.

My thanks too, of course, to Selina Walker, my UK publisher and editor, for your general brilliance and for being so lovely. To everyone else at Century in the UK – you are the best! Thanks especially to Lucy Hall, Rachel Kennedy and Alice Gomer, and to Jade Unwin and Evie Kettlewell, all of whom were working so hard and doing such wonderful things with *The Woman on the Ledge* while I wrote this book. You kept me going, for sure! Huge thanks once again to my eagle-eyed copy-editor Caroline Johnson, who went above and beyond to help me, to proofreader Gabriella Nemeth, and to Joanna Taylor and Venetia Butterfield for their editorial input and advice. My thanks to Glenn O'Neill for such beautiful, vibrant covers.

Thanks as always to my agent, Judith Murray, for also being brilliant and lovely, and to Mia Dakin, Kate Rizzo, Sally Oliver and everyone else at Greene & Heaton. Huge thanks to my US agent, Gráinne Fox at United Talent Agency, to my US publisher, Sarah Stein, and to Lisa Erickson and to everyone else at HarperCollins in the US. Thank you, once again, for believing in me.

To the wonderful readers, book bloggers, Bookstagrammers, booksellers and librarians who have supported me on this journey – you have been incredible. Authors never tire of hearing that a reader has enjoyed their book, and to see so many of you talking about mine and recommending it to others has been truly mind-blowing. Thank you so much!

A huge thank you to the wonderful friends and family who have become my little core of early readers: Tara Kaby, Ian Astbury, Simon Kingston, Karen Draisey and Amy Eastham (in spite of pregnancy sickness), and also to Rachael Hilliard and Catherine Scammell. Your feedback has been invaluable and has spurred me on so many times when I have been flagging. I am so grateful to you for giving up your time. Thank you, too, Rachael, for the help with the osteopathy storyline, and to Alison Lindenbaum for answering my questions – and for the treatment.

I am in the very fortunate position to have been able to get a second opinion on some of the legal aspects of the storyline from some of the best legal minds I know: James Turner and Alex Walsh Atkins, my colleagues at Tuckers Solicitors. The same goes for Laurence Wilson of Wilsons Solicitors, who gave me such helpful guidance on family law and procedure, and a big, big thank you to Sophie Walker and Anna Renou. Counsel's advice from a real-life Sarah-and-Anna team – I was so thrilled to have this! My thanks also to fellow author, former detective and police advisor Graham Bartlett for his expert guidance on International Arrest Warrants and extradition procedure. Your knowledge is immense, Graham, and you are such a fabulous resource for your fellow authors. Thank you so much to everyone here for giving up their time. While I believe all the legal aspects of the plot are true to life, any remaining errors are mine and not theirs.

Through my work as a lawyer I am also very fortunate to be in a position to meet and speak to forensic and other experts. Thanks so much to Chris Goddard of Collision Science for his specialist help with some of the technical aspects of the plot. It was so interesting to talk to you, Chris, and I loved how passionate you are about your work. It was inspiring. My thanks also to Debbie Rushton from Forensic Science for the introduction.

A special thank you goes to Tracey Budding, Clinical Nurse Specialist from Birmingham Women's and Children's NHS Trust, for sparing the time to talk to me and share such an enormous amount of knowledge about pre-term babies and neonatal care. I tend to do quite a lot of research for my stories, even though what ends up in the book is usually only a small fraction of the information I've been given, and this was definitely the case here. It may seem as though the extra material is superfluous, but this isn't the case at all; it all sits there at the back of my mind as I write and helps me to create a fictional world I can believe in. I was so impressed with the amount you knew, Tracey. Those little babies and their mothers are so incredibly lucky to have you, and we in the UK are all so lucky to have an NHS with people like you in it. Thanks also to Amanda Spiers for her help with GP procedure for babies, and to Mahala Bradford for her help with hospital procedure.

To Maja Rose Coates. The baby. Thank you, Maja, for the six-week-old photos and the three-month-old cuddles, and the chuckling and spitting up of sick, and for reminding me how heartbreakingly gorgeous Sam would be.

Thanks to my mother, Marsha, for Hope (and for Polly-anna and The Glad Game and for the drop scones and the buns we had for tea – like the Railway Children!) and for all the hugely interesting discussions we still have which inspire my characters.

And finally, thank you as always to my husband Mark, for being there through thick and thin, and for all the walks and talks which helped bring this story to life.